Virulence

E. W. Johnson, M.D.

Copyright © 2020 E. W. Johnson, M.D.
All rights reserved
First Edition

PAGE PUBLISHING, INC.
Conneaut Lake, PA

First originally published by Page Publishing 2020

This is a work of fiction. Names, characters, businesses, places, events, locales, and incidents are either the products of the author's imagination or used in a fictitious manner. Any resemblance to actual persons, living or dead, or actual events is purely coincidental.

ISBN 978-1-64701-361-5 (pbk)
ISBN 978-1-66240-825-0 (hc)
ISBN 978-1-64701-362-2 (digital)

Printed in the United States of America

To Kim, Amanda, and Emily. You not only kept me going, but the clinic as well, and you made every day better than it could have been. I will be grateful until my final breath.

After that, it's a crap-shoot.

Dedication

My deepest gratitude to the staff at Page Publishing. They have served as mentors, babysitters, wilderness guides and camp counselors. With patience and a gentle hand, they kept me on the path to bring this book to print.

Special thanks to Jason Milkowski for assistance with military issues. I still keep his phone number in my wallet.

Prologue

THE DEATH OF A LONG-CHERISHED dream, of any import, is a profound event. It parallels the loss of a loved one, and causes irreparable damage to the human heart. Following much the same pattern, there is denial, disbelief, a slow transition to acceptance, and then the eventual embrace of the grieving process. In a merciful world, this is a confined, finite process. For some, it is a nightmare frozen in time that has no ending.

In 1995, when *The Bible According To Mark Twain* was first published, it inflicted such a deep and painful wound that I fear there shall be no recovery. On his path to final judgement, fearing his personal resume would fail celestial scrutiny, Mark Twain felt compelled to steal the admission pass from a recently deceased Cardinal traveling along with him. While Mr. Twain was granted immediate entry into Heaven with his pilfered credentials, the Cardinal, amidst great protest, was forced to seek other accommodations.

That Samuel Clements holds court in Heaven causes me nothing less than pure joy. It is where he belongs, either as a learned advisor, or possibly a part-time consultant. That he 'borrowed' his entry ticket does not ruffle the few remaining Christian feathers that I still possess. Nor have I lost any measurable sleep over the final resting place of the victimized Cardinal. In the end, we all probably get what we deserve.

What plagues me to the deepest core of my being is not Mark Twain's rightful place in eternity, but the bitter certainty that it has utterly destroyed one of my most revered hopes. The great expectation and honor of one day meeting him face to face has now been reduced to zero.

1

It had been over five months since the discovery of the toxic waste site in Woodhaven, Washington. The initial shock waves that rolled through the community had dissipated, the disbelief had evolved to a quiet acceptance, and the shared resolve was to move forward, to focus on the future. It would never be exactly the same again, but a new normal now defined the town and its people.

The cleanup process had long been completed, and, true to form, the Army Corps of Engineers and the Shoreline management agency were still arguing over the best plan to protect the Columbia River. The concrete bulkhead and underground pumping system had been installed, and so far, no PCB contamination had been detected in the main waterways. It was temporarily reassuring, but close monitoring would continue for years, perhaps decades.

Lastly, with a seamlessly coordinated effort through the EPA and local government, fueled by federal emergency funding, every home, farm, and business in the old flood zone known as the Bottoms had been hooked up to the city water system.

Not one well remained in use. Some of the newly constructed pipeline remained aboveground, but it was safe. As were the crops, produce, and cattle within the spill region. There were no additional health risks to deal with, and no devastating financial hardships that would further penalize local residents.

The first three to four weeks after the PCB dump site had been unearthed were a nightmare of activity. The size of the small town had doubled with an influx of hazmat personnel, engineers, investigators, and reporters from every branch of media. Dr. Nolan had successfully avoided any contact with the press by having his staff run interference, and then referring all questions to City Hall or Sheriff Dent. It had worked to keep him insulated and out of the public eye, but his favored status with local government and law enforcement had been severely strained.

By the second month, the news stories had dwindled to a trickle, and printed articles were once again being used to light fires and cover the floor of birdcages. The cycle had run its course, and the appetite for new, fresh entertainment had shifted to other journalistic targets. Mercifully, Woodhaven had become yesterday's headline. By the third and fourth month, there was barely a mention or question voiced about what had happened.

And, there was no one in town more grateful for a return to the ordinary pattern than Dr. Nolan. His extracurricular activities had been set to rest, and his life was now back to the controlled chaos of practicing medicine. But it was a predictable, manageable insanity. It was direct, and simple, and just about patients again.

Now Wednesday near the end of June, his last scheduled appointment of the morning session was a local builder he had known for years. The man was nearly his age, gifted with humor, but a commanding figure at six feet five, prone to anxiety symptoms when out of his comfort zone. He was noticeably uneasy when Dr. Nolan entered the exam room.

"Jesus, Kenny, long time," Dr. Nolan said, shaking hands. "How many spec houses are you juggling?" He went to the corner sink to wash his hands.

"Five right now," the man answered. "One more starting next week. Trying to ride the market while it's still strong. Remember what happened in '08?"

Dr. Nolan nodded and sat down on a stool near his patient.

"Do I." He laughed. "My IRA vanished overnight, and I believe you only survived by doing home repair jobs. Feast or famine. I'm glad you're doing well again. Family all good?"

The man was beaming now, much more at ease.

"Oldest boy's working with me over the summer," he explained proudly. "Younger kids are all in sports."

"And your wife? Still abusing you on a daily basis?" Dr. Nolan asked.

"It's horrible," the man said. "She runs the business and just orders me around all the time. It's hell, Doc."

Dr. Nolan nodded again, trying to look sympathetic.

"That's because she's smarter than you, and a lot better looking," he noted. "Now, why are you here bothering me?"

"I almost forgot. My wife is smarter than me. She made me come in," he admitted. "I've got something growing on my head. Damn thing rubs right where my hard hat sits."

Dr. Nolan stood up and felt the man's scalp, all hidden beneath a full head of hair. There was a soft, pliable mass over the occipital area nearly two centimeters in diameter.

"You've got a cyst between the skin and your skull. Pretty common. Has it been getting bigger?"

"Yeah, and sore sometimes," the man answered. "What can you do?"

Dr. Nolan glanced at his watch. It was officially lunchtime, but his staff was still in the building. He knew that granting the patient a delayed appointment would allow his anxiety to reassert itself and sabotage any future treatment.

"It needs to come out before it gets infected," Dr. Nolan explained. "Fifteen minutes and we're done."

"Now? Right now?"

"No. First you get a haircut, then I numb you up, then we get rid of it. We're not barbarians."

"Jesus, I don't know," the man said, his agitation growing. "I've got to get back to the job-site."

"Okay, fourteen minutes." Dr. Nolan smiled. "This way you don't have to think about it. One-stop shopping. Now, either come with me to the procedure room, or I'm calling your wife." He purposely avoided using the word "surgery."

Dr. Nolan opened the door to the hall and waited. The patient stared at the floor, then stood and followed him to the surgery suite. Cat followed behind. She quickly had the patient situated on the hydraulic bed with two pillows supporting his neck.

Cat had been his head nurse for seventeen years. Nothing phased or distracted her. Dr. Nolan gave her a knowing glance, letting his eyebrows arch as a warning.

"Simple cyst. Give him a Friar Tuck haircut. Standard setup with 4-0 Ethilon," he said in a low voice. Cat already had the clippers out. In less than a minute, a shiny bald area four inches in diameter exposed the bulging nodule over the crown of the man's head.

"This is the only bad part," Dr. Nolan explained. He had filled a 10-cc syringe with numbing medicine. "This stings a little, but works fast." He could see his patient grabbing at the edges of the table.

"Isn't there some other way to do this?" the man nearly pleaded.

"We could pray for you," Dr. Nolan said, wiping the area with alcohol. "But that usually doesn't work. Now, hold still, or I'll have Cat dial your wife." He began infiltrating the surgical site, the skin turning stark white as the lidocaine and epinephrine took effect. Satisfied, Dr. Nolan went to wash up and put on sterile gloves. He stood watching as Cat scrubbed the area with Betadine. He placed a sterile drape over their work site, had Cat adjust the overhead light, then nodded for her to glove up.

Dr. Nolan studied the area where the cyst was bulging outward, nearly the size of a golf ball.

"Okay. You will not feel any pain," he told the man. "Just a little tugging sensation when we loosen it up around the margins." He had already made an elliptical incision through the skin. Slowly he made these deeper until the underlying fascia opened and exposed the upper curved dome of the mass.

"Man, I don't feel anything," the patient said, in genuine relief and amazement. "You've done this before, right?"

Dr. Nolan laughed.

"No. Never," he said, in a slow drawl. "But I read about it in a book once. It sounded pretty easy."

"Goddamn it, Doc. That's not funny," the man responded, but he was laughing too. Cat just shook her head, dabbing up any excess blood oozing from the incision.

Dr. Nolan took a thin, narrow pair of scissors from the instrument tray. Keeping them closed, he inserted them along the walls of the cyst, opening them to free the adhering tissues. Repeating this process, he was able to work around the entire circumference of the leathery pouch without causing it to rupture. Placing his fingers along both sides of the wound, he began applying pressure, the cyst slowing moving upward, almost popping out of its hiding place. He grabbed one end of it with forceps and held it out for the patient to see.

"That was in my head?! That's gigantic," he said.

"Men always exaggerate size," Dr. Nolan told him. "But it is pretty damn big. Your hat will definitely fit better."

"Are we done?" the man asked.

"No. Now you've got a big sinkhole on your noggin," Dr. Nolan explained. "We make sure there's no bleeding, then five or six stitches will close this up. For an extra fifty bucks, I'll cinch these up super tight and get rid of the wrinkles on your face."

"Great," the man said. "But what about the rest of my body?"

Dr. Nolan had already finished the first three sutures.

"You're screwed like the rest of us, sorry," he explained. "Age and gravity get us all." He completed the final stitches, pulled the sterile drape away, snapped off his gloves, then smiled broadly at his patient.

"That's it?" the man asked.

"That's it," Dr. Nolan assured him. "You did great. Cat will put a dressing over the area. Keep it dry for twenty-four hours, then come back in a week and we'll take the stitches out."

Cat finished taping a bandage in place, lowered the table, then helped him stand.

"Jesus, you guys are magicians," he said.

"No. I'm a magician," Dr. Nolan said. "She's an evil sorcerer. But she's also the best goddamn assistant I've ever had. Now, go home and tell your wife how brave you were."

The man nodded and headed back to the reception area. Dr. Nolan washed up again.

"Good job, Cat." He smiled.

"That cyst was gigantic," she said. "I'm glad you didn't have to cut it."

"Me too," he said. "Would have smelled for hours. Sorry about the delayed lunch."

"That was worth it. Pretty cool," Cat remarked. "I like when things go the way they're supposed to."

Dr. Nolan nodded his agreement. He took the chart from the counter and plotted a course for his office. Amanda ambushed him in the hall. She held out a small piece of note paper.

"You remember that EPA guy that was in charge of the clean-up?" she began. "He called while you were in surgery. Very polite. He'd like a call back. Said he's on eastern time." Dr. Nolan frowned, then checked his watch. He had not had contact with anyone from the Environmental Protection Agency since January.

"No hint about why?" Dr. Nolan asked.

"Not a word. You want me to call him back?"

"Not yet," Dr. Nolan said. "Let me get some coffee first. You guys lock up and go to lunch. Just leave the number on my desk. Thanks."

Amanda nodded, waited for Cat to finish cleaning the surgical suite, then grabbed Evie and headed outside into a warm and sunny spring day. At least they would get a break before the afternoon session.

Dr. Nolan salvaged the last half cup of coffee from the pot. He buffered it with an extra measure of milk, checked to make certain the front door was locked, then finally made it to his office. He sat staring at the phone number in front of him, remembering back to his first meeting with Arthur Campbell. He had basically set a trap for the EPA, but Mr. Campbell had turned out to be a caring, dedicated professional, quickly responding to the situation and the needs of the community. He made things happen.

So, what was this about? Just a courtesy call, an update? Was there a new problem? Had the ongoing testing indicated an additional threat?

It was nearly four in the afternoon on the east coast. He took a sip of his lukewarm coffee, winced at the acrid bitterness, then dialed the phone.

"That you, Sean?" Arthur Campbell answered on the second ring. "I still remember your area code."

"I'll bet you do." Dr. Nolan laughed. "I was just thinking about the day we met."

"Don't remind me," Mr. Campbell said. "It was a little uncomfortable getting blindsided like that, but it was well played. You guaranteed there would be no delay. I might have done the same thing."

"I usually prefer exigency over diplomacy," Dr. Nolan admitted. "Half the time it works, and half the time it doesn't. I just couldn't gamble on the bureaucratic machinery being in good working order."

There was a long silence on the other end of the line, too long.

"That's what prompted this call, Sean," Mr. Campbell said at last. "I was on a conference call with Dr. Pulliam at the Center for Disease Control this morning. You read about the outbreak of Legionnaires' in southern California about a month ago? They had a large team in the area for three weeks, then it just stopped. They did a full sweep and never found the source, not even a clue. They were going to stay on-site, but now they've got a Zika outbreak and some cases of dengue fever south of San Diego. They didn't have the manpower to cover everything. As much as they hate not finding answers, they had to pull their people out of the Imperial Valley."

Dr. Nolan had been listening carefully. He had seen two or three articles about the California outbreak, but was not well versed on the specifics.

"How many cases were documented?" he asked.

"Forty-seven dead, 117 exposures confirmed, all recovering," Mr. Campbell said. "And, then it vanished. No cases for the last 10 days."

"The CDC doesn't miss much," Dr. Nolan remarked. "They've isolated infection sources to air conditioners, water tanks, respiratory equipment in hospitals, even a mist machine in a small grocery store. I can see why they'd be frustrated. But, how does this concern me?"

Again there was a hesitation before the older man answered.

"After the call, I kept remembering how you set up your investigation in Woodhaven. You were methodical, focused, and a little unorthodox in some of your actions, but you never stopped looking, asking questions. About noon, I called Dr. Pulliam back in Atlanta and told him the story, then I made a suggestion."

"Okay. I'm getting lost here," Dr. Nolan said. "What does Woodhaven have to do with this Legionnaires' outbreak?"

"You, Sean," Mr. Campbell answered. "You've proven yourself to be a talented investigator. It seemed clear that a new approach and new eyes might be worth a try. And Dr. Pulliam was intrigued by the idea. They would be willing to credential you and any assistant you select for two weeks. They would make all their existing data available for review, and offer any assistance possible. They just don't have any people to spare."

Dr. Nolan leaned back in his chair and closed his eyes. It was an absurd proposal from every aspect.

"Arthur, I appreciate the compliment, but I'm not an epidemiologist," he explained. "I'm a jack-of-all-trades, small-town doctor with no specialized training in this area."

"That didn't stop you before," Mr. Campbell reminded him. "You defined the problem, found the answers, and nothing could stop you. Maybe that's the only skill you need. I just know forty seven people died, and there's no explanation."

Dr. Nolan could not focus on any single thought. A dozen questions and objections were spinning together in a dizzying haze.

"But my practice," he said. "I can't just leave."

"CDC has a family physician in Seattle who will cover the two weeks," Mr. Campbell explained. "She's got family in Portland, and was thrilled by the opportunity."

"What about my girls?" Dr. Nolan said next, more to himself. He was already considering a potential list of temporary house sitters that could stay with them. Now that school was almost out, the logistics would be much simpler.

"That's your call, Sean. If you can't help, I understand," Mr. Campbell said. "I realize this is a lot to ask, but it's a serious situation. At least give it some thought. Let it settle for a while, then call me tomorrow. Whatever you decide will be the end of it."

Dr. Nolan looked down at the notes he had been taking; 47 dead, 117 infected. Why had it just stopped?

I…I'll call you in the morning," Dr. Nolan said. "And, Arthur. Thanks for turning my day into a shit storm."

The older man burst into genuine laughter.

"What goes around, comes around," he finally said. "I'll be waiting."

2

Dr. Nolan jotted down a list of to-do items, most important to least. His first call was to the Morgan family, the owner-operators of the largest restaurant in town. Their oldest daughter had provided childcare in the past on rare occasions, and he trusted her to supervise his own children without hesitation. But he was not certain she was home on college break.

"Mrs. Morgan? Dr. Nolan. Sorry to bother you, but I was wondering if Kellie was back from school? Something has come up that may take me out of town for a few weeks."

"Not a problem, Dr. Nolan. She got home last week. All she does is fool around on her computer half the night, and then sleep in till the afternoon. Let me get her."

Dr. Nolan waited impatiently, tapping his pen on the desk. He pushed his chair back, strained to pull the large copy of *Harrisons Internal Medicine* from a nearby bookshelf, looked up Legionnaires' disease, and began to review. He was already three pages into transmission, diagnosis, and treatment before the phone came back to life.

"Hello? Dr. Nolan?" Kellie asked, still half asleep.

"Hi, kid. School going well?"

"Mm-hmm." Kellie yawned. "Glad to be home though. Mom said you might have a job offer?"

"Correct," Dr. Nolan said. "Two to three weeks, full time. You'd have to stay at the house and drive my girls to sports, go to the movies, whatever. Six hundred a week with a generous food and entertainment budget. You interested?"

"God, yes," Kellie answered, suddenly awake. "I hadn't lined up any work yet. When does this start?"

Dr. Nolan crossed the first and most important line off his schedule. He glanced up at the calendar.

"It's not official yet," he told her, "but probably Saturday morning. I've still got two more logistical problems to solve, but I'll know by tonight. You have an e-mail address?" He scribbled down the contact number.

"Cool," the girl said. "How old are your girls now?"

"Fifteen and thirteen," Dr. Nolan said. "And that brings up the big rule. Any teenage boys show up, you have to be willing to shoot them. Nothing too serious or lethal. Just wing them."

Kellie laughed.

"You sound just like my dad," she said.

"That's why I like your old man. He's a genius," Dr. Nolan quipped. "I'll call or send an e-mail later. And thank you."

"No, thank you," Kellie said. "It'll be fun."

Dr. Nolan hung up, sighed deeply, then dialed a local travel agent he had used in the past.

"Sherrie. Hi, Dr. Nolan. Sorry about the short notice, but I need to end up in the town of Imperial, California, by Saturday afternoon. I need a hotel for two weeks and a rental car, too."

"Wow, what's the occasion?" the woman asked. He could already hear her on the computer.

"Just business," he answered. There was no reason to add any explanation about the forty seven fatalities or what he was actually doing.

"Just you?" she asked.

Dr. Nolan hesitated for just a moment. That was going to be the next challenge to face.

"No. Two one-way tickets, two hotel rooms."

"Okay," the woman said. "Name?"

"Eileen Carson," he said.

"Got it," the travel agent said. "I don't see any direct flights. Give me about an hour to sort this out. I assume you prefer a fairly decent hotel?"

Dr. Nolan laughed.

"I don't want bed-bugs or chiggers," he said. "But, not the Ritz either. Nice, but not fancy."

"Understood," the woman said. "One hour."

The phone went dead, but Dr. Nolan sat with it pressed against his ear. He had just committed his sister-in-law to be his research assistant on a two week trip to investigate an outbreak of a deadly disease. There was no possible way to navigate the collected evidence already accumulated by the CDC without her help, and no credible path forward that did not depend on her assistance. She had been an essential part of his search for the toxic dump site, and this was even more challenging. Now, all he had to do was tell her.

He partially dialed her number, hung up, partially dialed again, hung up a second time, then took a deep breath and completed the call. He was on shaky ground.

"Hello," Eileen said cheerfully.

"Saint Eileen," Dr. Nolan began, "how are you doing? Long time no talk to." He cringed as he said the words.

"I just saw you and the girls two days ago," she reminded him, already suspicious.

"Oh, right, right," he said. "I was just wondering how you were feeling?"

"Aside from hot flashes from the medicine I have to take, I feel fine," she said. The tamoxifen was a necessary component of her breast cancer treatment.

"No nausea?" he asked.

"Just hot flashes and sweats," she answered. "I can live with it or die without it. Pretty easy decision."

"But, other than that you feel good? Strong? Back in the groove?"

"Yes, Sean, perfectly fine," she answered, a little defensive. "Why so concerned?"

"Oh, you know, just glad you're back to normal. How about I pick up something after work and come over with the girls? Anything sound good?"

Eileen knew him well enough that she could read how uneasy he was.

"I've got a roast in the oven big enough to feed a small army," she said. "Just show up when you can, and maybe by then you can get to the point. You either did something or want something. Which is it?"

"Both," he admitted. "But it's complicated. I don't want to do this over the phone."

"Boy, this must be good," Eileen said.

"And, you've got to make me one promise," Dr. Nolan added.

"What?" she asked.

"When I explain all this, I don't want you to murder me in front of my daughters. I don't want that to be their last memory of my time here on earth."

Eileen laughed, but her curiosity was in full bloom.

"I promise," she said. "So, now I get to spend three hours letting my imagination run wild. This better be worth it."

"It will be an evening to remember," Dr. Nolan assured her. "All I ask is that you hear me out, then say yes or no. One of those answers will break my heart, but your decision will stand without any repercussions. Okay?"

"Fair enough," Eileen said. "You have a nice way of setting the table, Sean. See you later."

Dr. Nolan replaced the receiver and nearly crossed out the third notation on his list, then reconsidered. Eileen's participation was not a settled issue. He needed to convince both she and Mike that it was a worthwhile endeavor.

He heard the lock turn in the front door. Amanda peeled out of formation at the reception desk, and Cat passed his office on her way to the nurses' station. She saw the medical book open on his lap and the paperwork on the desk.

"You didn't eat anything, did you?" she asked, already knowing the answer.

"Got busy and forgot," he said.

Cat shook her head. She searched the side pocket of her purse, tossing him a granola bar.

"You're a good mommy." He smiled. "Thanks."

"You need a mommy. You work on that and I'll make coffee. Show starts in ten minutes," Cat said. She put her things away and headed for the back room. The phones were already ringing.

"You call a travel agent?" Amanda yelled. "Line two." It was her way of erasing any illusion of privacy.

"Dr. Nolan," he said. "What did you come up with?"

"Portland to San Diego, then a turboprop to Imperial. Rental car is Alamo. Two suites at the Courtyard Inn," the woman announced proudly.

Dr. Nolan noted the itinerary, then read off his VISA number.

"Good work," he said. "I may have to cancel Eileen Carson's ticket. Is that a big problem."

"Penalty fee is all," the woman said. "Let me know as soon as you can if something changes. I'll print all this out and drop it by the clinic on Friday."

"You do good work, Sherrie," Dr. Nolan said.

"Pleasure, Doc. See you Friday."

The first of the afternoon patients were already in rooms when Dr. Nolan came out of his office. Cat and Evie both stared at him, anxious to learn details about his upcoming trip.

"Okay. Okay. Patients first," he said. "After work, I'll sit down and explain everything to you, and Cienna and Aubriel. I only want to do this one time. Agreed?"

They both nodded and went back to work, but the suspense was torture. In all the years Cat had served as his head nurse, there had only been two or three days when he missed time.

The flow of patients continued at a steady, unbroken pace, with no unexpected emergencies. Cienna and Aubriel had arrived after school, both doing homework in his office. Their father told them about dinner at Mike's and Eileen's, but they were not aware of anything out of the ordinary until after clinic business had been completed.

Dr. Nolan brought two extra chairs into his office and placed them facing his desk, and his staff stood and waited behind them.

"This is a sudden change from normal, but there's been a disease outbreak in California that took the lives of forty seven people. The Center for Disease Control has been there for three weeks without finding an answer, and now they have to respond to a new problem somewhere else. I've been asked to come down and review the situation and see if I can see anything that might have been missed. Like giving a second opinion."

He paused, meeting his daughters' eyes, not yet certain if they understood.

"I'll be gone for two weeks," he continued. "I'm hoping your Aunt Eileen will help with reviewing all the test data, because you all know how talented I am with computers. I've already spoken to Kellie Morgan about staying at the house, and the CDC is going to send down a doctor to cover the practice. But I can't do this without everyone in agreement. If this creates a problem here, then I won't go."

He waited, looking first to his daughters, and then to his staff. It was Aubriel who broke the silence.

"Cool! So, you'll be like a detective again. Just like when you found the spill site in the Bottoms," she said, smiling broadly.

"And I can take care of the animals for you," Cienna offered.

"And, we get two weeks of peace and quiet," Cat added. "It will seem like a vacation."

Dr. Nolan smiled. There had been no counter argument or protest. They were giving their permission for him to leave.

"I'll be in phone contact every day," he explained. "And we'll be available if any problems or questions come up. Kellie Morgan will hold down the fort at home, and Cat will be in charge here. The fill-in doctor will get crushed if you guys don't smooth the waters."

"So, when do you leave?" Cat asked.

"Saturday morning," Dr. Nolan said. He stood up, then hugged each of his daughters in turn. It would be the longest separation between them since they were born. It occurred to him that the time was nearing when their lives would diverge to different journeys, and a flickering sadness touched at him.

"Two weeks isn't so long," Cienna said, more to herself.

"Now I've got to convince your aunt to help," Dr. Nolan said. "This might be a deal breaker. You guys ready?"

Dr. Nolan nodded to his staff. There would be time to go over the details of his absence later. Any impending tests or referrals would require attention and close follow-up, but he had full confidence that Cat would function as his surrogate. She was that good.

The sun was still hovering above the hills to the west as they drove toward Mike's and Eileen's home.

"Eileen doesn't know about this yet," Dr. Nolan said. "I thought it would be safer to bring it up during dinner."

"But, it's so cool," Aubriel repeated.

"She might find it chilling," their father explained. He pulled into their driveway and parked behind Uncle Mike's truck. Before Dr. Nolan had turned off the engine, Aubriel was already out the door, running toward the house, joyfully yelling the news.

"Dad wants you to be a detective again! Just like before!"

3

Eileen and Mike were seated at the kitchen table when Dr. Nolan and Cienna entered the room. Aubriel was sitting next to her aunt, still smiling. Eileen was not smiling. She looked up, crossed her arms, then regarded Dr. Nolan for a long moment.

"Sherrie Masters called about an hour ago to remind me I need my passport at the airport," she informed him. "Seems I'm going on a two week trip. And, now I hear we're off to solve some big mystery. What else don't I know about?"

Dr. Nolan felt his cheeks burning. He sat down across from her. He looked to Uncle Mike for support, but the other man just stared down at the table.

"Forty seven people are dead in California from an outbreak of Legionnaires' disease. The CDC asked me to come down and try to help," Dr. Nolan said, trying to keep the words steady. "I knew I couldn't do it alone, so I was hoping—"

"Yes," Eileen answered, cutting him off in midsentence. "You told me on the phone you wanted a simple yes or no. It's yes."

Aubriel clapped her hands.

"This is like a TV show. You guys could make a movie," she exclaimed.

"I'm not moving to Hollywood," Mike announced. "Not a good place for farming. I'll loan her out for two weeks, but then you've got to bring her back."

Eileen finally unfolded her arms, granting Dr. Nolan a reprieve. She interlaced the fingers of both hands and leaned toward him.

"All you had to do was ask." She smiled. "I've been blessed my whole life. Where I live. The family I have. My children. If I can be of any use helping someone else, it's the least I can do."

Dr. Nolan nodded with a boyish grin on his face.

"I just couldn't do it over the phone," he admitted. "It's a pretty bizarre request, and I was afraid either you or Mike would object. If your answer was no, it would have ended the discussion. I need your computer skills and your talent for finding clues."

Eileen looked at Mike and raised her brows, her eyes asking the question.

"I don't know," Mike said, shaking his head slightly as he spoke. "I don't like the idea of your running off with my wife for two weeks to some tropical location. Who's going to feed me and darn my socks?"

"Chauvinist." Cienna laughed.

"And proud of it," Mike responded. "Two weeks on my own could be the end of me, and we've got harvest in a month. But, I s'pose I can get by."

Eileen put her right hand over his forearm and gave him a squeeze.

"What's darning a sock mean?" Aubriel asked.

"Means you're too cheap to buy new ones," her father explained. "Uncle Mike wears his until they walk away to escape further torture."

"That's no joke," Eileen added. "I've had to burn some in the fireplace before. Dead animals don't smell that bad."

Cienna and Aubriel were laughing.

"Those are working man's socks," Mike protested. "They don't just give those away! You've got to earn them! Why is everyone picking on me all of a sudden?"

"Because it's fun," Cienna explained.

Mike tried to look injured, but his eyes were sparkling.

"You really burned up some of my socks?" he asked Eileen, feigning disbelief.

"It was that or give up breathing," she said. "But, I think we can afford new ones."

"I'm just a poor farmer," he lamented. "We can't be wasting money on frivolous store-bought dry goods."

"Then maybe you should sell that new John Deere tractor that cost the same as our house," Dr. Nolan suggested. "You know, the one with air-conditioning and surround sound stereo."

"That's blasphemy!" Mike shouted. "That's an essential piece of farm equipment. You can borrow my wife, but don't you even think about my tractor."

Eileen patted his hand, offering assurance.

"Your tractor's safe, dear." She smiled. "You sure you're okay about this trip?"

Mike looked at her and nodded.

"Like you said before, we owe a lot of thanks. This sounds like a good thing."

Eileen stood up and kissed his forehead.

"Good answer," she said. "Now, you two girls help set the table and stop laughing at your poor, mistreated uncle."

Over dinner they kept their conversation to family and local topics. When they had finished, Dr. Nolan's daughters left to do kitchen duty, and the three adults wandered out to the back.

"So, Saturday morning, eh?" Mike said.

"Early," Dr. Nolan answered. "Most of the day will be wasted just getting there."

Eileen was looking up at Orion's Belt.

"You have any ideas on how to do this, Sean?"

Dr. Nolan smiled.

"Just beginning to think things through," he said. "The CDC is the best. I've got to approach this in a different way. We don't have a big team of field operatives to work with, so we have to narrow the scope. I'm just not sure how yet."

"But, this is safe, right?" Mike asked.

"It's safe," Dr. Nolan told him. "That's the other strange part of this. No new cases for nearly two weeks. Either the source died out on its own or somehow got cleaned up. I think that's what bothers them the most. No answer."

"Well, you did pretty good looking for poison," Mike said. "Now it's just smaller."

Dr. Nolan nodded.

"A lot smaller," he said.

4

It was just past 8:00 a.m. when Dr. Nolan dialed the cell number for Arthur Campbell.

"What took you so long?" He laughed, knowing from caller ID it was Dr. Nolan.

"Had to sleep on it and work out some details on this end. But, I'd be happy to take a second look if they still want me."

"Figured you would," Mr. Campbell said. "In fact, I just won a fifty dollar bet with Dr. Pulliam. Told him yesterday afternoon you'd be willing to do it."

"Do I get half?" Dr. Nolan asked, joking.

"Then I doubled down," Mr. Campbell said. "I've got a hundred on the second wager."

"And what's that about?" Dr. Nolan asked.

Arthur Campbell did not answer right away.

"I'll tell you when this is done," he said at last. "The suspense will keep you on your toes."

"There's already enough suspense. How do we work this? I've got a dozen questions," Dr. Nolan said.

"Not my area. I'll give you Dr. Pulliam's private number," Mr. Campbell explained. "He was already setting things in motion."

"You were pretty sure of yourself, it sounds like," Dr. Nolan said.

"No. Not at all, Sean," Mr. Campbell answered. "I was sure of you. There's a big difference."

Dr. Nolan smiled at the answer. He copied down the phone number for Dr. Pulliam in Atlanta.

"Okay, Arthur. I'll call you when I get back and find out about the bet," he said. "Is this gambling addiction a new problem, or a lifetime habit?"

Arthur Campbell laughed again.

"With you involved, I don't see this as gambling," he explained. "This is like taking candy from a baby."

He was still laughing when he hung up. Dr. Nolan was intrigued by the show of humor, but lost in the one sided reasoning. He shrugged it off and dialed the Center for Disease Control, surprised when no receptionist ran interference.

"Dr. Pulliam," the voice answered.

"Oh, hello. Sean Nolan calling. I was given your number by Arthur Campbell at EPA."

"Good. Good of you to help," Dr. Pulliam said. "This is outside protocol, but I can't keep people in the Imperial Valley any longer. Too many other hot spots. Arthur was raving about you as a natural-born investigator. Gave me a run-down on what you did last year with almost no staff."

"Thank you," Dr. Nolan said. "But I had help. It was a team effort."

"Well, it was one nice job. You up for another challenge?"

"I am," Dr. Nolan answered. "But you know epidemiology isn't my specialty."

"I know your training, and Arthur says you're like a racehorse with blinders. You focus on the finish line, and you don't let anything distract you. He also said you tend to run over things that get in your way."

"Are you okay with that?" Dr. Nolan asked. "A more charitable observer might say I exhibit extraordinary enthusiasm at times."

Dr. Pulliam laughed.

"I can accept that," he said, "as long as you stay within the legal confines of the agency rules. You will be credentialed through us. You have the right to search and test any reasonable suspect locations. But if someone refuses, you have to get assistance from the local authorities. No John Wayne heroics."

Dr. Nolan thought back to the long search to locate and identify the toxic dump site. He could only recall about a half dozen felonies and misdemeanors.

"I always try to follow the law," he said truthfully. It just didn't always fit the situation.

"Good," Dr. Pulliam said. "This is a federal branch, but we've already done a security clearance on you. Anyone you want with you?"

"My sister-in-law. Eileen Carson. She helped me with research and computer work here in Woodhaven."

"You have a date of birth, address, phone number?" Dr. Pulliam asked. He took down the information. "You book a flight?"

"Saturday morning," Dr. Nolan said. "The connecting leg gets us to Imperial Airport at two fifty in the afternoon."

"Okay. I'll have one person stay and meet you when you land," Dr. Pulliam said. "They'll have a copy of everything that's been done, all the victim data, test sites, everything. The hospital lab in El Centro has been trained to do rapid Legionnaires' testing, but there's been nothing for two weeks now. If you get samples, they can run them in less than an hour."

Dr. Nolan was taking notes.

"Official paperwork?" he mumbled.

"Right. We'll have ID cards for you and, uh, Eileen Carson. Time's short, but we need a quick background check on her as well."

"She's never even had a traffic ticket," Dr. Nolan said.

"Just procedure," Dr. Pulliam explained. "There will be a health department contact number, too, but they're in San Diego. And busy. You heard about the Zika and dengue cases?"

"A few days ago," Dr. Nolan said. "Doesn't sound good."

Dr. Pulliam half snorted in disgust.

"Damn oversight committee won't admit climate change is a real threat, and the fucking mosquitoes are moving up from South America loaded with diseases we're not ready for. It's already happening right in front of them, and they keep ignoring the problem."

"Your hair gray?" Dr. Nolan asked.

"And thinning," Dr. Pulliam answered. "At some point, I'll just start pulling it out. Now what else?"

"Money," Dr. Nolan said. "How do you want to handle this?"

"This happened so quickly, we haven't had time to cover everything. Can you just keep receipts and submit it all when you're done? Anything within reason. These checks won't be coming through payroll, if you get my drift?"

"I do, and I will," Dr. Nolan said. "Oh, a map. Since we're showing up on a weekend, can your people get me a big map of the area?"

"How big?"

"Four to six feet. I've got to see the problem area to understand it."

"Okay. Big map. Last chance, Dr. Nolan. Any final wishes?"

Dr. Nolan read over the pages of notes covering his desk.

"Only one," he said. "Arthur told me he had a bet going with you, but he wouldn't elaborate. Any hints you can offer?"

Dr. Pulliam laughed.

"I already lost one wager," he explained. "I didn't think you'd drop everything and volunteer for this assignment. So, then Art needles me into another bet. Well, actually a two-part bet. If I lose this, I just sign over my paycheck."

"And you're not going to tell me either, right?"

Dr. Pulliam thought for a moment, his tone serious again when he answered.

"Let's just say that if he wins, I'll pay up with a big smile on my face."

"No wonder you guys are friends," Dr. Nolan said. "You're both dickheads."

"In two days, I'll be your boss." Dr. Pulliam laughed. "Then you have to call me Mr. Dickhead."

"That I can promise," Dr. Nolan said. "And thanks for all the information. Should be interesting."

"That we both agree on," Dr. Pulliam said. "Good luck."

Dr. Nolan hung up the phone. He gathered up all his paperwork and placed it in a manila envelope. The first patients were already in exam rooms, and the morning passed in what seemed like minutes. Before going home at lunch, another thought entered his mind. He asked Amanda to track down Sheriff Dent. Line two was blinking on his desk phone before he had finished his last chart entry.

"Robert, how's the cop business?"

"Peaceful. Just like it's supposed to be," the sheriff answered. "You staying out of trouble.?"

"Yeah, but just on a temporary basis," Dr. Nolan said. He gave an overview of what had happened in the Imperial Valley and his contact with the CDC.

"These guys must be desperate to bring you in." Sheriff Dent laughed. "They know how you operate?"

"That's insulting, Bob. I'm a highly trained professional," Dr. Nolan reminded him.

"You're a train wreck," the sheriff countered. "You said Eileen was going with you?"

"I need her to keep things organized," Dr. Nolan admitted.

"You need a babysitter is more like it. At least she'll keep you reined in," Sheriff Dent said. "Why you bothering me?"

Dr. Nolan stretched out the phone cord and kicked his door closed.

"You know anybody down in that area, Bob? Someone you trust. We're going to be strangers in a strange land."

Sheriff Dent had passed through the southwestern desert region a few years ago, travelling all along the border as far as Yuma during a conference on immigration and drug trafficking.

"I don't know any local or state officers down that way, but I do have an old friend in Border Patrol. We did our military service at the same time. He's rock-solid. You want me to make a call?"

"If you would," Dr. Nolan said. "I'd feel better knowing we had a contact person in the vicinity. Just in case."

"Okay. I'll get back to you tomorrow," the sheriff said. "Two weeks, right?"

"Give or take," Dr. Nolan said. "Why?"

"Just imagining how nice and quiet things will be without you around," the sheriff said, still piqued over the media referrals Dr. Nolan had directed his way after the waste site discovery.

"It hurts me deeply to hear you say that, Bob. Won't you miss me? Just a little?"

"I'll suffer through it," the sheriff said, but he was smiling. "You ever been down that far south before?"

"No. San Diego once," Dr. Nolan said.

Sheriff Dent leaned back in his chair and propped his feet on the desk.

"There's an old joke about hot places," the sheriff told him. "It goes, 'It may not be hell, but you can see it from there.' That's where you're headed."

"That bad?"

"That bad," the sheriff assured him. "Have a nice trip."

Dr. Nolan hung up, went to the door, and looked over at Cat.

"Can you look on your computer and see what the temperature is in Imperial, California?"

She nodded, typed in the request, then grimaced.

"One hundred and two degrees," she said.

Dr. Nolan leaned his forehead against the doorframe and closed his eyes.

"Fuck," he said.

5

Friday was a hornet's nest of past, present, and future. Dr. Nolan struggled to balance his current patient load with any unfinished business, all while trying to schedule new tests two to three weeks ahead. He tried to fashion a work calendar for his replacement, but his thoughts raced through a kaleidoscopic landscape at a pace he could not control.

At five thirty, he asked his daughters for privacy and brought his staff into the office, closing the door behind them.

"Well, that's a wrap." He sighed. "The new doctor, Kendra Henderson, will be in Portland by later tonight. She'll take call starting about midnight, so, Amanda, you need to update the voice message on the phone. You also need to keep her clinic load to three people an hour until you see how she handles things."

Amanda nodded. She wrote down Dr. Henderson's cell number and gave copies to Cat and Evie.

"And emergencies?" Amanda asked. "There's no way she can tackle what you let in the door."

Dr. Nolan smiled at the veiled compliment.

"Roll with the punches," he suggested. "If she seems the least bit uncomfortable, direct those patients to the hospital. Don't scare her to death on the first day."

"And, last resort, you'll be available?" Cat asked.

"Twenty-four seven," Dr. Nolan answered. "And let's dispense with any false impression. Cat, you're in charge. Not the doctor. You run the clinic and guide her along. There's nothing you haven't seen or done in all these years. Just hold her hand and try not to let her kill anybody while I'm gone."

They all laughed nervously, but it was not really a joke. An experienced, well-trained nurse was a priceless commodity. Cat had kept him out of trouble on numerous occasions.

"We'll be fine," Cat said. "And your daughters will be fine. We've got everything covered on this end. We're more worried about setting you loose on the outside world."

"Eileen will be there to manage any chaos," Dr. Nolan said. "I wouldn't even attempt this without her along."

"Good luck," Cat said. "We don't understand what you're taking on, but we get the why. You have a plan?"

Dr. Nolan stood up. He wanted to hug each of them, but settled on a handshake.

"Only pieces so far," he admitted. "I'm hoping for divine inspiration. Thank you for making this possible."

They filed out, each with their own assigned duties to prepare for the next week. Dr. Nolan put his stethoscope around his neck, picked up the *Harrisons Internal Medicine* textbook, gathered his daughters, then left by the back door without saying goodbye. It was only going to be a two week absence, but he had to fight back a tear as he locked the door.

It was a mile down the road before he could breathe normally again.

"What's dinner?" Aubriel asked, hoping for takeout.

"Ham in the oven," he said. "Macaroni and cheese with Caesar salad after I take care of the animals."

"Whoa," Cienna said, "what's the occasion?"

"Last supper," their father joked. "And, this will give you leftovers. Kellie is coming over about nine."

Cienna and Aubriel fell silent the rest of the way home. They were proud of what he was doing, excited to have Kellie stay with them, but each feeling uneasy about him leaving. He was the one constant in their universe.

"I'll go with you," Cienna said as he got ready for barn chores. "I need a refresher course."

He counted out the six Fig Newtons and handed her the plastic bag.

"Most important thing to remember." He smiled. "This is the highlight of their day."

They went out, stopping to scrub and refill the water trough, then headed for the barn. Cienna watched as he fed the donkeys and goats, cleaned the floor, then sat to pet them, talking nonstop about everything and anything as he rubbed their chests and necks.

"Now I know why you smell so bad when you get back to the house," she said.

Dr. Nolan just smiled.

"Okay, your turn," he said. "Come sit here and hand out their treats."

Cienna took his place, the animals mobbing her when they saw the bag of cookies appear in her hand. One of the goats was trying to crawl up on her lap.

"I think they like me." Cienna laughed, trying to keep her balance.

"If you forget the Fig Newtons, they'll turn on you with a vengeance," he warned her. He sat down next to her, one of the donkeys laying its head across his knee.

"You've had these guys since before I was born, huh?" Cienna asked.

"Almost twenty years," her father said. "I should have just stuck to miniature donkeys. They're cheaper and don't talk back."

She pushed against him with her shoulder.

"Very funny, Daddy dear." She laughed. "And Mom loved these guys, too?"

"Oh, man, did she," he answered. "She'd come out and brush them, take them for walks with her. Just didn't like them in the house. These were her babies, too."

They sat in silence for a time, the last sunlight fading through the open doorway.

"I look through the box of pictures you keep in the desk upstairs sometimes," Cienna confessed. "Helps me remember."

"Me, too," her father said. "Just remember to put them back where they belong when you're done. That's the memory drawer."

Cienna leaned her head against his shoulder.

"You still keep her picture on your nightstand. When does that go in the memory drawer?"

It was a fascinating question that momentarily stunned him. His young adult daughter was delineating the past from the present, separating now from a painful history. He was struck by the authentic maturity of her statement, and he could not design a coherent answer.

"Someday," he said, almost in a whisper. "When did you become so philosophical?"

"I'm growing up, you know," she said. "You worry about us, and we worry about you. That's all."

"Man, are you ever," Dr. Nolan said. "And, that reminds me. I don't want you to feel bad about Kellie staying here. If you were one year older, able to drive, I would have left you in charge. It just wasn't the right time yet."

"No. I get it," Cienna assured him. "But next time…"

"There is no next time," Dr. Nolan said. "I'm never leaving again. Honest to God."

Cienna jumped up, laughing, and ran to the gate.

"We'll see about that," she said. "Now let's go eat. You've got packing to do."

He followed her outside, slowly walking back to the house with his arm around her shoulder.

"And, don't forget Callie," he reminded her.

"Dad, I've got it covered. Quit worrying." She giggled.

"Okay. Okay," he lamented.

"Jeez! What took so long?" Aubriel whined.

"I had to show your sister how to milk the cow," her father explained.

"We don't have a cow," Aubriel said.

"That's why it took so long," he answered, washing his hands at the sink.

Cienna laughed.

"You're both whacky," Aubriel said. "And I'm starving."

"Twenty minutes," her father said. "You put a pot of water on to boil, and I'll go change."

Aubriel acted the part of a mistreated child, but did as requested. The water was just beginning to percolate when he returned to the kitchen.

"Blue box macaroni?" Aubriel asked.

"Is there any other kind?" her father responded. He finished the salad, had them set the table, sliced the ham, then sat together as a family. They avoided any reference to his upcoming trip, either by design or desire. It was enough just to share time together.

They were just finishing the dishes when Callie started barking, followed by a knock on the door. Cienna and Aubriel raced each other to the foyer, shrieking with excitement. Kellie Morgan had arrived early, a suitcase in one hand, and a backpack in the other filled with CDs and videos.

"Wow. Hi. I've got every season of *Game of Thrones*," she announced. "What do you guys want to do first?"

"Music first," Aubriel voted. "Do you have any Sam Smith, Sia, Billie Eilish?"

To Dr. Nolan, it was all a foreign language. With his daughters busy combing through music options, he waved Kellie into the kitchen.

"Man, you're all grown up." He smiled. "Thanks for stepping in here. There's three hundred dollars in the envelope in the kitchen window for food and whatever comes up. The girls have my cell number for any problems. You have any questions or worries?"

"None at all," the girl said. "This will be fun. Like a two week slumber party."

"I hope you're right," Dr. Nolan said. "I'll be checking in every day, but I trust you to keep them safe."

Cienna and Aubriel were shouting for her from the living room.

"Okay to make popcorn?" Kellie smiled.

"Help yourself. I tried to stock up on essential snack items." Dr. Nolan laughed. "Whatever I forgot will fall to you."

"Cool. No worries," Kellie said. "You're leaving early, I hear."

"Around four. You can either share a bed with one of the girls or fold out the couch. Whatever works."

Kellie had Cienna help her find the popcorn and set the microwave, then they all migrated back to the great room. Dr. Nolan felt like he had already left. He readied the coffee maker for the morning, took Callie out for a walk, remembered to retrieve the Garmin from his car, then went to the stairway.

"I could use a hug," he informed his daughters. They ran over, gave him a quick squeeze, then returned to more pressing business. His going-away party was over.

Half smiling, he went up to his room, pulled a dusty suitcase from the rear of the closet, wiped it off with a washcloth, then tossed it on the bed. This was not an expedition that required formal attire. He found two pairs of Levi's in a drawer, one with the tags still fixed in place, and a pair of comfortable chinos. Along with underwear and socks, he managed to locate three T-shirts that were stain free and without holes. He placed his running shoes in between his medical books and the Garmin, then threw in a Tiger Woods golf cap for good measure. He would travel in slacks and a dress shirt, but anything else needed would have to be purchased.

He moved the bag onto the floor and set the alarm for 3:00 a.m. He would get four hours of sleep if he was lucky. Peeling off his sweats, he crawled into bed, the music downstairs loud enough to send bass vibrations through the walls. On any other evening, it would have been an unbearable annoyance. On this night it was soothing, a reassurance.

Dr. Nolan patted the bed next to him with his left hand. Callie was not allowed on the furniture, and she looked at him with her head tilted to one side. When he beckoned a second time, she tentatively reached up with one front paw, then the other, finally jumping up and lying next to him, a wide grin showing. He stroked her head over and over again.

"I know you were listening tonight," he told her. "Kellie thinks she's in charge, and Cienna thinks she's in control. I didn't want to hurt their feelings, but I'm actually leaving you in charge. It's up to you to keep an eye on everything. I know it's asking a lot, but I believe your wisdom and judgment are unequalled. What do you say?"

Callie nodded, then rested her muzzle on his chest. Dr. Nolan fell asleep with his hand draped across her neck. He awoke in the same position when the alarm sounded, the room pitch-black and strangely foreign. It took only a minute to refocus, and he made no attempt to hit the snooze button. He showered and shaved, dressed, finished packing his personal items, then quietly made his way down the stairs. Callie had given him a brief raise of her head, but quickly fell back to sleep. His two daughters and Kellie were huddled on the sleeper sofa together sharing an oversize comforter. They did not stir or notice his passing.

Dr. Nolan stood at the kitchen window, his eyes staring into the darkness, his vision fixed on something far away. He finished two cups of coffee, took one last look at his girls, then left the house without making a sound. The drive to Mike's and Eileen's seemed odd at such an early hour, and he only passed one other car on the road, a peaceful contrast to his usual commute.

When he pulled into the Carson farm, it seemed that every light in the house was in full blaze. Mike met him in the driveway, grabbed his suitcase, and tossed it in the back of his Jeep Cherokee.

"You awake, Doc?" Mike asked, smiling broadly.

"Partially," Dr. Nolan answered. "How can you be so cheerful in the middle of the night?"

"Hell, I'm usually out in the fields before this," Mike said. "This is late."

Eileen came down the steps with her own suitcase. Mike took it from her and placed it in the car, then opened the rear passenger door.

"You got everything? Ticket? Passport? Phone? Purse?"

"Double-checked," Eileen answered. "Even remembered the charger for the computer. If I forgot anything it's too bad now."

Mike had insisted on driving them to the airport. He was animated and nervous, keeping up a monologue all the way down to the curb at the departure area of the terminal. Eileen and Dr. Nolan barely said a word.

"Made good time," Mike announced. He sprang out of the car and carried their luggage to the outside check-in counter. Dr. Nolan unzipped his bag and pulled out his hat.

"Thanks, Mike," he said. "And thank you for letting me have my research assistant."

"It's all good. All good," Mike said. He hugged Eileen, then held her face gently between his hands and kissed her goodbye. He tried to say something to her, but suddenly he was crying. Turning away quickly, he almost jogged back to the car, pulling out into traffic without looking back.

"Big, tough farmer." Eileen smiled. "I knew he would do that."

"I think it's nice," Dr. Nolan said. "You ready?"

"I don't know what for," Eileen said, "but I guess this is how it starts."

The air terminal was eerily quiet at such an early hour. Even the TSA check-point was nearly deserted. They grabbed coffee at the Starbucks kiosk and found their assigned gate with thirty minutes to spare. Boarding on time, at least a third of the seats were unoccupied. Dr. Nolan settled in next to the window, put on his hat, pulled it down over his face, and leaned against the cabin wall.

"You nervous?" Eileen asked.

"No."

She thought for a moment, retightening her seat belt.

"You figure out how you want to go at this?" she asked.

Dr. Nolan reached up and lifted the bill of his cap just far enough to make eye contact. He was smiling at her.

"You ever watch the old Jack Benny show?" he asked.

"I remember it," she answered.

"The character he played was a penny-pinching miser. In one skit, a robber jumps out of an alley, points a gun at him, and says, 'Your money or your life!' Jack just stares at him. So the robber says it again, only louder, 'Your money or your life!'"

"So?"

"So, Jack just stares at him, then finally shouts, 'I'm thinking!'"

Dr. Nolan pulled his cap down again and sighed.

Eileen nodded, a smile on her face. She folded her hands in her lap, going back over the retold story.

"I get the joke," she said, "but how does that help you pick a starting point?"

The plane began to move backward, the whine of the engines suddenly louder.

Dr. Nolan did not answer. He was sound asleep.

6

They arrived in San Diego well before noon. Dining in one of the more upscale restaurants in the main terminal made the hour-and-a-half wait for their connecting flight pass quickly. Dr. Nolan even managed to track down a tourist guidebook detailing local facts and visitor destinations in and around the Imperial Valley. He read through it as they ate, making star notations in the margin space marking items of interest.

"The town of Imperial is over five hundred feet below sea level," he informed Eileen, handing her the book. "Not a good place to hide out during the next great flood."

"I read an article about the Dead Sea once," Eileen said. "At a mile below sea level, you can't dive down in the water. You just pop up like a cork."

Dr. Nolan laughed, envisioning pale-skinned travelers bouncing around like fishing bobbers.

"Probably reduces the risk of accidental drowning, though. There's always a bright side," he added.

"What's ours?" she asked. "This seems a lot bigger problem than Woodhaven was. And, we don't have all my relatives to lend a hand."

Dr. Nolan looked at her and nodded.

"This isn't big," he said. "It's monumental. Somehow, we've got to turn it into a small, manageable model we can work with. You ready?"

The second leg of their journey was much shorter. The smaller commuter plane took off exactly on time, gained altitude, then banked east and away from the ocean. In the span of minutes, the green valleys and foothills transitioned to jagged brown mountains, the vegetation dead or dying. The mosaic of swirling rock and wandering canyons stretched for miles, then the plane throttled back and nosed downward, the last peaks vanishing.

In their place, where there should have been only desert, a vast flat checkerboard of green fields unveiled themselves, reaching as far toward the horizon as vision allowed. Access roads and variations in crops were the only division markings in the living quilt of the valley, a tapestry of agriculture magically conjured from barren earth by the sorcery of irrigation. It was the final gift of the Colorado River before it vanished back into the soil.

Bouncing through turbulent air from heat fueled updrafts, the plane banked twice more, leveled out, then touched down smoothly at the Imperial Airport. The terminal was much larger than Dr. Nolan expected, then he remembered it was the county seat, and only four miles from the much larger city of El Centro. It was a pleasant surprise, and somehow comforting.

Exiting the landing ramp into the air-conditioned concourse, a young man was waiting, a handwritten cardboard placard held up with the initials "CDC" written in black felt pen.

"You must be the welcoming committee?" Dr. Nolan smiled, shaking hands. He introduced Eileen.

"I'm the last of the original ten people sent out here," he said. "I'm Dr. Freiberg. Nice to meet you both. And, thanks for stepping in. This has been a frustrating situation, to say the least. We were pretty much out of ideas anyway. Then all the resources got pulled out from under us."

"Yeah. Zika and dengue. I heard from Dr. Pulliam yesterday," Dr. Nolan explained. "Sounds like a nightmare."

"The beginning of one," Dr. Freiberg agreed. "Let's find somewhere to sit. I've only got half an hour to catch my flight out."

He carried a large suitcase in each hand as they followed him to the open food court area. Choosing a table in the far corner, he lifted one of the bags up and flipped the latches. Removing folders, some red, and a larger number bound in yellow, he constructed two towers of paperwork.

They sat down, Eileen and Dr. Nolan on one side of the table and the younger man across from them, only his face visible above the wall of patient information.

"Oh, I almost forgot," Dr. Freiberg said, reaching into the hidden compartment of the suitcase. From an envelope, he retrieved their official identification cards, complete with hazy photographs that had been relayed from the Department of Motor Vehicles.

"I look this bad?" Dr. Nolan asked Eileen.

"Usually worse," she said. "Don't be vain. This young man is short on time."

"Okay, so, quick overview." Dr. Nolan smiled, placing the card in his wallet.

Dr. Freiberg looked to both sides to make certain no one was too near. He placed his hand on the red charts in front of them.

"Forty seven terminal outcomes in less than three weeks. Children, teenagers, young adults, middle age, elderly. No pattern. Locals and tourists. No pattern. No common thread. We tested every drinking fountain, drainage ditch, water tank, air conditioner, faucet, mud puddle, and dog dish in a forty mile radius. And all we came up with was a thousand or so negatives."

Dr. Nolan could see how tired the young physician was, and he was certain they had been diligent in their search.

"That's a big head start for us," Dr. Nolan told him. "We won't be wasting time duplicating your investigation. And no new cases, right?"

Dr. Freiberg nodded.

"Thirteen days and counting," he said. "It just vanished."

Dr. Nolan pointed to the taller stack of yellow charts.

"I take it these are confirmed cases that recovered?"

"Correct. One hundred and seventeen that we can verify. Dr. Pulliam explain about any testing you need done?"

"Hopefully none," Dr. Nolan said. "But, he told me to use El Centro Memorial. They can get results in an hour. How many ERs and urgency care centers in this area?"

Dr. Freiberg took a moment to do the math.

"Two major hospitals, four community hospitals, and about a dozen urgent care centers," he said. "But, every suspected Legionnaires' case is immediately referred to Memorial. That's still in effect."

Dr. Nolan listened, scribbling down notes on a napkin.

"Good. Good. We'll stop by there later and check in. Anything else?"

Dr. Freiberg looked at them both.

"I wish I had more answers for you." He sighed. "A lot of hours went into this. Ten people working twelve to fourteen hours a day with no break. All for nothing."

"On the contrary," Dr. Nolan corrected him. "You've eliminated the majority of exposure sites, and you've narrowed down the playing field to two teams. Dead people and lucky people."

Dr. Freiberg gave him a painful smile.

"Sad, but true," he said.

"How long have you been doing this?" Dr. Nolan asked.

"Almost three years," the younger man said.

"You like it?"

Dr. Freiberg reacted with a genuine smile.

"Excuse my French, but I fucking love it," he said. "I can't even imagine private practice in a hospital setting. I get to travel, solve mysteries, and sometimes help save lives. What could be better?"

"Probably a bigger salary," Dr. Nolan joked. "You and I are both on the lower end of the professional income average, and I love it, too. I'll let Dr. Pulliam know you all deserve a pay raise."

"Not likely, but thanks for the thought," Dr. Freiberg said. He glanced at his watch. "Shit. I've got to run." He shook their hands again.

"You want this suitcase?" Dr. Nolan asked.

"Nope. It's all yours," Dr. Freiberg said. "When you're done, leave everything with Infectious Disease at Memorial. They'll get it back to us."

"Good luck," Dr. Nolan said. "And thanks for the briefing."

Dr. Freiberg picked up the other suitcase, began to walk away, then stopped and turned.

"Pulliam told me what you did back home. Pretty cool," he said.

"Even a blind dog finds a bone sometimes." Dr. Nolan smiled.

"Let's hope you find another one. Happy hunting." Dr. Freiberg disappeared down the corridor.

Eileen had been mostly silent as the two physicians spoke. She was staring at the neatly stacked column of red charts.

"These were all people," she said.

"They were indeed," Dr. Nolan answered.

"What a terrible waste." She sighed.

Dr. Nolan began filling the suitcase again.

"They're here now to help us figure out what happened. They're our witnesses. We need to listen to what they tell us. That's what you concentrate on. Okay?"

He had to remind himself that dealing with life and death on an intimate level was not a part of her daily routine. This was foreign, and ugly, and not easily suffered. There were children hidden in those files, and she felt it with a mother's heart.

"I just need to get busy," she said.

"Okay. Let's get busy then." Dr. Nolan smiled.

They went to baggage claim, picked up their luggage, then dragged everything to the car rental desk. All the arrangements had been made through the travel agency.

"All in order," the clerk said. "Just need a driver's license and credit card. Nissan Rogue suitable for your needs?"

"As long as it has air-conditioning, it will be perfect," Dr. Nolan said. He signed the rental agreement and was given the keys.

"Lot's just across the street to the right." The attendant smiled. "Number nine. Enjoy your stay."

They gathered their bags, then Dr. Nolan set his down. He went back to the counter.

"Do you have road maps?"

The clerk smiled, reached under the counter, and handed him a Triple A map neatly folded.

"Can I have a few more?" Dr. Nolan asked.

The man blinked and nodded.

"A few? One? Two?"

"I think about twelve," Dr. Nolan said. "That will be a good start."

"Twelve maps?" the man repeated.

"Correct. One dozen. Nice even number," Dr. Nolan told him.

The man slowly leaned down, brought up the entire box of maps and counted out twelve.

"Will that do it?" he asked.

Dr. Nolan shook his head, putting three or four of the maps in each pocket.

"For now. Thank you kindly." He rejoined Eileen.

"What was that about?" she asked.

"Step one of a long journey." He smiled.

They went out through the main doors into the afternoon sun. The ambient temperature was 105 degrees, and standing in a sea of concrete and asphalt, nearer to 120 degrees.

"Holy shit," Dr. Nolan said. The air was actually moving. Physically palpable waves of heat rippled around them. Even the act of breathing becoming a deliberate effort. He could feel sweat trickling down his back.

"A little balmy," Eileen remarked.

They navigated the crosswalk, located their rental car, tossed all three bags in the rear compartment, then got in and put the air on high. Both of them were breathing heavily.

"And people work in this," Dr. Nolan said. "We need to stay well hydrated until we get used to this."

"I don't want to get used to this," she answered. "Can I change my mind and go home?"

"Not a chance. Misery loves company." Dr. Nolan laughed. He put the car in reverse and backed out of the parking space. "We can't check into the hotel until five. Let's take a road trip." He collected all the maps from his pockets and handed them to Eileen.

"Where to?" she asked.

"South to El Centro first," he said. "We need to find a Walmart or Target. I live to shop, you know."

"As long as they have air," Eileen said. "What are we buying?"

Dr. Nolan had seen the supersized map of the area on the bottom of the suitcase holding the charts provided by the CDC.

"Same as Woodhaven," he explained. "We're going to collect puzzle pieces and build a picture. You have a pen?"

"Always," Eileen said.

"Okay. Twenty legal pads. Rolls of yarn, all different colors. Gel pens, also multiple colors. Rolls of tape. And tacks. Lots of tacks."

Eileen was making a list.

"Okay, what else?" They had arrived at the main highway. Dr. Nolan turned right, quickly reaching the town of Imperial. It was double the size of Woodhaven. Not a large city, but not small either.

"You need a hat," he told Eileen, "or you'll burn your face off. Sunblock. Those shirts that keep you cooler. What are those called?"

"Dri-Fit," Eileen offered, starting to laugh.

"Anything else?"

"Those cups that keep liquids cold. And water! Lots of water." He paused to take a breath. They passed City Hall and the courthouse, then he noticed a number of bail bondsmen and legal aid offices, most advertising help with immigration problems.

"This is quite a list," Eileen said. The car followed the highway again, gas stations and strip malls, more and more residential for a few miles, then back to commercial as they neared El Centro. It was a much larger metropolitan area, complete with tall buildings and a dense business center. On the southern border, he spotted a Target sign.

"Salvation," he sighed. He circled the parking lot three times, searching for a spot as close to the entrance as possible.

With her list in hand, Eileen headed off to track down the office supplies. Dr. Nolan took a second cart, loaded up a case of water, located the stay-cool cups, then picked three pastel shirts from the rack that guaranteed an improved level of comfort. He wondered if they made underwear out of the same material. The sunblock was positioned prominently near the checkout stands. He waited there for Eileen, paid with his credit card, then headed back to the car. It was an oven. Even the steering wheel was nearly unbearable to grasp.

Dr. Nolan headed south again, the city giving way to large areas of farmland on either side of the highway. They also began to pass more and more poorly kept homes, small and drab, yards cluttered with derelict trucks and old appliances. He was remembering the guidebook he had read in San Diego.

"Fastest growing area in the state, and the poorest," he told Eileen. "Forty eight percent agriculture. How much of the workforce is Hispanic, I wonder?"

"How many white people do you know that would want these jobs?" she asked.

They passed under Freeway 8, jogged east to 111, continued for about ten miles, then pulled to the shoulder. Dr. Nolan kept the air running. He unfolded one of the road maps and rotated it into position, looking in all directions. The valley basin seemed endless.

"I meant to ask you before. How's your Spanish?"

"Not very good," Eileen admitted. "What about you?"

Dr. Nolan laughed.

"I can ask a lot of questions about medical symptoms, but if I get more than a yes or no response, I just smile. If we have a lot of cases with Hispanic patients, we're going to need a translator."

He was trying to get some sense of the geography. The Mexican border was less than an hour south. Yuma was southeast. The Coyote Mountains and Ocotillo were due west. But everything in the distance was just a glaring white blur. There was nothing to use as a measuring tool.

"Okay. That's enough for now," he said, giving her the map. "Time to shower, eat, and start working." He completed a U-turn and headed back north toward Imperial.

"Tonight?" Eileen said.

"No time to waste," Dr. Nolan quipped. "How many of the workers down here are illegal, any guess?"

"At harvest time, probably a lot," Eileen answered. "Even in Washington, when the berries are ripe and you need pickers, sometimes you don't look too close. It's the same everywhere."

"Don't you worry about getting fined?" Dr. Nolan asked.

"Not really. They've all got ID, and they're good people, willing to work. Sometimes the papers are good, and sometimes they're not. We try to be careful, but if the crops are going to die in the field…" She shrugged.

Dr. Nolan nodded. He had given medical care to hundreds of illegal workers over the years, never refusing anyone who needed his services. Often, they paid their bill in cash, and just as often they used forged papers and never paid him at all. It was not anything he ever lost sleep over.

"You're the farmer," Dr. Nolan said. "You know anything about this area? What they grow?"

"Mainly fruits and vegetables," she answered. "Not so much grain or grass seed. Grape vineyards and almonds are up north where it isn't so damn hot."

"Those are the smart crops," Dr. Nolan remarked. "But water is becoming a problem everywhere. I read an article about how deep they're drilling wells now. The costs are in the millions."

"Exactly right," Eileen said. "And, even that's a temporary fix. The big wine producers started buying up land in Oregon and Washington years ago. They know what's coming."

"I'm not nihilistic just yet," Dr. Nolan told her. "But, this is global. Food crops are losing protein and nutrient levels, and every year there are more people to feed. I follow the science, the proposed changes in agriculture, all of it. And nothing changes. We only seem motivated to move when the monster bites us in the ass."

"It worries me," Eileen agreed. "Sometimes so much, I just tune it out. Mike and I have talked about just quitting, letting it go. But, it's in his blood. The land, the rhythm of it. He understands it."

Dr. Nolan nodded. He knew exactly what she meant. As much as he enjoyed complaining, the seven day a week cycle of farming was Mike's passion. It was a battle and partnership with nature that defined his value and purpose.

They made their way back through El Centro and Imperial, turning once again onto the entry road to the airport. The hotel was only a few blocks down. Now after six, the peak temperature had subsided to the low nineties. Their rooms were side by side on the third floor, facing directly into the setting sun. The mornings would be cooler, but it was a small consolation.

Dr. Nolan set the suitcase of files on the settee at the foot of the bed. The room was larger than normal, earning title as a suite by having two armchairs and a small desk. There was the standard television, a tiny refrigerator, and a coffee maker in the alcove outside the bathroom.

He went next door to Eileen's room.

"Shit, I've got to get coffee and cream," he said. "Why don't you take a nap for a while. This is the beginning of some long days. You think of anything else?"

Eileen sighed, already tired from travelling.

"Food later," she said. "I'll call Mike and let him know we're safe and sound, then stretch out for a while."

"Okay, I'll give you two hours," Dr. Nolan said. "Enjoy the air-conditioning."

He went down to the lobby, the night clerk cheerfully writing directions to the local Safeway and Starbucks. In half an hour, he was back with two pounds of medium roast Kenyan coffee, a quart of milk, and an assortment of half stale doughnuts from the bakery department. All of the essentials were accounted for.

He called home to check on his daughters, but could only leave a recorded message. He was glad they were out doing things, but not hearing their voices was a disappointment. It made the room lonelier and more confining.

After setting the coffee maker on a ten cup maximum, he stood near the entry door to survey their work space. There was only one wall that was not compromised by art work or windows. Inch by inch, he managed to turn the queen size bed sideways, leaving a foot of access to conduct business. Dumping the files out on the bed, he took out the large area map supplied by the CDC, fixing it to the plaster with multiple strips of tape. The names of the towns and their physical relationship was just beginning to seem familiar.

The first cup of coffee in hand, he took all the red files and threw them back into the empty suitcase. He rummaged through the plastic shopping bag from Target, selected a blue felt pen, picked up one of the legal pads, scooted one of the armchairs close to the bed, sat down, selected a yellow file randomly, and began to read.

These were the survivors, the fortunate group that had escaped a critical illness. By simple luck, or will, or timely care, or a combination of all three, they had postponed death. But each folder was a unique story, a personal drama that documented their abrupt loss of health, the treatments that turned the enemy away, and their slow recovery. There were demographics, test results, lab data, admission histories, and daily care notes. And, between the written lines was the emotional narrative, the questions, the fear, the hope, the anguish of both patient and care-giver.

The second half of each file was a precise and detailed outline of the CDC inquiry. A complete medical profile was followed by symptom occurrence, progression of the illness, and the diagnostic evidence to support hospitalization. With the exposure to infection window two to seven days, every potential contamination site had been tracked down, tested, and tested again. It had been a meticulous, methodical, painstakingly professional investigation. Dr. Nolan nodded as he followed their pathway, his admiration growing. He could find no flaws or weak points in their action plan.

By the fourth cup of coffee, he had completed the review of eleven charts. Ten of them were now in the suitcase with their red counter-parts. One was sitting alone on the desk.

The soft knocking on the door startled him. He stood, stretched, then went to let Eileen into the room.

"I'm sorry I slept so long," she said, her eyes widening as she looked around. It was as if a bomb had exploded. Files were everywhere, the furniture was in disarray, and there were crumpled wads of legal paper littering the floor.

"That's okay." Dr. Nolan smiled. He shoved a cake doughnut in his mouth, refilled his coffee cup, and poured one for her.

"You realize it's 3:00 a.m.?" she asked.

Dr. Nolan checked his wristwatch.

"Jesus, so it is," he said. "I'm going to dock your pay for being late. Or early. Or something."

Eileen laughed, closing the door behind her.

"I didn't know I was getting paid," she said. Her gaze went to the map on the wall. A single sheet of yellow paper was pinned next to it. "Looks like you started without me. You want to fill me in?" She squeezed behind the bed to see what he had written in blue ink. There was a name, address, date of birth, and every location the person had visited the week before becoming ill.

Dr. Nolan placed the second chair near his, motioned for her to sit, then handed her a legal pad.

"We can't do this," he explained, sitting down and propping his feet on the mattress. "It's too much, and we don't have time to waste. We're looking for ground zero, the one point in the universe where this started. There's no person-to-person transmission. Every one of these people had to visit or pass by a single, shared location. The CDC couldn't find that one common denominator, but we have to."

"But, you just said we can't do it, that it's too big. What do we have, about 160 people?"

"I said we can't do that." Dr. Nolan smiled. "So, we make it smaller. First, we get rid of the dead people. They're hard to interview and often forgetful. There is no new information they can offer us, so that eliminates forty seven targets."

Eileen nodded.

"That's a fourth eliminated. What else?"

"We throw out tourists, and only concentrate on locals," Dr. Nolan explained. "The guidebook said tens of thousands of visitors come through this area every week. They're sightseeing, riding four-wheelers in the sand dunes, rock hounds. We don't have the manpower to be tracking them down all over the country. The thought also occurred to me that the illness ratio was lower in that group. Why?"

Eileen did not follow.

"You tell me." She shrugged.

"Because they bring supplies with them," he said. "They're camping out, not congregating in high traffic areas. Only about half the cases occurred in travelers. I've barely scratched the surface, but any patient not living in the Imperial Valley is out, back in the box."

"Okay. Now we might be down to half," Eileen noted. "Is that doable?"

Dr. Nolan shook his head.

"Still too many," he said. "Remember, all we have to do is find the one communal crossing point. The only way I can make this small enough for us is to limit our search to local males, over sixty years of age, who either smoke or have lung disease."

Eileen just blinked at him.

"Okay. I'm no doctor, but I'm totally lost now. How does that work?"

Dr. Nolan put his feet back on the floor and leaned toward her.

"Smokers get lung infections quicker than healthy people," he explained. "That means we shrink the exposure window to two to five days prior to their illness. Second, older men don't drive much. That's fewer target sites. We just need to go through these files, take out the ones that fit this profile, then interview them again, see if there's a common thread."

"That's what you've been doing?" she asked, nodding to the map.

"I've gone through eleven charts. Ten are out. One keeper. And, when you find a match, write down their contact information and stick it on the wall."

Dr. Nolan picked up one of the files on the bed and handed it to her.

"Okay. Men. Smokers. How old?" she asked.

"Sixty or older," Dr. Nolan decided. "I'll make more coffee."

Slowly but steadily, the mountain of charts melted away, most back in the suitcase, but a rare few making their way to the desk. With each matching pattern, a new sheet of paper was pinned on the wall near the map. When they had finished, thirteen patients had been identified that met Dr. Nolan's criteria.

He went to the window, a blinding flood of light assaulting them as he opened the heavy drapes. It was almost noon.

"Much more manageable." He sighed, looking at the printed names. "We've got one in Calipatria, two in Brawley, one in Westmorland, three in Imperial, four in El Centro, one on a farm near Holtville, and one in Calexico." He yawned and stretched his back.

"Wait a second," Eileen said. She was looking back through the discarded files. "I just had two other people sick on a farm near Holtville. Young women." She located the first one. "Dahlquist Farm. Hispanic worker. Twenty-four." She gave the chart to Dr. Nolan. He immediately scanned back to the CDC report. They had interviewed the woman twice. There was no travel history, and the farm was thoroughly tested, even the sprinklers out in the fields.

"Here's the other one," Eileen said. "Also a worker. Age eighteen."

Again Dr. Nolan examined the CDC report. The girl was living on the farm and had not been off the premises. After two days in the hospital, she had been released on oral medication.

"This is an outlier in the pattern," Dr. Nolan noted. "But the CDC saw that. With three clustered cases, they went over that place with a magnifying glass. Nothing. They even checked a second time."

He wrote the names of the two young women on the same piece of paper that marked the older male worker who had been treated. It made no sense.

"I'm too tired to think anymore," Dr. Nolan said. "You hungry?"

"Starving," Eileen answered.

"Give me ten minutes to shower and change," he said. Eileen went to her own room to freshen up, equally drained after nine hours of reading files.

Dr. Nolan took an extra five minutes to shave. Remembering the oppressive heat, he dressed in chinos and a pastel green pullover shirt from his Target shopping spree. The concierge gave them directions to a restaurant in downtown Imperial that served breakfast all day. It was only in the midnineties.

"I must be getting acclimated," Dr. Nolan said. "This is almost bearable."

"Good for you," Eileen said. "I'm sweating like a pig."

"It's probably all that coffee you drink." Dr. Nolan laughed. "Maybe you should cut back a little."

"As soon as you stop making me work all night," she said. "Aren't you tired?"

"Past it," he said. "But after I eat it'll be time for a nap. You should rest, too. But first, I need you to set up one or two visits with survivors on our list. Close by if possible."

"Will do," she answered. "Phone calls I can handle."

"And remember, we're officially under CDC auspices. No one can actually refuse to talk to us," he explained.

They found the restaurant one street over from the main thoroughfare.

"Hamburger. Fries. And a chocolate shake," Eileen told the waitress. Dr. Nolan ordered a more classic selection of bacon and eggs, and more coffee.

"How can you do that?" Eileen asked.

"Old habits die hard. In medical school, every third night was on call. We typically went thirty to thirty-two hours without sleep. Coffee kept us and our patients alive."

"And you can just lie down and go to sleep?"

"Like a baby." Dr. Nolan smiled.

Eileen just shook her head. When her milkshake came to the booth, she held it against her cheeks, the cold a welcome relief. The red flush of her face and neck began to fade.

They were both ravenous. Neither had eaten a normal meal for over a day, and there was little conversation across the table. As he pushed his empty plate away, as predicted, Dr. Nolan gave a wide yawn.

"You're amazing." Eileen laughed. "Let's get you back to the hotel, and this time I'll work while you rest."

"Damn good plan," he said.

He had managed to park in the shade, so the car was only about 130 degrees. With the air on full, he looped around the block, passed the courthouse, then slowed near the legal aid offices.

"Give me a minute," he said. "I'll leave the car running so you don't spontaneously combust."

Even though it was Sunday, he could see people in the building. He pulled up to the curb and went in, the large room only moderately air-conditioned. There were a half dozen lawyers and clients spaced out at the desks behind the counter. He waited patiently behind one Hispanic gentleman, then was greeted warmly by an older woman manning the check in station.

"And, how may I help you today?" she asked. Near or past sixty, her smile was genuine and easily given.

"I hate to bother you, but I'm Dr. Nolan with the CDC," he explained. "We're here for two weeks, and I think we may need the help of a translator. Do you have a list of people that might be willing to work with us for a few hours here and there?"

"We do indeed," the woman said. "We need them in court almost every day. A lot of our clients speak some English, but it's best to be precise. Let me see. Give me a minute."

The receptionist left and went to one of the side offices. Dr. Nolan stood with his hands on the counter. To the left were two very young male attorneys, both Caucasian, both speaking fluently with their Hispanic clients. The last desk was occupied by a portly black woman in her late fifties, her booming laugh audible over the mixed conversation in the room. He looked to the right and caught his breath. The woman at the first desk was strikingly beautiful. Dressed in jeans and a white blouse, her dark skin, raven hair, and brown eyes highlighted her smile. She was athletic, gracefully at ease in her carriage, and appeared to be in her mid to late thirties.

"Sorry. Sorry. I've got the book. Are you looking for men or women?" the receptionist asked.

"A woman, preferably. Someone calm and reassuring. Not threatening. Someone older," Dr. Nolan said. He was still staring at the woman that had caught his eye.

"Hmmm. Let's see. There's three names I can give you. All good. All experienced."

"Someone like a grandmother," Dr. Nolan added. "Comforting."

The receptionist nodded.

"I put a star next to Mrs. Ramirez." The woman smiled. "She's worked with us for years. She'd be perfect."

"I can't thank you enough," Dr. Nolan said. He put the list in his pocket. A family with two small children had come in and were standing behind him. He smiled and moved aside, gave her a wave, then moved to the door. At the last second, he turned, went around the counter, and approached the woman at the first desk. She was in animated conversation with an older

Hispanic man. He was small in stature, and heavily weathered from years of manual labor. Dr. Nolan reached out and shook his hand.

"Por favor. Momentito," he said, his accent horribly awkward. The woman looked up from her computer.

"Yes?"

"Are you married?" Dr. Nolan asked.

"What?"

He tried to smile.

"I haven't slept since early Saturday," he said. "I've had way too much coffee, and since I saw you I can't quite think properly. I asked if you were married."

"And who are you exactly?" she asked.

"Oh, sorry, Dr. Sean Nolan with the CDC."

She smiled ever so slightly.

"Is this your normal technique, Dr. Nolan?"

"Oh, I don't have a technique," he answered.

Her smile gained conviction.

"Why don't you come back and ask again when you've had some sleep," she suggested. She held his eyes without wavering.

"Okay. I can do that," he said. He shook hands again with the Hispanic man, then walked back to the front, leaving without looking back.

He was whistling when he got back in the car.

"You seem cheerful," Eileen noted.

"Got a list of interpreters," he announced. He whistled all the way back to the hotel.

7

Eileen called on his cell phone and woke him at 4:15 p.m. Dr. Nolan had never reached the comforting arms of deep sleep, but the rest period had revived his purpose.

"Sorry, but we've got two appointments," she said. "One at five o'clock. One at seven o'clock."

"No. It's okay," he yawned. "We're not getting paid to lounge away the day. I'll shower and meet you downstairs in twenty minutes. We staying local?"

"Yeah, but bring Garmin," she told him. "I'm no good reading maps in the dark."

"Okay. Twenty minutes." He jumped in the shower, choosing cold water to shock him fully back to reality. After brushing his teeth, he put on the tangerine orange Dri-Fit shirt from Target, found the direction finder in his suitcase, and, as a last touch, placed the stethoscope he had brought along around his neck. It was both a security blanket and a recognizable emblem of his role.

Eileen was waiting. She had retrieved two cups of coffee from the first-floor cafeteria.

"Bless you, my child." Dr. Nolan smiled, accepting the offer. It was bitter, stale, made with low quality arabica beans, but it was hot, and it had caffeine.

Still in the mid-eighties, Dr. Nolan started the car, plugged in the Garmin, allowing it a few minutes to reboot.

"Where first?" he asked.

"North to Brawley," Eileen said. "Fellow's name is Anthony Trenholm. Talked to his wife for quite a while. Nice lady. Says he hasn't been okay since he got home from the hospital. Just sits a lot. But, he was more than happy to talk to us."

Dr. Nolan typed in the address written down on Eileen's notepad.

"He's lucky he didn't get fitted for wings," Dr. Nolan explained. "It will take months before he gets back to normal."

The nasal female voice on the Garmin instructed him to turn left on Highway 86. The town was only a few miles north. It was nearly the same size as Imperial, the commercial center quickly giving way to well-kept residential housing, and then just as quickly becoming more low income areas as they moved farther from town. Two miles further up the road, the Garmin ordered a series of turns into a poorer neighborhood, then announced their arrival.

"Okay. You take notes," he told Eileen. "See what else his wife can add, and jump in if you think of something I'm missing."

They went up and knocked on the door, the high-pitched barking of a small dog answering. The house was a small rectangle, everything in place, but the early signs of neglect beginning to show. Areas of paint were peeling, a window screen was torn at the bottom, and the air-conditioning unit was rusting near the fan outlet. The yard had not been weeded or mowed in weeks, and areas of grass were browning away.

Mrs. Trenholm smiled to greet them, a frenzied terrier-mix guard dog dancing around her ankles.

"Are we safe?" Dr. Nolan laughed. "She looks like she could rip my leg off."

"All bark," Mrs. Trenholm explained. "Just good company. Come in. Come in."

Dr. Nolan let Eileen lead the way. The living room was small and dark, the curtains all tightly closed. There was a small couch, a coffee table, one lamp, and a Lazy Boy chair facing the corner television. Mr. Trenholm was seated there, his legs propped up, not turning to look at them.

"This is Eileen Carson, and I'm Dr. Nolan from the CDC. Thank you for letting us barge in like this, but we have a few more questions."

"Not a problem. Not at all," Mrs. Trenholm said. "Come meet Tony. Can I get you anything? Something to drink?"

Dr. Nolan arched his eyebrows at Eileen. It was the perfect opportunity to interview each of them separately.

"Ice water for me," Eileen said. "Do you have any coffee on hand? Dr. Nolan drinks it night and day."

"No, but I can make some," the woman offered.

She introduced them to her husband, then the two women adjourned to the kitchen. Dr. Nolan sat down on the edge of the sofa closest to Mr. Trenholm. The man was in his seventies, still pale and tired looking, the lines in his face deeply etched, dark purple half circles beneath his eyes. On the wall were family photos, and a single picture of Mr. Trenholm in uniform.

"You ex-military?" Dr. Nolan asked.

The man glanced at the image and nodded.

"Sixty-four to '66. Nam," he said.

For the first time, he looked at Dr. Nolan and forced a smile.

"That was pretty rough duty," Dr. Nolan said. "Thank you for your service."

The old man lowered the leg rest and turned toward him slightly, giving a nod.

"I had easy duty," he explained. "Tactical air ground crew. We kept the planes flying and ready for missions."

"Wasn't any easy duty," Dr. Nolan said. "I'm glad you made it through all that."

"Worst was watching all the kids fly in," the old man said. "Then, in the dark of night, we'd load the caskets. All of them covered in flags. All going home again." He stared off at the distant memories, still painful and raw.

Dr. Nolan let the silence stand for a moment. He leaned down and gave the dog a back rub.

"I was reading your hospital file last night," he said at last. "You're still a tough guy. That kind of pneumonia usually kills people. You remember much about it?"

Mr. Trenholm sat back again.

"Shaking chills, then I couldn't breathe," Mr. Trenholm said. "My wife called the ambulance, and that's about it. They had to stick me on a breathing machine for five days. Seemed like a bad dream."

"And, how are you doing now?" Dr. Nolan asked.

Mr. Trenholm shrugged.

"I'm as useless as that day," he said. "I try to do anything, and I get shaky, have to sit down and rest. Like a baby."

"That's normal," Dr. Nolan explained. "I tell my patients it takes three to six months to recover from a major illness or surgery. Men just get a little irritated about the slow pace. We don't like limitations."

Mrs. Trenholm called from the other room.

"Tony, you want anything?"

"Coors," he yelled, then looked at Dr. Nolan. "Hosers bought Coors. Isn't that something?"

Dr. Nolan nodded. It took a second to understand the Canadian reference.

"Part of the global economy." He smiled. "Even American car companies have been bought out."

"Ain't right," Mr. Trenholm said. "That should be sacred."

Eileen and Mrs. Trenholm returned with a tray. Dr. Nolan mixed milk into his coffee, and Tony settled into a comfortable position with his ice-cold beer in hand.

"Thank you," Dr. Nolan said. "We just have a few questions. We went over the CDC interview from the hospital, so this won't take long. The main focus is on any travel in the five days before you got sick."

"You mind if I smoke?" Mr. Trenholm asked. He was already lighting up a cigarette before anyone answered.

"It's your house," Dr. Nolan said. "And, I'm not here to give any lectures. But, you do know those goddamn things will stunt your growth?"

Mr. Trenholm laughed and started coughing.

"I'm tall enough," he said, once he regained his breath. The small dog jumped into his lap and nestled down.

"Let's see," Dr. Nolan read over Eileen's notepad. "The CDC report says you went to the local store three times, Home Depot in El Centro, the Moose Lodge two nights, a gas station here in town, a golf course in Imperial, and an Ace Hardware store. That sound right?"

Mr. Trenholm nodded, taking another puff of his cigarette.

"Water heater element burned out," he told them.

"So, you never travelled north of here? Not once?"

"Nothing there I care about," Mr. Trenholm said. He took a drink of his beer.

"How about you, Mrs. Trenholm?" Eileen asked. "Anything you remember?"

The older woman thought back.

"That's nearly a month ago," she said. "I wasn't at the hospital when the other people talked to him. I don't drive anymore. Have to get the neighbor to take me places. Let's see. A month ago. What about your hearing aids?"

"What!?" her husband yelled, exaggerating the joke.

"The VA in Yuma." She laughed. "When did you go down there?"

"Hell, I don't know," Mr. Trenholm answered. He looked at Dr. Nolan. "All those years around jet engines, VA had to pay for hearing aids. Then the damn things hurt my ears when I wear them. Better to be half deaf."

Dr. Nolan looked to Mrs. Trenholm for help.

"You have any way to pin down when his appointment was?"

The woman stared at the floor, then suddenly smiled. She went to the kitchen and brought back a wall calendar. Using her finger as a guide, she read through all the scribbled notes marking the days back to late April.

"Here. Here." She pointed. "April 19th, 11:00 a.m. Audiology." Eileen wrote down the time, then rechecked the day he was admitted to the hospital.

"Six days before," she said, looking at Dr. Nolan.

"I tell you some damn Canadian company bought Coors!" Mr. Trenholm asked, looking at the label on his beer can.

Dr. Nolan smiled and nodded. It was not uncommon for patients recovering from severe illnesses to have cognitive lapses.

"Mr. Trenholm. Tony. Can you remember how you got to the VA? What roads you drove on? Any other places you stopped?"

"It's just down and over about seventy miles," the older man said. "I don't recall, but I stay off the freeway. Too fast for me."

"What about stops?" Dr. Nolan asked. "Did you eat anywhere? Get out of the car?"

The older man shook his head.

"Ate at the commissary," he said. "Only stopped to pee. Twice, maybe."

Dr. Nolan leaned closer.

"Where did you stop, Mr. Trenholm? It could be important."

"Peed in the bushes. Along the road, I guess. I don't know," he answered. There was no point in pushing him further.

"Okay, good. That helps," Dr. Nolan said. He smiled at both Mr. and Mrs. Trenholm. He stood up and shook the older man's hand, then gave the dog a rub on its head. "Thank you for letting us come into your home. You've been very helpful."

He and Eileen made their way to the door. Mrs. Trenholm followed them out on the porch.

"I'm sorry he didn't do better," she apologized. "Ever since he came home, he forgets what he says and does sometimes."

"You both did great," Dr. Nolan assured her. "Try to get him reading or doing crossword puzzles, look through old picture albums. And get him out walking. He needs to exercise his mind and his body. It's a slow process, but everything will get better."

"I hope so," the woman said. "I think your visit was a good thing."

"It was for us," Dr. Nolan said. He thanked her again, helped Eileen into the car, then sat thinking.

"For a minute, I thought we were close to some answers," Eileen said, disappointed.

"We did get some answers," Dr. Nolan told her. "How many survivors live north of here?"

Eileen checked her paperwork.

"One in Calipatria, one more in Brawley, and one in Westmorland," she said. "Why?"

"Most of the cases are to the south, and now we know Mr. Trenholm went that way before he got sick," Dr. Nolan explained. "The CDC already tested everyplace he went here. They just didn't know about the trip to the VA. Who's our next patient?"

"Ummm. Patrick Mayfield," she said. "Just north of Imperial. I figured it would be easier close to the hotel."

"Good thinking," Dr. Nolan said. "And closer to dinner. We'll try to stay on a more reasonable diet plan from now on." He reprogrammed the Garmin, tracing their path back to the main highway.

"What's on the agenda tomorrow?" Eileen asked.

"Try to set up a meeting with the patient in Westmorland first," Dr. Nolan said. "And I'll see if we can get an interpreter. The farm thing is driving me crazy. It was gone over twice, but why three cases from one location? It's like a flashing red light, but when they looked, there was nothing there."

"But Mr. Trenholm sure didn't go visit some farm out in the desert," Eileen said. "So what's the connection?"

"That's the sixty-four-thousand-dollar question." Dr. Nolan smiled. "Let's see if Mr. Mayfield knows?"

The Garmin took them to an upscale housing division with a gated entrance. The homes were newer, nicely landscaped, and most had pools in the backyard. It was a stark contrast to their previous stop.

Mr. Mayfield turned out to be a vivacious, friendly, second-generation Irishman. He welcomed them with a flashing smile, escorting them to the back patio area. It was now down in the mid-seventies, and just comfortable. Eileen was served ice water, and more coffee was on brew for Dr. Nolan. They took seats around the dining table. Dr. Nolan noticed water and fresh footprints around the collar of the pool.

"You back to swimming?" he asked the man.

"Twice a day," Mr. Mayfield said proudly. "I'm up to twenty laps. Hasn't been easy." He pulled an inhaler from his robe pocket and took a single dose, holding it for five seconds before exhaling. "Sorry."

"Not at all," said Dr. Nolan. "Albuterol?"

"Duoneb," Mr. Mayfield nodded. "Then Symbicort twice a day. Bad asthma. That's why I moved here, and then I almost die from Legionnaires' disease. Just got off the oral prednisone two weeks ago."

"You seem well on the road to recovery," Dr. Nolan complimented him. "It helps when people work at it."

"Getting there," Mr. Mayfield said. "First day home, I did one lap and had to lean on the edge of the pool for ten minutes. It's a scary feeling when you can't get air. Makes you think about dying."

Dr. Nolan nodded. He knew from the medical file that Mr. Mayfield had been on a ventilator for nearly a full week.

"I'll bet you had a sore throat for a while." He smiled.

"Sore? I couldn't even talk when they took that tube out of me. My wife thought it was heaven. I had to write notes to her."

"It was heaven," said Mrs. Mayfield, coming out to join them. She and her husband had white wine, Eileen her ice water, and Dr. Nolan a full carafe of fresh coffee. He took one sip and sighed.

"Mexican beans," he said. "Either Chiapas or Oaxaca. Perfect roast."

"Very good. It's Chiapas," Mr. Mayfield said. "I got hooked on good coffee because it helps me breathe better. Some chemical."

"Methylxanthine," Dr. Nolan said. "And tons of antioxidants. Discovered in Ethiopia by goats. That's why I love goats."

They all laughed.

"Well, that explains everything," Eileen said. "You enjoy your coffee, and I'll ask questions, or we'll be bothering these people all night." She pulled out her notes. "We've gone over the previous CDC reports, but new information seems to indicate the infection source may be to the south of here. All of your contact sites were local, and they all tested negative for the bacteria that caused this. We wanted to check again and make certain nothing had been missed."

Dr. Nolan was watching him closely. He held eye contact with Eileen, then looked down and to the left, away from her.

"I couldn't talk to them much," he began. "Everything was all mixed up."

"Is there something you could add now?" Dr. Nolan asked. "It could be critical to our understanding of what happened here."

Mr. Mayfield was still looking down.

"If I remember something, would it cause trouble? Would I be in trouble?"

"Not with us," Dr. Nolan said. "This isn't a criminal case. It's a health issue. We only want to prevent trouble, not cause it."

Mr. Mayfield nodded, and his wife put her hand on his shoulder.

"So, is this kind of off the record?" he asked.

"I keep a lot of things off the record," Dr. Nolan admitted. "All I care about are answers."

Mr. Mayfield nodded again, then looked up.

"My inhalers," he said. "They're not covered by insurance. The two I use cost over a thousand dollars a month, and my wife is on medicine, too. We cross into Mexicali once a month and fill our prescriptions. I thought I could face some federal charges or something if I told anyone."

Dr. Nolan understood the predicament Mr. and Mrs. Mayfield faced all too well. For years he had been helping his own patients obtain medication from Canada.

"No one will know about this but us," Dr. Nolan promised him. "Now, what route did you take?"

"Down on 86, and back on 111," he said. "There was a wreck or something."

"And did you stop anywhere?" Dr. Nolan asked.

"I don't know," Mr. Mayfield said. "It was six weeks ago. Maybe."

Dr. Nolan felt his heart skip with the answer, but showed no emotion. It was never going to be simple.

"That's an enormous help," he told the Mayfields. "And none of this will be written down. You have my word."

Mr. Mayfield was openly relieved. Dr. Nolan stood and shook his hand, then walked back through the house to the door.

"Thank you," Mr. Mayfield said.

"Other way around," Dr. Nolan told him, then he turned to Mrs. Mayfield. "And thank you for the great coffee. It was a pleasure meeting you both."

Back in the car, Eileen was beaming.

"Not a bad night's work," she said.

"Not bad at all," Dr. Nolan agreed. "You get to pick the fanciest restaurant in town now. It's on the CDC."

8

Dr. Nolan got back to his room just before 10:00 p.m. The plan was to get a decent night's sleep and start again early in the morning. He called to check on his daughters. They were glad to hear from him, but the short absence had not yet exacted any emotional expenditure. They were having too much fun with their new live-in house mother. He listened, smiling, as they recounted movies, shopping, and makeup seminars.

"No tattoos," he warned them. "And no piercings."

"Oh, Dad, don't worry." Cienna laughed. "We're doing fine. Call tomorrow."

That was it. He had been dismissed, no longer an essential fixture in their day. He was relieved, and just a momentary feeling of loss cast a cloud. Accepting the fact that he was no longer the center of their universe was not a welcome reality.

He sighed, then put his phone on the charger, scrolling his messages. A call had come in earlier from a Sergeant Ted Neely with Border Patrol. He was the local resource contact given to him by Sheriff Dent. Dr. Nolan copied down the number and placed it in his wallet, making note to call back tomorrow.

After a quick shower, he took some of the tacks and yarn to the map and strung outlines from their interview points to destinations in the south. It was not an impressive or complex web, but it was a framework. The visual certainty of it gave him something tangible, a measure of substance. It was not much, but still reassuring.

He found the phone numbers given to him by the receptionist at the legal office. First thing in the morning he would try to find a translator. It was even more pressing now that they visit the farm near Holtville. There was no logical construct to explain three cases of Legionnaires' in the same small area if it was not the source. But the CDC had done the appropriate testing, and it would still not resolve all the loose ends. The two surviving patients they had spoken to had never been near Holtville.

He propped the pillows on the bed and lay down, looking up at the map. Their target zone was smaller, but it was still thousands of square miles. And, somewhere inside those boundaries, an invisible enemy was hiding, one that had already murdered forty seven people.

He fell asleep with the lights on, deeply and soundly at first, but then the dreams began. Moving fragments, faces, voices, the two patients they had visited earlier, hospital beds, ventilators. He saw his daughters cuddled together on the couch the morning he left. How long ago was it? Just two days? The young woman at the legal aid agency, her skin like coffee and cream, her eyes uncertain, suspect, annoyed, amused. And, then she started coughing. A harsh, unremitting cough that ended with blood across her hand.

He woke suddenly, drenched in sweat. It was just before 5:00 a.m., the eastern sky beginning to lighten. He grabbed the suitcase of files from the CDC and tossed it on the bed. One by one, he picked out the red charts, skimmed over the first few pages, then threw them on the floor. With only a few left, the frantic search ended. He sat down and read the collected data from cover to cover, the life ending story of an old Hispanic worker who lost his battle with Legionnaires' pneumonia. His place of employment was listed as Dahlquist Farm. Now there were four cases from one location.

Dr. Nolan showered again, shaved, dressed in jeans and a flaming pink T-shirt, gathered up five charts and an extensive list of test sites already covered by the CDC. He was just reaching for the door handle when he heard a knock.

"Room service." The young lady smiled. She took one step into the entry, her smile vanishing, replaced by a look of shock. The bed was sideways in the center of the room, the floor littered with colored folders and crumpled paper, dirty clothes draped over furniture, coffee cups and empty pastry wrappers on the desk, and an enormous map taped to the wall decorated with strands of yarn.

Dr. Nolan felt his cheeks reddening.

"I…um…I was working late," he explained. "Maybe tomorrow would be better. After I straighten up a little."

The woman nodded, backing into the hallway, more than eager to move on to other challenges. Dr. Nolan followed her to Eileen's room, a sheepish grin on his face. The housekeeper kept giving him furtive glances.

Eileen was nearly ready. She held the door open for the woman and her cart.

"This young lady thinks I'm a pig," Dr. Nolan said from the doorway. "She was scared to go in my room."

Eileen said something to the girl in Spanish, and they both laughed.

"I know what you said," Dr. Nolan lied. "That was cruel and malicious."

Eileen nodded.

"The truth hurts sometimes," she said. "I need ten more minutes."

"Okay. I'll be downstairs. They have some kind of breakfast thing." He took the stairs, grabbed coffee and a raspberry Danish, then took a table near the windows. It was early, but he was too impatient to wait. He dialed the number of Mrs. Ramirez, the interpreter most recommended to him.

"Mrs. Ramirez, hello. Dr. Sean Nolan from the CDC. I'm sorry to call at this hour, but I'm in desperate need of an experienced translator. The legal aid people said you were their best resource."

The woman spoke flawless English, but clearly had a Spanish tone in her syntax.

"Oh, I'm honored, doctor. I was told you might call," she said, her voice warm and pleasant. "But, I have court this morning. Maybe one hour. There's no way to ever know."

"That's not a problem," Dr. Nolan said. "We need to visit workers on a farm near Holtville. This afternoon would be perfect, but it might run a little late. Is that a possibility?"

The woman hesitated for a moment.

"I can bring something to eat," she said. "I'm used to odd hours. For years I am on call to social service, the courthouse, the police. It will be fine."

"If we run late, we can stop at a restaurant on the way back to town," Dr. Nolan said. "But, then you have to pay the bill."

Instead of laughter, the phone was silent.

"I would have to pay for dinner?" the woman asked, obviously confused.

"No. No. I'm sorry. Bad joke," Dr. Nolan apologized. "We pay for everything. I was trying to be funny."

"Oh, a joke. I see now," the woman said. "Good. What time were you thinking?"

"Two o'clock," he said, refraining from any more banter. "Where can we meet?"

"Since you know where the legal offices are, I will park there," she said. "Blue Toyota Camry."

"Perfect. My partner and I will be looking forward to working with you," Dr. Nolan said. "Thank you very much." He hung up before adding any other misdirected comments.

Eileen sat down across from him with a plate of bacon and waffles.

"You sleep?" she asked.

"Some. Last night was very helpful, but I've started off today on the wrong foot," Dr. Nolan explained. "The cleaning staff thinks I'm a barbarian, and the translator thinks I'm a moron."

"Keeping the bar low like that can work in your favor, though." Eileen smiled. "There's nowhere to go but up."

"Well, that's certainly true," Dr. Nolan admitted. "You have any luck with the patient in Westmorland?"

Eileen shook her head.

"Called twice last night, and then again a few minutes ago. No answer. Just a recording," she said. "What do you want to do?"

Dr. Nolan frowned.

"Let's drive up there anyway. Get more used to the area. If we can't locate him, we'll come back and swing by Memorial Hospital in El Centro. We don't meet up with the translator until two."

"Sounds good. You talk to your girls?"

"Yeah. They don't miss me much," he said. "Having too much fun."

"Don't be a baby," Eileen said. "They'll miss you plenty in a couple of days. Wait and see."

"Maybe I'm obsolete," Dr. Nolan told her. "I'm a barbarian, a moron, a big baby, and I'm obsolete. Hell of a combination."

"And, I'm working for you." Eileen laughed. "What does that make me?"

"A loser," Dr. Nolan said. "Pure and simple. Oh, shit, I almost forgot. Take a look at this." He pushed the single red file over to her side of the table. She read it as she finished her food.

"Same farm? Why no interview?"

"Died without regaining consciousness," Dr. Nolan explained. "Turned out his ID was phony. They don't even know his real name. Nothing. No family. No history. Nothing."

"That's pretty heartbreaking." Eileen sighed. "Somewhere, somebody cared about him. A wife, kids. Maybe a brother or sister."

Dr. Nolan nodded. It was heartbreaking, and a stark condemnation of a system that would create such an inhumane scenario.

"We'll ask about him today," Dr. Nolan said. "Maybe one of the other workers knew his real name, where he came from?"

"Good," Eileen said. "You ready to hit the road, you obsolete moron?"

"Yeah, but I still drive," he said, getting up and stretching. "That I can still manage." They gathered their files and went out to the car. It was eight fifteen and only eighty-three degrees.

They headed north on Highway 86 again, turning west toward the Salton Sea on 78. Westmorland was only a short drive past Brawley, but a much smaller and more depressed community. There were fewer farms, and more desert. Out of the town itself, the neighborhoods and homes were older, dirtier, smaller, and sadder. Dr. Nolan recalled his reading: fastest growing area and the poorest.

The Garmin led them to a quiet street of plain, square, single story homes. There were no manicured lawns or landscaped estates. The front yard of Mr. Atley's house was cracked earth, and the concrete walkway was buckled and irregular, numerous sections of the ancient cement just missing. An old Impala sat in the driveway, the garage door open and displaying a jumbled tangle of furniture and discarded debris.

Dr. Nolan knocked on the door. He could hear a dog whining and a television, but there was no answer. He knocked a second time, tried to look through the living room window, then came back down the steps. He circled around to the driveway and followed pavers to the back. The yard was fenced, accessible through a metal gate. Eileen followed close behind.

Dr. Nolan knocked on the back door once, then louder a second time. Now the dog was barking. Still no answer. He slowly tested the latch. It turned freely in his grasp, and he opened it a few inches, ready to call out Mr. Atley's name. Before he could speak, the house itself exhaled a breath of heavy, foul, putrefied air. Dr. Nolan winced, opened the door just far enough for the small dog to escape, then closed it again.

"Hello, kiddo," he said softly, kneeling down to level himself with the animal. Some degree of pug ancestry, the dog was black with huge eyes and a broad forehead. Just the sight of it made Dr. Nolan laugh. He let it smell his hand, then began to rub it's neck and back.

"What's wrong?" Eileen asked, still near the gate.

"Just a little delay," he said. He looked over the yard, finally locating a metal bowl. He filled it from the faucet near the door. "I'll bet our friend is thirsty. Right, kiddo?"

The dog began drinking immediately, not pausing until the dish was empty. Then she came back to Dr. Nolan, half cowering.

"It's okay, kid," Dr. Nolan said, picking the dog up and cradling it in one arm. "Let's go out and sit in the nice, air-conditioned car, shall we." He led Eileen back to where they had parked, putting the dog in the back seat.

"What's going on?" Eileen asked again.

"I want you to wait here for a few minutes and dog sit," Dr. Nolan told her. "You have any perfume?"

"In my purse," she said. Dr. Nolan retrieved her bag from the front seat, then found a napkin in the glove box. When she handed him the small spray bottle, he soaked part of the paper tissue, tore off two pieces, rolled them up, inserting one in each nostril. He handed her the car keys.

"Get out of this heat and just wait for me," he said. He held the door open until she complied. Going first to the garage, he found a pair of cotton garden gloves, put them on, and returned to the back of the house. This time he stood to the side, opened the door wide, then waited a full minute before entering.

Death had its own distinct odor, and old death an even darker signature. Dr. Nolan had met them both before, and they were unmistakable in their proclamation. It was obvious that Mr. Atley was no longer among the living.

Dr. Nolan walked through the galley kitchen, the sink cluttered with dirty dishes, four empty Jim Beam bottles on the counter. He stopped briefly to open the refrigerator, noting the half quart of milk was still within date.

He passed through the dining area, then found Mr. Atley sitting in an overstuffed chair in front of the television. Wearing only boxer shorts, he was a dark purple color, his lower legs and feet black from pooling of blood. He was swollen and bloated from early decomposition, and insects had already claimed him as a fertile breeding ground. Dr. Nolan had not wanted Eileen to ever have such memories or visions.

On the side table was a glass of scotch, a large ashtray filled to capacity with cigarette butts, some unopened mail, and the remote control. A breathing medicine for patients with emphysema was on his lap. From all appearances, Mr. Atley had just gone to sleep.

Judging from the condition of the body and the dog activity in the room, it appeared death had visited one or two days ago. Dr. Nolan went down the hall to the bedroom. Not surprisingly, the bed was neatly made. Patients with severe respiratory problems often slept in a sitting position. He checked the nightstand and bedside trash can, but there was nothing of note.

The medicine cabinet in the bathroom was also a disappointment. There was a bottle of baby aspirin, one blood pressure medicine, and one heart medication. Both had labels from a local pharmacy. The garbage can held nothing more than used Kleenex and a discarded razor blade.

Back in the kitchen, Dr. Nolan found dry dog food in the broom closet, along with a box of Milk Bones. He set these on the counter, then looked through the cupboards and drawers. In the one near the phone he found some plastic poker chips emblazoned with a logo, and a half dozen slot machine tokens. These he placed in his pocket.

The garbage can under the sink was last. There were maggots climbing out from the organic material inside, and he used the handle of a scrub brush to sort through the paper. Beyond a receipt from a nearby grocery and a copy of the *Watch Tower*, there was nothing of interest. Reclaiming the pet food, he went out in the yard and threw the gloves aside, removed his perfumed nose plugs, then splashed water on his head and face from the faucet. He tried to wash his hands, but without soap he still felt contaminated. He waved them in the hot air until they dried, not wanting to touch his jeans.

Able to breathe again, he took the dog food back to the car. He motioned to Eileen to lower the window, then gave his new friend one of the Milk Bones. The dog was dancing all over the back seat.

"This dog stinks," Eileen said. "Thanks for making me babysit."

"I did you a favor," Dr. Nolan explained. "His owner smells a lot worse. You want to call 911 and tell them we have a deceased resident out here. I need to take a walk."

"Jesus, are you kidding? Just call them and say what? We broke into this guy's house and found him dead?"

"That's about it." Dr. Nolan smiled. "Remember, we're with the CDC. We had a reason to be here."

"Oh, right. Okay," Eileen said. While she notified the local police, Dr. Nolan walked to the end of the street and back, breathing in and out as deeply as he could, trying to exercise every polluted atom from his system. The nausea he had felt was finally fading away. He even welcomed the wave of perspiration, cleansing the pores in his skin.

Eileen rolled the window down and handed him a bottle of water.

"Ten minutes," she informed him.

He drank half the water in one swallow, the other half more slowly. Then he handed her the empty bottle and walked over to the rusting Impala. There was nothing in the console or glove box, but a gas receipt was on the floor just under the passenger seat. It was from a convenience store in Calexico, and the date read April 14.

He rejoined Eileen, the air-conditioning almost too efficient. A shiver went through him.

"Can you check and see when Mr. Atley was admitted to the hospital?"

Eileen read through his file.

"April 20th," she said.

He handed her the printout from the gas station.

"Good work. Six days. That fits, right?" she asked.

"Perfectly. And it's south again, just like the others. At least we know for certain he was on Highway 111 for a while."

The police cruiser pulled into the driveway and parked behind the Impala. Dr. Nolan got out, introduced himself, showed his official ID, then gave a rundown of Mr. Atley's untimely demise.

"You need a mask to go in there," he warned the officer.

"That bad?"

"Worse than bad," Dr. Nolan assured him. "And, I've got his dog. It's so ugly, it's cute, but I can't take it with me. We're bunked up in a hotel."

The officer nodded.

"I'll take it to the local vet. They should be able to find her a home. You sure you don't want to go back in there with me?"

"Positive, thanks," Dr. Nolan said. "A little bit of Mr. Atley goes a long way." He got the dog and transferred it to the back seat of the patrol car, giving the animal one last pet. "Sorry, kid. Things will get better now." The dog stood up and put its paws on the glass, watching him leave.

"We done?" Eileen asked.

"Yeah, but I need another shower and different clothes. I'm almost out of shirts."

"The hotel has a laundry." Eileen laughed.

"The maid might have gotten me evicted," Dr. Nolan said. "She wasn't very happy about the interior decorating."

"Don't worry. I explained your lack of sleep, and told her you were a big tipper," Eileen said.

They were headed back to Imperial.

Dr. Nolan laughed.

"Let's just hope the CDC has a sense of humor."

9

At their hotel, Dr. Nolan asked if the same housekeeper was on duty who had visited his room. He and Eileen waited in the lobby, only a few minutes passing before she responded to her pager. The look on her face as she approached them confirmed that the visual image of his storm-tossed suite was still a vivid memory.

Dr. Nolan smiled, then took the gambling chips and tokens from his pocket and held them out for her to see. Her eyebrows arched up as she did a quick count of the value. It was over four hundred dollars.

"Do you know where these came from?" he asked her.

She took one of the gold-colored slot machine coins and examined the logo.

"Si. Yes. It is from the big casino in Mexicali," she explained. "Just across the border. They have shows, dancing, music."

Dr. Nolan nodded. It explained why Mr. Atley had gotten fuel so far south. He gave all the chips and tokens to the maid.

"This is for the big mess I made upstairs. I'll straighten up some before tomorrow, but leave the furniture and map where they are. Okay?"

"Yes, sir. Thank you," she said. "Tomorrow."

Upstairs, Dr. Nolan placed a new yarn marker on the map, leading first to Brawley, then bifurcating onto either 86 or 111, then merging again halfway to Calexico. Their search area was now down to two major highway corridors, and all the possible side roads and branch points that joined them. It was potentially thousands of miles to cover.

"I'll go call Mike, and you change," Eileen said.

"Gladly," Dr. Nolan said. After a quick shower, he put on the last of his clean clothes, loading everything else into a large bath towel. Whether real or imagined, the lingering presence of Mr. Atley had been eliminated. He could breathe again.

After reclaiming Eileen, he dropped his laundry at the services desk, and they headed back out into the white sun. It was already ninety four degrees.

"The worst is yet to come," he announced, glancing at his watch. There was over an hour of free time until they were scheduled to meet Mrs. Ramirez.

"I suppose you want to go shopping again," Eileen joked, getting into the car. She was already uncomfortable in the heat, her face the color of a Roma tomato.

"Not till next year," Dr. Nolan said. "Once every six months is my limit. Let's check in with the hospital in El Centro. It's not that far from where we're going."

Fifteen minutes later they were in the parking lot of Memorial Hospital, a modern six story building with a central hub and two large wings devoted to patient care. They went in together, found the emergency room, identified themselves, then waited to speak to one of the duty physicians.

A young woman in blue scrubs and running shoes came out to greet them.

"I'm Dr. Schriver," she said, shaking hands. "Fran." She looked at their CDC credentials.

"Dr. Sean Nolan, and Eileen Carson, one of my investigators," he said. "Actually, my only investigator. You heard about the Zika and dengue outbreak."

"Unfortunately," Dr. Schriver said. "We're getting updates daily. We've had too much fun here already."

Dr. Nolan nodded toward her lower abdomen.

"How far along are you?" he asked, smiling.

"Good eye, Doctor," she said. "Just over six months. I didn't think I was showing."

"Your first?"

"God, yes." She laughed. "It would have been crazy trying to start a family during training. Now I just do three twelves a week. Lots of time off."

"Good plan," Dr. Nolan said. "I waited, too. My daughters are fifteen and thirteen now. But I'm dumb enough to work five twelves and take call on weekends."

Dr. Schriver cringed.

"Your wife must love that," she commented.

Dr. Nolan did not let his smile falter.

"I'm Mom, too," he said. "Long story."

Dr. Schriver nodded, but asked for no additional explanation.

"And, how about you?" she asked Eileen.

"Two girls and a boy." She smiled. "All grown and gone. Just waiting for grand-kids to spoil."

"Well, we've got the generations covered." Dr. Schriver smiled. "Why don't you come in back and we'll talk."

They went through the ER, past dozens of curtained exam bays, then found an empty table in the lounge. Dr. Schriver took three bottles of water from the refrigerator.

"I know you're busy," Dr. Nolan said. "We just wanted to check in and make sure everything was still quiet."

"Sixteen days, I think." Dr. Schriver nodded. "It was like a war zone for three weeks. We even had people on ventilators in the hallway. Then it just stopped. The CDC team that came in was wonderful. Even checked the respiratory equipment in the hospital. Showers, bath pools, air ducts, drinking fountains. They went through this part of the valley twice that I know of."

"And, no cases were ever reported from south of the border?" Dr. Nolan asked.

"Nothing official," Dr. Schriver said, giving a shrug. "But who knows? Nothing confirmed, anyway. We get tons of tourist travel, but it was mostly locals. You guys getting anywhere?"

Dr. Nolan shook his head.

"We've only been here three days," he said. "We have identified some new travel information that fits a few of the time windows, but the area involved is the size of Rhode Island."

"And there's just the two of you?"

"Yeah, but we're hot stuff, especially in this climate." Dr. Nolan laughed. "Anything else you can think of?"

Dr. Schriver stood up, subconsciously placing her right hand over her lower abdomen.

"All I can do is wish you luck," she said. "We've already had too many fatal cases."

"And, that number went up today," Dr. Nolan informed her. "We found one of the survivors dead this morning when we went to interview him. His recovery kind of stalled out."

Dr. Schriver walked them out to the reception desk.

"Lab's still geared up for testing, just in case," she told them. "Happy hunting."

They shook hands, then returned to their baking car.

"She was nice," Eileen said. "It's refreshing to run into a physician who's empathetic, courteous, professional, soft-spoken…"

"Okay. Okay." Dr. Nolan laughed. "I kind of get your subtle inference. Women doctors are actually becoming the dominant force in ER work. Back in my day it was a rarity. I like it."

"Women rule," Eileen said. "Now, find me ice cream before we meet the translator."

"Okay, boss," Dr. Nolan said. He pulled into a strip mall, located a Baskin Robbins, and came to the car with a chocolate sundae.

"Does this improve your opinion of me?" Dr. Nolan asked, fitting his seat belt.

"A little," Eileen said, savoring the cold. "I hate taking that damn tamoxifen."

"You can hate it as much as you want," Dr. Nolan said. "Just keep taking it. I'm tired of training new assistants."

"See, your empathy is ass backwards," Eileen noted.

"But still charming," Dr. Nolan said. He navigated back to Imperial, parking just south of the legal aid office. He was about to go inside and look for the dark haired lawyer when a blue Camry pulled into the curb. He bent down, smiled, and waved at the woman behind the wheel.

Mrs. Ramirez got out and locked the doors with the electronic key.

"Are you the CDC doctor?" she asked, coming toward him.

"I am indeed, and you must be the world famous translator, Mrs. Ramirez," Dr. Nolan said. The woman smiled and shook his hand. She was absolutely perfect, almost a model provided by central casting to fit the role he envisioned. Mid-sixties, she was about five feet two, a little overweight, her hair tightly bound back with gray along the temples. She wore a blue print dress, an enormous white purse draped over her right shoulder, and her smile was warm and genuine. She was everybody's grandmother.

Dr. Nolan showed her his CDC identification card, then took her arm, helping her into the back of the Nissan behind the driver's seat so she could have eye contact with Eileen. He introduced the two.

"Nice to meet you," Eileen said. "You came highly recommended."

"That is kind to hear," the woman said.

Dr. Nolan pulled out into traffic and headed south.

"You're an angel," Dr. Nolan told her. "I'll fill you in while we drive."

"You speak Spanish?" Mrs. Ramirez asked Eileen.

"Muy poquito," Eileen answered.

"And you, Doctor?"

"Muyier poquitier," he said. "I can ask small, easy questions. We need someone that will hear everything, understand nuances, even read between the lines. I think there may be illegal workers involved, and they won't feel comfortable talking to two white strangers."

Mrs. Ramirez nodded.

"This time of year, there will be many such workers," she agreed. "Now there are more from South America. Even I have trouble understanding them sometimes. What is this about?"

"You know about the sickness a few weeks ago that made so many people ill? Three…no…four people on this one farm were infected," Eileen told Mrs. Ramirez. "When the CDC first interviewed them, they didn't answer very many questions. We need to know where they came from and where they might have been exposed to the bacteria."

Mrs. Ramirez nodded. Dr. Nolan could see her apprehension through the rearview mirror.

"There's no danger from the illness now," he assured her. "You work with lawyers and their clients, right? This is the same. We ask questions, try to find answers, clues. Kind of like detectives."

The smile was returning to her face.

"And to see if they lie to you, yes? You want to know their feelings?"

"Yes. Exactly," Dr. Nolan answered. "Are they answering honestly or not."

"The lawyers and clients lie to each other all the time," Mrs. Ramirez said. "It is a funny business. Oh, and that reminds me. I did not speak with you about my fee."

"Jesus, are you kidding?" Dr. Nolan whined. "We have to pay you?"

Mrs. Ramirez sat stunned, not knowing what to say.

Eileen met her look, then closed her eyes and shook her head.

"He's being silly," she explained. "Some type of infantile humor disorder. How much do you usually charge?"

Mrs. Ramirez started laughing.

"The court pays twenty-four dollars an hour," she said. "Is that all right?"

"No," said Dr. Nolan. "Make it fifty dollars. I have an expense account."

Mrs. Ramirez sighed deeply and relaxed.

"I think I will like this job," she said.

At El Centro, they turned onto the freeway and headed east. An exit sign for Holtville doubled back and twisted through a two lane road until they slowed at the city limits. It was a small collection of stores and fast-food restaurants, no building taller than two stories. It disappeared behind them as quickly as it materialized. Dr. Nolan pulled over and programmed the Garmin.

A series of direction changes finally pointed them to the northeast. They passed large, modern farms with a mixture of new and old homes, some near the road, others distant shadows down long, dusty driveways. And, in between, there were more and more dilapidated, ramshackle buildings that served as houses, here and there clothes on a line, a parked truck, a dog sleeping in the shade of a tree, tiny glimpses of life.

Dry desert reached fingers of sand and soil along the pavement, long ago buckled and cracked from the merciless heat. Tumbleweeds and stunted mesquite dotted the landscape, and then suddenly would transition to vibrant green fields of thriving crops. Dr. Nolan kept their speed below forty, riding the waves of rolling asphalt. The Garmin finally ordered them to slow and turn to the right.

An arched, wooden gateway announced in white letters they had reached Dahlquist Farm. A steel arm blocked their entry, a security pad on the left. Dr. Nolan buzzed the key marked office.

"Yes," a man's voice answered, somewhat annoyed.

"Hello. Dr. Sean Nolan with the CDC. We're here to follow up on the patients that were treated for Legionnaires' disease."

There was a long pause before the voice answered.

"Wait there," was all that was said.

Eileen sighed, then turned to Mrs. Ramirez.

"You have children?"

"Two, boy and a girl. Both grown," Mrs. Ramirez said. "My son is in the Navy, and my daughter just finished school to be a lawyer." Her pride was visible in her smile.

"And Mr. Ramirez?"

"Passed five years ago. He had been ill for a long time," Mrs. Ramirez answered, far enough in memory that it caused no outward pain.

"Company coming," Dr. Nolan whispered.

A well-worn Jeep Wrangler came at them half buried in a cloud of dust. It pulled off on the shoulder of the driveway, and a man in jeans and a gray T-shirt approached their car. He was in his forties, unshaven, and not welcoming.

"What's this about?" he asked again. Dr. Nolan showed him his ID card. He was not going to allow it to become a discussion.

"Center for Disease Control," he repeated. "By court order we have to follow up on all recovering patients from the recent epidemic."

The man bent lower, looked at Eileen and Mrs. Ramirez, then went to the gate control. As the metal barrier swung open, he nodded them forward, not speaking. Standing sideways, Dr. Nolan could make out the unmistakable outline of a pistol at the back waistband of his jeans.

Dr. Nolan smiled and put the car in gear.

"Thank you," he said as they passed.

"Wow," Eileen said. "Not exactly a warm and fuzzy reception. And, what court order do you have that I don't know about?"

"Judge Judy on TV." Dr. Nolan smiled. "She gave the order."

Mrs. Ramirez laughed. She was beginning to enjoy his humor.

A half mile down the road was an immaculate two story farm house surrounded by old shade trees. Just beyond were three enormous open buildings and a steel silo standing thirty feet tall. Two of the structures appeared to be processing facilities, and the third was filled with tractors, trucks, and very new looking equipment. Everything appeared to be clean and well kept.

At the far end of the equipment compound was an enclosed area with a number of vehicles parked outside. Dr. Nolan considered it a likely starting point.

They had just gotten out of the car when the door to the office opened, a cherubic-faced man near fifty smiling as he approached. His blond hair was thinning and in retreat, but he still moved with assurance and command. He was wearing tan pants, a short sleeved dress shirt, and slip-on loafers.

"Hello. Hello." He smiled, shaking hands. "Come in out of this heat. You have any trouble finding us?"

"It was just getting through the gate that slowed us down," Dr. Nolan said, smiling.

"Oh, sorry about that," the man explained. "We have a fairly big payroll every week. Lot of cash on hand. Just a precaution. I'm Keenan Dahlquist, by the way."

"Dr. Sean Nolan. And this is Eileen Carson from the CDC, and our translator, Estelle Ramirez. Quite a place you have here."

"It's actually my father's farm," the man explained, "but I took over the management about four years ago after he broke a hip. Just about two thousand acres. Melons, sugar beets, asparagus, broccoli. Keeps us busy."

"My husband and I do strawberries and raspberries in Washington," Eileen said. "But only 120 acres. Your operation is huge. How many workers?"

"Oh, varies with the season," Mr. Dahlquist said. "Thirty to over a hundred."

"You have trouble getting help? We sure do. Sometimes we lose crops because we can't get enough pickers."

Kennan Dahlquist nodded. He brought chairs over and arranged them around his desk.

"Not a problem here," he answered. "We treat our people well. That was always my father's number one rule. They helped make him successful. We pay above average, we feed them twice a day, and we even have some housing units. Even have a day care area."

Dr. Nolan listened, nodding as Mr. Dahlquist spoke. He took note of the term "our people" used over and over. Not employees or workers, but more of a possessed commodity.

"You must have been worried when the Legionnaires' outbreak started?" Eileen asked. "Especially when four people came down sick."

"Worried? I was terrified," Mr. Dahlquist admitted. "Not only for our people, but it could have shut down the whole harvest. The CDC saved us. They came in and tested everything, made sure there wasn't a problem here on the property. They were here two, three times. Man, they even tested toilet tanks."

Dr. Nolan smiled.

"We don't miss much," Dr. Nolan said. "It was just odd to have four cases in one place, didn't make sense. But, it also didn't fit with all the other cases in the valley. Not unless they were all working for you."

"We're not that big." Mr. Dahlquist laughed. "I didn't even know how you caught that bug until they explained it to me. We're more used to E. coli and salmonella, germs that can affect crops. This was a new one."

"And, a lethal one," Dr. Nolan added. "The fellow who died, and at least one of the women who got sick turned out to be illegals, correct?"

Mr. Dahlquist looked him directly in the eye and nodded.

"It happens," he said, just as a matter of fact. "Fake ID is available all along the border. Both here and there. We screen as best we can, but everyone has the same problem. People need work, and we need people."

"We've been burned before, too," Eileen said. "And now we've got the idiotic law that stops teenagers from working in the fields."

"It's funny in a way," Mr. Dahlquist said. "I grew up working this land since the age of ten. Didn't hurt me. Now the kids just sit in the house and watch TV or play with their phones. It's all gone crazy."

"And they eat too many calories, drink too much pop, and get fatter and fatter," Dr. Nolan said. "It is crazy."

They fell silent for a moment.

"So, what can we help with?" Mr. Dahlquist asked, slapping his knee. "Anything at all."

"We need to examine the three survivors and do a follow-up interview," Dr. Nolan explained. "Part of the protocol."

Mr. Dahlquist looked at the wall clock.

"Tell you what. We provide dinner at five o'clock. I can give you a quick tour, we'll go say hello to my dad, and then you can eat here and talk to our people. How's that sound?"

Dr. Nolan looked at Eileen and Mrs. Ramirez. There was no objection.

Mr. Dahlquist led them out to a Cadillac Escalade. Dr. Nolan took the back seat with Mrs. Ramirez, letting Eileen sit up front. They headed out slowly over a series of one lane dirt roads, the farm a flat canvas of ever changing color, a right turn after a mile, then another right turn, then another, the processing area again ahead in the distance. Along the western border of the cultivated tracts were two single level, cinder block structures, each with six small, individual living quarters. An even smaller building stood between them.

"These are the housing units," Mr. Dahlquist explained. "You want to stop?"

"Please," said Dr. Nolan.

They pulled in and parked. Mr. Dahlquist left the engine running, and the two women stayed in the air-conditioned car. Mr. Dahlquist led Dr. Nolan to an end unit, knocked to make certain it was empty, then opened the door. The room was square with a cement floor. Two single beds were against opposite walls. There was a small metal sink, a walled off toilet stall, a small wardrobe for clothes, two metal folding chairs, and two windows, both covered with metal bars. The room was clean, private, and recently painted.

"Very nice," said Dr. Nolan.

Mr. Dahlquist led him out, then showed him the two communal showers in the smaller building, one for men, and one for women.

"Like I said. We take good care of our people," Mr. Dahlquist told him.

"I'm impressed," Dr. Nolan admitted.

They went back to the car.

"We've got time to say hi to my dad before dinner. If I don't take you up there, I'll never hear the end of it. He was very grateful for how the CDC responded when things got bad."

Back in the soothing climate of the big Cadillac, they drove past the commercial buildings to the farm house. Mr. Dahlquist led the three visitors up the steps, the door already open and inviting.

"Come in. Come in," said the senior Mr. Dahlquist, a wide grin on his face. Medium height and build, he held a cane in his left hand, but his handshake was still strong and powerful. Dr. Nolan noticed the thick, weathered skin, the gnarled fingers and numerous telling scars from years of physical labor. Balding now, his blue eyes were still alert and focused.

"Thank you for seeing us, Mr. Dahlquist. Quite an empire you've built here," Dr. Nolan said.

"Ben. Ben. Mr. Dahlquist was my grandfather." The old man laughed. He led them to a sitting room, a noticeable limp and sideways shift to his gait. It was obvious to Dr. Nolan that arthritic changes had not only compromised his hips, but his knees as well.

They all took seats, and Dr. Nolan introduced Eileen and Mrs. Ramirez.

"Your team saved us," Ben Dahlquist said. "We could have lost a whole season when that damn sickness broke out. They tested everything and got us back in business in just a few days."

"They're very good at what they do," Dr. Nolan said. "They keep little fires from becoming big ones. I'm glad it worked out."

"They're heroes to me," the old man said. "Can I offer you something to drink?"

"It's okay, Dad," his son interrupted. "I've invited them to meet the crew and stay for dinner. We've only got a few minutes."

"Oh, good, good." The older man nodded. "I love these people. Hard workers. Helped me build this farm and keep it growing." There was genuine admiration in his voice.

"How many years have you been here?" Dr. Nolan asked.

"Born in this house," Ben Dahlquist said. "Been remodeled here and there, but this is the original homestead, 1878. Tough sledding back in those years. Irrigation changed everything. Didn't really amount to much until the late fifties." He sat, nodding to himself, recalling memories. "You come back sometime and I'll show you pictures. Used to plow and harvest with mule teams."

"I would love that," Dr. Nolan told him. He liked Ben Dahlquist. Authentic and proud of his life's work, he reminded

Dr. Nolan of his elderly patients back home. They were his greatest joy.

"You don't speak Spanish, Dr. Nolan?" the old man asked, nodding toward Mrs. Ramirez.

"I speak Spanish and Croatian equally well." Dr. Nolan laughed. "The problem is, I keep getting them mixed up. Mrs. Ramirez was kind enough to offer her assistance."

Ben Dahlquist slapped his knee, laughing in response.

"Well, we don't hire too many Croatians," he said. "You look like you're in good hands."

"Okay, folks," Keenan Dahlquist said, holding up his wristwatch. "We need to get over to the plant. Dad, I'll see you later."

They all stood, shook hands with the senior Mr. Dahlquist, and thanked him for his hospitality. He did not follow them to the door.

"Offer stands, Dr. Nolan," he called after them. "You come back anytime."

"Thank you. I will." Dr. Nolan smiled.

They took the car back to the office area and parked. Dr. Nolan retrieved his stethoscope and three legal pads from their Nissan, then Kennan Dahlquist escorted them to one of the open processing buildings. Three long rows of tables had been set up in the open half of the structure, folding chairs spaced along them. Large fans pushed some cooling air around them, but it was still thick and humid. They could smell a pleasant mixture of spices and cooking food as they entered.

"Twice a day, six days a week," Mr. Dahlquist explained. "Sundays we don't work."

"You set up your own kitchen?" Eileen asked.

"Come take a look." Mr. Dahlquist led them to the far end of the room. A partition wall opened into a fully equipped cooking facility. The stoves, ovens, refrigerators, and freezers were all stainless steel. They were industrial quality, and the room was organized and spotless. Five Hispanic women were busy completing their preparations. They looked up and smiled, but said nothing.

"This is just like my kitchen at home," Dr. Nolan remarked.

"Liar," Eileen said. "You have a microwave and a hot plate. You wouldn't know how to use any of this."

Mrs. Ramirez was laughing.

"Just a touch of home," Mr. Dahlquist said. "Our way of thanking them for all they do."

He took them out, seating them at the head of the front table. Dozens of workers were beginning to arrive as the day shift ended. They washed up at a sink along the wall, then took chairs in small groups, glancing at the visitors and keeping their voices low. When most of the available spaces had been filled, Mr. Dahlquist introduced their guests, explaining that after dinner they wanted to interview some of them. There was a silence in the room, here and there a nod.

"They get a little uneasy when strangers show up," Mr. Dahlquist explained. "But, they'll be available to you."

"I understand," Dr. Nolan said. "I make myself nervous. We'll be fine. Mrs. Ramirez will see to that."

"Good." Mr. Dahlquist smiled. "You'll have to forgive me, but I've got hours of payroll and farm orders. Feel free to do whatever you need to do. And, if there's any questions, I'll have our ranch foreman stay available."

Dr. Nolan stood and shook his hand.

"You and your father have been wonderful hosts," he said. "Thank you."

"Pleasure," Mr. Dahlquist said. "Foreman's name is Dell Sprague. He let you in the gate earlier. I'll have him come over." He gave a half wave, then headed back to his office.

The kitchen staff began bringing out large platters and bowls of food, setting up an assembly line on tables against the wall. All of the workers stayed in their seats, looking at Eileen, Mrs. Ramirez, and Dr. Nolan.

"I think we're supposed to go first," Eileen whispered.

"I hope this isn't like the food testers that kings and queens employed," he whispered back. "They usually had short careers."

He stood up, smiled to the group of workers, then escorted the two women to the serving line. There were plastic plates, silverware, napkins, and an impressive array of tamales, quesadillas, mole sauce, black beans, rice, salad, and assorted cold drinks. The workers started to line up behind them.

"This is amazing," Eileen said, filling her plate.

"But, no coffee," Dr. Nolan said. "I'm not eating here again."

"Jeez, it's a hundred degrees in here," Eileen said. "You're impossible."

Back at their table, it was the same protocol. No one would eat before they started, but with the first bite, the room became a beehive of activity, laughter, and conversation. They were now just members of the collective.

"This is excellent," Dr. Nolan said.

"Authentic Mexican food," Mrs. Ramirez said. "Not like the restaurants. Big difference."

"Give the Dahlquists credit," Dr. Nolan said. "This is very thoughtful, and not cheap."

"Pays to keep good employees," Eileen said. "No farm survives without them."

Dr. Nolan nodded, but did not respond with words. He was busy eating.

10

Keenan Dahlquist sat at his desk, going over shipping vouchers. His secretary had left for the day, and the droning hum of the air conditioner was the only sound in the room. He brushed away an annoying fly that kept practicing touch and go landings on his neck.

The door opened, a wave of hot air flowing in and rustling his paperwork.

"Shipment ready?" he asked, not looking up.

"All loaded," Dell Sprague replied. Two double trailers were waiting in the first packing shed, their large wooden cargo boxes filled with dried sugar beets. By midnight, they would be across the border in Mexicali, delivered to the only processing plant in the region.

"And the return trip?" Mr. Dahlquist asked.

"Fully booked," his foreman answered. "What's with the tour group?"

Kennan Dahlquist finally looked up at him.

"Goddamn CDC again," he said. "Some kind of follow-up visit. I thought this was all over and done with."

"You worried about trouble?"

"Always," Mr. Dahlquist answered. "After dinner, they're going to interview the workers that were ill. I want you to stay close and make sure no one gets too friendly."

"And, if they do?"

"Be creative," Mr. Dahlquist said. "That's why you get paid the big money."

Dell Sprague smiled and nodded.

11

THE WOMEN FROM THE KITCHEN staff began collecting the dinner dishes. The questioning glances from the assembled workers were beginning to multiply.

"Okay, Mrs. Ramirez," Dr. Nolan said from behind a smile, "you ready to earn your keep?"

"I will do my best," she answered.

Dr. Nolan put the stethoscope around his neck, then stood and led Mrs. Ramirez to the front of the table area.

"Just repeat what I say, as closely as you can," he told her. "And give them that big smile, okay?" She nodded.

Dr. Nolan had her introduce themselves, making it clear they were from the Center for Disease Control.

"We have nothing to do with immigration or the police. We only want to keep you safe and healthy, nothing else. Your help could save other people from getting sick."

He paused, giving Mrs. Ramirez time to translate. Still smiling, he tried to make eye contact with as many people in the audience as possible.

"When the sickness came, we know that three of you became ill and recovered. Can those people raise their hands please?"

Slowly, an older man at one of the tables held up his hand, then two of the women near the kitchen followed.

"Bueno. Good," Dr. Nolan said. "We need to check and see how you are doing. Second, the man who died, did anyone know him? Did he have any close friends? We would like to be able to contact his family."

There was no response. Most of the workers looked down at the tables, a few others peeking to see if anyone would acknowledge the request.

"No one knew him?" Dr. Nolan repeated.

Again, there was only silence and averted eyes.

"Okay." He sighed, then whispered to Mrs. Ramirez, "I guess he wasn't very popular."

She tried not to laugh, but did anyway.

He looked out at the workers again.

"All right. Thank you very much. We would like the three people who raised their hands to stay for a few minutes. The rest of you can do whatever you do. And, thank you for letting us share dinner with you."

Many of the workers smiled and nodded, but they wasted no time in vacating the building. In less than a minute, the large room was nearly empty. Dr. Nolan noticed that the man who had unlocked the gate for them earlier was in the room, leaning against the wall behind them.

"How do you want to do this?" Eileen asked. She was holding the charts supplied by the CDC.

"Let's see if anyone speaks English. You and I can start there. Mrs. Ramirez will have to interview the others." He directed everyone to the table nearest the kitchen.

The male survivor, Louis Garcia, was in his early forties and did speak English. Dr. Nolan shook his hand, then had him take a seat about twenty feet away from the others. The two women, one of them very young, were adamant that they only spoke Spanish.

Dr. Nolan reviewed their files. The names on the records were Maya Sorento and Lucia Coleta. He held a brief consultation with Eileen and Mrs. Ramirez.

"Let's keep the two women together for now," he suggested. "Be charming, go slow, and see if you can get one of them to talk to you. We want to know how they got here and any place they might have visited before they got sick. Okay?"

Dr. Nolan had the group of women sit near the kitchen door. As they seated themselves, the ranch worker moved closer, still leaning against the wall.

Dr. Nolan went back and sat across from Mr. Garcia, not wanting to make him feel cornered or threatened. He shook hands again.

"Thank you for your help," he began. "Are you feeling back to normal?"

"Good. Si. Yes. Very good," he answered. "Some cough still."

Dr. Nolan nodded. He looked at the personal information sheet in the CDC chart. It was almost blank.

"I see you are forty four. Have you worked here long?"

"Yes. Long time now," Mr. Garcia answered.

"And where did you work before this?" Dr. Nolan asked.

"Another farm. Wherever they need me," Mr. Garcia said.

"And, where was that? How long ago?"

"I don't remember. No se," he said, not at all comfortable.

"Okay." Dr. Nolan smiled. "Before you got sick. Two weeks before. Dos semana. Do you remember going anywhere? To town, to the store, to visit anyone?"

Mr. Garcia looked down and shook his head from side to side.

"I live here," he said.

Dr. Nolan tried not to show any frustration.

"Do you send money back to your family?" he asked the man. Mr. Garcia smiled and nodded at the mention of his family.

"Si. Every week. From here," he said. "I have not left."

Dr. Nolan knew he was not telling the truth, but there was nothing to be gained by confronting him.

"Okay. Thank you," he said. "Can I listen to your lungs?" Mr. Garcia nodded. Dr. Nolan came around the table, had the man take half a dozen deep breaths, then patted him on the shoulder.

"You are very lucky to be alive," he told the worker. "Thank you again."

"De nada." Mr. Garcia smiled and bowed his head.

Dr. Nolan made a hand gesture to indicate he was free to go, then gathered up his papers. There were no new entries. He watched the man leave, then looked over to where the four women were talking. Eileen tipped her head ever so slightly in the direction of the younger girl.

Dr. Nolan wandered over and introduced himself.

"El medico," he said. "Let's have this young lady move to the next table so I can examine her, and Mrs. Ramirez can stay here."

With more hand gestures, they managed to separate the two women. Eileen's Spanish was adequate enough to keep things moving. Dr. Nolan exaggerated and slowed every step of his evaluation. First, he looked at her throat, then checked the lymph nodes in her neck, taking more time to listen to her heart and lungs. The ranch worker was watching intently.

"Learn anything?" he whispered to Eileen, pretending to write in the woman's chart.

"Mmm, hmm." Eileen smiled. "And I think Lucia speaks pretty good English. Too bad we have an audience."

"Maybe I can help with that," Dr. Nolan said. He stood up, thanked their subject, then approached their silent guardian. "Hi, I'm Dr. Nolan. You are?"

"Dell. Dell Sprague. Mr. Dahlquist sent me over to help."

"Perfect." Dr. Nolan smiled. "I need coffee. Can you help me ask the ladies in the kitchen if there's any coffee?"

The man glanced at Mrs. Ramirez, and then at Eileen, but he was trapped. He walked with Dr. Nolan to the kitchen. Dr. Nolan acted grateful as his new acquaintance asked one of the women to make coffee, a task he could have accomplished on his own. Mr. Sprague turned to leave.

"Have you worked here long?" Dr. Nolan asked, stopping him.

"Six years," Mr. Sprague answered. "Worked my way up from field boss to supervisor."

"Big place," Dr. Nolan said. "Farming is half computer work now, isn't it? Weather, water use, fertilizers?"

"It is," the man said, now more engaged. "Used to have gigantic sprinkler systems," he explained. "Now, it's all drip hoses underground. All runs on timers. We know to the gallon where it all goes. Computer even makes adjustments for temperature and humidity."

"Jesus, I thought my job was technical. Now you have to be a scientist and a computer geek just to farm." Dr. Nolan laughed.

"Mr. Dahlquist is the computer guy," the man admitted. "I just make sure everything keeps running." He was slowly moving back toward the other room.

"Hey, let me ask you something," Dr. Nolan said.

One of the women held out a cup of coffee. "Oh, God bless you. Smells good. This other worker, no one knew him. Do you think he was an illegal? Maybe had fake papers?"

Dell Sprague hesitated.

"I don't know. People come and go all the time," he said. "I turned over all his stuff to the coroner. That's all I know."

Dr. Nolan sipped his coffee and nodded.

"Just seems odd that with all these workers, no one knew much about him. Was he staying in one of the housing units?"

"Yeah. I think so. Why?"

"Oh, most of them have two beds, that's all. He must have been sharing the room," Dr. Nolan noted. "You know who the other worker was?"

Dell Sprague was becoming noticeably agitated. He shifted his weight from foot to foot.

"No idea," he said flatly. "I'm not their den mother. Anything else?"

"No. Thanks for your help," Dr. Nolan said. He followed the other man out, just as Mrs. Ramirez was giving the young woman she had interviewed a big hug. There were tears in the young girl's eyes.

"We all done?" he asked, looking at Eileen and Mrs. Ramirez. They both nodded, gathering up their papers. He turned to the young girl, smiled, and held out his coffee cup.

"Un mas, por favor?"

She was short, her slightly round face framed by black hair, her dark eyes fringed in red from crying. He held her gaze for a long moment, then she bowed, took the cup, and disappeared into the kitchen.

Dr. Nolan leaned forward, trying to read the notes Mrs. Ramirez had jotted down on her pad. The young woman returned, bumping into him and spilling some of the coffee. She apologized over and over.

"No problema," he said. "Gracias."

"You folks done," Dell Sprague said, not really a question. "I'll lead you out to the gate."

He followed them back to the parking area, then climbed into a jacked-up silver Ram truck with oversize tires and a roll bar. The dual mufflers sounded like a roaring lion. He drove slowly past them, then sped up when he was certain they were close behind.

At the road, he opened the gate with a remote control, pulled over and let them go by, not bothering to wave. Dr. Nolan checked the rearview mirror, a sigh of relief when no headlights appeared behind them. He took a drink of his coffee.

"Well, ladies, my guy is an illegal worker. He's never been anywhere, never leaves the farm, and is afraid to talk. How about you, Eileen?"

"Almost the same," Eileen reported. "I did find out she came from the Yucatan Peninsula area. Wouldn't say when she arrived, and says she never leaves. Obviously illegal."

Dr. Nolan sighed. He glanced at Mrs. Ramirez in the rearview mirror.

"Two down," he said. "So, what did you find out, big shot?"

Mrs. Ramirez smiled broadly and looked at her papers.

"Real name Maya Alicias. Fifteen years old. Her brother was murdered for refusing to join a street gang in Guatemala. Her parents scraped together all the money they could and sent her north."

"Whoa, nice work!" Dr. Nolan shouted. "Now, when did she arrive, and where has she been?"

"That's when she started crying," Mrs. Ramirez explained. "She was scared. Scared to death. I think if I could spend more time with her I could do better."

"Better! You did great," Dr. Nolan told her. "Will you marry me, Mrs. Ramirez? I assume you can cook?"

Mrs. Ramirez was laughing, a high-pitched rolling wave that filled the car.

"You are a crazy man," she said.

12

They delivered Mrs. Ramirez back to her car just before 9:00 p.m. Dr. Nolan escorted her to the safety of her Toyota Camry, then gave her a big hug.

"You're a superstar," he told her. "Write out a bill for your services, but we might need you again. Are you up for it?"

The woman smiled.

"It was a good day," she said. "Just call if you need anything."

He watched her pull away from the curb and head south, then walked up the sidewalk to the legal aid offices. The lights were still on and the door unlocked. Only one of the young male lawyers was still working, and he was chest deep in documents.

"Can I help you?" he asked, barely glancing up from his papers.

"Uhhh…the woman that works here. Dark hair. Athletic. I don't see her," Dr. Nolan said, clearly ill at ease.

"And you are?"

"Oh...sorry. Dr. Sean Nolan with the CDC. I spoke with her the other day."

The young man put down his pen, looked up, the beginnings of a smile on his face.

"Elena Cantrell," he said. "Left about half an hour ago." Dr. Nolan had neglected to ask her name at their first meeting.

"Oh, I see. Okay. No problem," Dr. Nolan said. "Well, thanks." He turned to leave.

"You like challenges, Doctor?" the young lawyer called after him.

Dr. Nolan laughed and nodded.

"I thrive on them," he answered, but did not elaborate.

"Good. She's driven, focused, tough as a five-dollar steak, and has no social life. She outworks all of us. Just saying."

Dr. Nolan regarded the young man, perhaps just thirty years of age, wondering if he had tried to date Elena Cantrell himself.

"Forewarned is forearmed," Dr. Nolan said. "Thanks for the heads-up."

He went out and rejoined Eileen. The temperature had fallen into the high seventies, but she still had the air-conditioning on at full force.

"What took so long?"

"Oh, had to check on something," Dr. Nolan said. He buckled in and headed toward the hotel.

"Quite a day." Eileen sighed.

"We didn't waste much of it," he answered. "Like before, one piece of the puzzle at a time. Tomorrow morning, I want you to check with the coroner's office and see if they have any information on the deceased worker. Then you and I are going to take a drive in the country."

"Business or pleasure?" Eileen asked.

"All business," Dr. Nolan said. "We're going down 86 to the Mexican border, and back on 111. I want to check every test site on the CDC list, just to make sure nothing was overlooked."

"That's one hell of a list," Eileen reminded him.

"That it is," Dr. Nolan said. "What did you think about our visit to the Dahlquist place?"

Eileen thought for a moment, trying to separate the objective and subjective sides.

"I liked the dad," she began. "But, I don't know. Junior seemed nice, the farm was amazing, and all the workers seemed scared."

"Maybe they're all illegal," Dr. Nolan suggested.

"Maybe," Eileen said. "But those two girls were different. More fragile. Something."

Dr. Nolan had not interacted with them for any length of time. His efforts had been directed at keeping the foreman occupied.

"I liked the old man, too. He's the real deal," Dr. Nolan said. "Junior was eager to show us all the positive things he could squeeze into a one hour tour, but then sent someone to keep an eye on us when we spoke to the workers. Seemed a little odd."

"Our workers get nervous when strangers come around," Eileen offered. "But, even after it was clear we weren't a threat, something was still off, out of normal. I don't know how to say it."

"Women's intuition?" Dr. Nolan smiled.

"Don't joke," Eileen said. "It works."

"I'm being serious," Dr. Nolan told her. "Mrs. Ramirez felt it too. Something."

They parked at the hotel and went to their rooms. Dr. Nolan's laundry was neatly folded outside his door.

"Tell Uncle Mike hi for me," Dr. Nolan said as she unlocked her room. "And rest up. Another long day tomorrow."

"You better go clean your room," Eileen reminded him sternly. "And give my love to the girls."

Dr. Nolan did as he was instructed. An hour later the charts were packed away, the litter of papers collected, and all the wrappers and dishes dealt with. Except for the bed and the map, it was back to normal. He studied the route they would take in the morning, showered again, got into bed, then phoned his daughters.

Now four days away from home, they were beginning to miss him. He listened to an update on their day, told them how much he loved them both, then reassured them he would be back before they knew it.

It was a good call.

13

Keenan Dahlquist watched the two trucks leave the farm just after 11:00 p.m. The round trip to Mexicali and back would take over six hours. If everything went as planned, they would return before sunrise.

He went to his desk, turned off the computer, then downed the last of his Chivas Regal, wincing slightly as it burned his throat. He picked up his keys, locked the door, then climbed into his Escalade. Backing out, he turned away from the main driveway. He slowly navigated down the one lane dirt road that led to the workers' housing units.

Pulling up to the last one on the north side, he shut off his car. Guided by moonlight, he went to the door, a chain running from the latch to a steel spike embedded in the frame. Searching for the right key, he undid the padlock and went in without knocking.

Maya Alicias was lying in a fetal position on the bed with her face toward the wall. She had heard the car engine, the footsteps, the key in the lock. She held her eyes shut tightly, pretending to be asleep, praying she was somewhere else.

Keenan Dahlquist did not speak. He stood looking down at her for a moment, then began to unbutton his shirt.

14

At breakfast the next morning, Eileen informed Dr. Nolan that the coroner had received nothing on the deceased worker. There were no identification papers, no personal effects, no letters, no clothing.

"Well, that's a shock," Dr. Nolan said sarcastically. "One more lie to add to the others. The foreman told me he turned everything over to the medical examiner."

"Why lie about that?" Eileen asked.

"Probably thought we wouldn't check," Dr. Nolan answered. "Simple."

Eileen finished her toast.

"You ready for tedious?" she asked. The list of sites the CDC had tested along both highways was five pages long.

"Best we start early. I'll grab some water." Dr. Nolan bought four bottles of Disani from the vending machine in the lobby, then they headed out. The heat was already oppressive.

"Can you imagine working in this?" Eileen asked.

Dr. Nolan laughed.

"We are working in this," he reminded her.

"I mean real work," she chided him. "Outside work."

"Not for ten minutes," he admitted. They drove south through El Centro, then began the slow, painstaking process of matching every store, shop, office building, gas station, rest stop, restaurant, strip mall, and public structure to the CDC list. There was not a single location open to the outside world that had not been tested. Dr. Nolan marveled at the man hours expended.

South of El Centro, the public access points began to thin out, sometimes with miles between checkpoints. By the time 86 merged with Highway 111, their targets were fewer and fewer.

"Let's check the right side down to Calexico, then the other side coming back up," he suggested. "I'm getting whiplash."

The last few miles were barren desert and more low income housing, only beginning to improve as they neared the outskirts of the city. At the first commercial area, they turned around and headed back north.

"Sorry, but I've got to make a stop," Dr. Nolan said. "That's what I get for drinking all that damned water."

Eileen laughed.

"Me, too," she said. "Try to find a gas station that looks civilized."

He passed up one option, opting for a newer, more brightly painted competitor a mile up the road. An old, boarded up building to the right appeared to be its predecessor, but the gas pumps had long been removed.

"Check the list first," Dr. Nolan said.

"Let's see. Mobil station. Address matches. Must have a small store inside. Tested both bathrooms. Water fountain. Ice maker. Three refrigerator units. Mop sink in back. No standing water sources identified."

"Okay. Done and done," Dr. Nolan said. "You want something from inside?"

"Anything with vanilla ice cream," Eileen said. "Just don't tell Mike."

Dr. Nolan promised secrecy. After using the "hombre" facilities, he walked through the small convenience shopping space, noting it was clean and well managed. He picked out two Hagen-Daz bars and rejoined Eileen.

"Eat fast or you'll be wearing this," he warned her. It was 104 degrees. The short break was welcomed. Dr. Nolan pointed at the sky through the windshield. Billowing white and gray cumulous clouds were building to the north, vertical columns expanding as they rose and grew in size.

"Looks like rain," Eileen said, a tinge of expectant joy in her voice.

"Not likely," Dr. Nolan reminded her. "This area gets three inches of rain in a year. Our luck isn't that good. Where next?"

Eileen sighed and looked at her notes.

"Card Lock a mile ahead. Commercial. No employees," she said.

"Okay. Party's over." Dr. Nolan smiled.

North again, hour after hour, they verified every potential contamination site along the route. By late afternoon, they had made their way back to Brawley. Dr. Nolan reversed course onto Highway 86 again, looping south to Imperial and their home base. He got out of the car, stretched, then instinctively ducked down as the first cannon blast of thunder and lightning exploded above them. The sound and blinding electrical discharge were nearly simultaneous.

"Shit! Let's get inside," he said. They half jogged to the lobby, barely inside when the next cycle erupted, this time a slight delay between sight and sound.

"It's moving away," Eileen said. "And no rain. Just dry lightning."

"Look at the bright side. At least it won't start any brush fires like back home. There's nothing to burn," Dr. Nolan joked.

"Too optimistic for me," Eileen said. "I'm done. If you don't mind, I'm going to turn in early. I'm exhausted."

He could see her fatigue. In just five days, they had covered a lot of territory.

"Good idea," he said. "We can take a fresh look at everything in the morning."

They rode the elevator up, the last of the storm moving off to the east, the thunder now like a bowling ball rolling down the alley, but without the pin strike. Dr. Nolan sat near the window in his room, reviewing what they had learned, irritated by what they had not. He turned on CNN, unable to stand the daily update of political buffoonery for more than a few minutes. He paced back and forth, then peeled off his clothing, showered in cool water, shaved, brushed his teeth, put on his only dress shirt, and regarded himself in the mirror. Not horrible, he thought.

Picking up his discarded jeans, he searched the pockets for his car keys, his fingers surprised when they touched on a folded piece of paper. He moved to the table lamp to read it. There were just three printed words: "Por favor ayudenos."

He knew the first two meant "please," but had never seen the last word. Eileen was probably asleep and in need of uninterrupted rest. He put the note in his shirt, skipped down the stairs, once again driving to the legal aid office. Elena Cantrell was at her desk, head down, eyes focused on court papers spread out in front of her. Dr. Nolan sat down in the vacant chair across from her.

"I finally got some rest," he said. "Are you married, or not?"

The woman looked up, already smiling before she made eye contact.

"Your technique seems unchanged," she said, laying down her pen. "Has this ever worked?"

"I'm just trying it out." Dr. Nolan smiled. "You think it needs refinement?"

"Maybe, just a little." She laughed.

"Look. I'm terrible at this," he admitted. "You're obviously intelligent, cultured beyond my level, and not difficult to look at. Have dinner with me."

"This just keeps getting better and better," she said. Her eyes were dancing with light. "But I won't eat till later. Sorry."

"That's perfect," Dr. Nolan said. "That's exactly when I was going to eat."

She laughed again, looking at him for a long moment.

"Eight o'clock," she said. "Now go away."

"That's where I was going. Away. Until eight." He stood up to leave, then remembered the note. "Oh, one last thing. What does this say?" He handed her the slip of paper.

She looked at it and frowned.

"Where did you get this?" she asked.

"Can't tell you," Dr. Nolan answered. "What does it mean?"

"It says, 'Please help us.'"

Dr. Nolan nodded. He took the note back and stared at it. When they were finishing at the Dahlquist Farm, the young girl had bumped into him when she brought the coffee. It was the only possible source.

"Okay. Thanks. Thank you," he said. "I'll be back at eight. Thank you." He went out and stood on the sidewalk, not certain what to do. He held the slip of paper between his thumbs and index fingers, only the size of a message from a Chinese fortune cookie. But this was real.

He placed it in his wallet, then searched for the phone number belonging to Mrs. Ramirez. Further up the street was a small café. He went in, sat at the back booth, ordered coffee, then dialed her home.

"Mrs. Ramirez. Dr. Nolan. I'm sorry to call so late, but we have a little emergency situation here," he explained. "I know it's short notice, but are you available in the morning? Say ten o'clock?"

"What happened?" the woman asked.

"I found a note in my pocket that asked for help. I think it was written by the girl from Guatemala."

"She asked me for a pen," Mrs. Ramirez said. "I thought it was to write down her name and village. Why didn't she just say it?"

"Too afraid. I don't know. But we need to go back. Tomorrow."

He could hear paper being shuffled.

"I have court," Mrs. Ramirez said. "I will call someone to take my place. The girl knows me a little. It is best for me to be there."

"Bless you, Mrs. Ramirez," Dr. Nolan said. "My marriage proposal still stands, if you promise to take cooking lessons."

"Be careful." She laughed. "I might just agree."

"Perfect. Ten o'clock. Same place?"

"Yes. Yes. I will see you then," Mrs. Ramirez promised.

Dr. Nolan checked his watch. He considered calling Sheriff Dent's friend at the Border Patrol office, but to tell him what? Just chat about a dozen possible scenarios? There was no justification for contacting anyone at this point, let alone law enforcement. It would all depend on what the girl was willing to tell them.

He had the waitress refill his coffee cup, wasted thirty minutes trying to think of witty dialogue, then walked back to the legal aid building, already nervous. Elena Cantrell was on the phone, smiling and engaged in an animated exchange. She held up one finger, finished her call, grabbed her briefcase, and joined him near the door.

"Where would you like to go?" he asked her. "It's your town."

"Something light," she said. "Anything heavy this late will give me bad dreams."

"I may do that anyway," Dr. Nolan warned her.

"We'll see. I'll drive," she said. She led him to the parking lot at the side of the building, unlocking the doors of a well-worn Honda Civic.

"I thought lawyers drove Mercedes," he said.

"I'm just a poor paralegal," she answered. "I took the bar exam two weeks ago. Now I wait."

They got in, headed north, then turned into a restaurant close to the airport. He held the door for her at the entrance, a gesture that did not go unnoticed. Only half occupied, the hostess led them to a large booth along the wall with no other diners nearby. She ordered a New Zealand Chardonnay, and Dr. Nolan more coffee.

"So, are you?"

"What?"

"Married?"

Elena smiled and shook her head. She was stunningly attractive.

"Was," she finally answered. "Long time ago. And what about you? I don't see a ring, and there's no tan mark indicating a recent change."

"Very good," he complimented her. "My wife passed away. Ten years now."

"I'm sorry," Elena said.

"So am I," Dr. Nolan said. "It's been the hardest on my two daughters. They ended up with me as mother and father."

"How old are they now?"

"Fifteen and thirteen," he told her. "But, I'm much more interested in your story."

The waitress came and took their order, she a Caesar salad with chicken, and he a Crab Louie.

"Okay. Old story," she began, her hands folded on the table. "Fell in love, married too early, worked to put my husband through school, got pregnant, became a boring housewife, got cheated on, got divorced, and then concentrated on raising my daughter. She's in her last semester at San Diego State."

Dr. Nolan clapped his hands softly.

"Bravo," he said. "That tells me a lot, but where's the you part? What were you doing all that time?"

She held his eyes.

"My job. Raising my child," she said. "I worked as a transcriptionist in a big law firm, took classes to become a paralegal, waited for Sophia to begin college, and then I did, too. Night school for four years. Just finished in January."

"That tells me much more." Dr. Nolan smiled. "You should be very proud."

"I actually am," Elena admitted.

The arrival of their food created a shift to less weighty issues for a time. Dr. Nolan studied her, the grace of her hands, the way she held her head, the comfortable eye contact. There was no hint of timidity. She was confident and self-assured. The scars that she bore were well hidden and not for public display.

After dinner, she ordered a second glass of wine and sat back, smiling again.

"Now, it's your turn," she said. "Besides being a notorious womanizer, what other secrets do you have, Dr. Nolan?"

He could feel his cheeks redden.

"Sean, please," he said, giving a small shrug of his shoulders.

"Just a small-town doc with two daughters at home," he said. "Not very exciting. Work too much, and rarely play hooky. Pretty much like a Boy Scout."

Elena laughed out loud, then leaned toward the table.

"I took the liberty of checking on you just a tiny bit," she confessed. "I don't believe you would fit in well with the Boy Scouts. Some of your recent escapades seem to be, how should I say it? Proactive."

He stared down at his coffee cup, not certain what information she had access to.

"Well, there have been moments," he admitted, not wanting to say more.

"My mother thinks you're charming and funny," Elena said, a teasing in her voice.

Dr. Nolan looked up quickly, caught totally off guard. He searched memory files at a frantic pace, finally reaching one conclusion.

"You can't be serious." He smiled.

"I am," Elena affirmed. "That was her on the phone tonight. She said you asked her to marry you."

"Twice," Dr. Nolan corrected her, "but only if she's a good cook." He was still shocked by the revelation. He shook his head in disbelief. Mrs. Ramirez, his gifted translator, was Elena's mother. "I guess this is one of those small world moments."

"Not such a stretch," Elena said. "She does a lot of work for our office. So, when you requested a list of language specialists, she was the top choice. Pretty simple."

"But, now I'm stuck with a spy on my staff," he lamented. "I won't be able to rearrange the truth more to my liking. She'll rat me out."

Elena laughed at his protest.

"Don't worry. She's been trained to hold a high standard of confidentiality. She's very professional."

"Is that where you inherited your independence and drive?" Dr. Nolan asked.

Elena nodded.

"She came here as a field worker forty five years ago from a Mexican village where women were treated like cattle. She educated herself, married, raised a family, and now works as an interpreter. Pretty amazing."

"She is," Dr. Nolan agreed. "And, I think her daughter is pretty special, too."

Elena tipped her wine glass at the compliment, then looked at her watch.

"This is getting late for me," she said. "Early court tomorrow."

"I have a full day, too," Dr. Nolan added. "I have a date with your mom."

They paid the bill and went back to her car. The drive to where he had parked his own vehicle was awkward and silent. When she pulled into the curb, he sat staring ahead.

"Thank you for tonight," he said at last, still not looking at her. "It's been a long time since I've spent an evening with anyone. Like this. Just talking. It was nice."

"It was," she said. "Maybe we should try this again."

Dr. Nolan sighed deeply.

"I don't know," he said wistfully. "I've never dated a mother and her daughter before. This could get complicated."

Elena laughed, reached over, and squeezed his left hand, her touch lingering just a moment.

"If it helps," she said, "I'm a pretty good cook myself. Had a good teacher."

Now Dr. Nolan laughed.

"See what I mean. It just gets more complicated by the minute. I've got some thinking to do."

"When you figure it out," Elena told him, "you know where to find me. And, don't keep my mother out too late."

"Yes, ma'am," he promised. He did not want to leave, but was not yet ready to pursue any other options. Getting out of the car, he gave a small wave as she drove off, holding his hand up as more of a salute. He had interacted with lawyers on numerous occasions. There had never been a single instance when he wanted to kiss one of them.

15

Mrs. Ramirez was ready and waiting precisely at 10:00 a.m.

"We are going to the same place?" she asked from the back seat. Dr. Nolan handed her the note he had found in the rear pocket of his jeans.

"I'll try to get you alone with her," Dr. Nolan explained. "Show her the note, then make it clear that we will help in any way we can. You have to get her to trust you."

Mrs. Ramirez nodded.

"Do you want me to call ahead?" Eileen asked.

"No. I'm timing this so we get there at lunch break. The more people around, the better. You and I will try to run interference and keep any watchdogs occupied."

"What if she wants to leave with us?" Mrs. Ramirez asked.

"I believe it's still a free country," Dr. Nolan said. "And if anyone objects, we can use Health Department rules to take her out. We'll make up something about testing at the hospital."

"But, all legal, right?" Mrs. Ramirez asked, a little concerned.

"Mostly, I think," Dr. Nolan told her. "But, if we do get into trouble, I know where we can get a great lawyer."

The high-pitched laughter from the older woman filled the car, further confusing Eileen. Dr. Nolan was forced to explain the connection.

"So, while I was sleeping, you were out on the town, eh?" she quipped.

"It was research," Dr. Nolan protested. "Since I had asked Mrs. Ramirez to marry me, her daughter wanted to make certain my intentions were honorable."

"And, did you pass the test?" Eileen asked, winking at Mrs. Ramirez.

"I don't know," Dr. Nolan said seriously. "I think we may have to meet again. But, I did find out firsthand that Mrs. Ramirez is a terrible cook. Nothing but TV dinners and Top Ramen."

Mrs. Ramirez was a wonderful audience for his frenetic, meandering monologue. She was laughing again.

"You are the biggest liar I have ever known that wasn't on his way to jail," she told him.

"Day ain't over," he said, smiling at her in the rearview mirror.

Most of the drive was taken up by a litany of inane commentary delivered by Dr. Nolan, the goal to keep Mrs. Ramirez relaxed and distracted. She was the most essential member of their team, and he did not want her attention diverted. They arrived at the gate of Dahlquist Farm just before noon, the mood changing back to a serious atmosphere as they stopped at the computer pad.

"Yes?"

"I'm sorry to bother you again, but this is Dr. Nolan from CDC. There were a few questions about immunization status that we failed to ask on our last visit. Just take a few minutes."

The pause was an eternity. Dr. Nolan kept checking his watch, drumming his fingers against the steering wheel. After eight minutes, the gate buzzed and swung open. They drove onto the property, no one visible as they parked at the office. There was no welcoming committee.

Dr. Nolan took notice that Keenan Dahlquist's Escalade was parked nearby. They knocked on the door and waited for an invitation before entering.

"Dr. Nolan," Mr. Dahlquist said, his voice betraying annoyance. "I thought we were all up-to-date on everything. You're catching us at a very busy time."

"I sympathize," Dr. Nolan said. "But, you know these government forms. If we don't get everything filled out, then we'll be sent back again. It was my fault the questions weren't answered."

Mr. Dahlquist looked up. There was no warm smile or nod. He kept his eyes fixed on Dr. Nolan.

"This can be done quickly?" he asked.

"Very," Dr. Nolan assured him. "That's why we came at lunchtime. We didn't want to disrupt the work schedule."

Mr. Dahlquist narrowed his gaze, then gave a small nod.

"And what exactly do you need?"

"Just immunization questions from the three workers who became ill. Mumps, measles, pertussis. All routine."

"You can have a few minutes, but then my people have to get back to work. Oh, and the one girl quit."

Dr. Nolan took a slow breath, not showing any emotion.

"Which one would that be?" he asked.

"One of the kitchen staff," Mr. Dahlquist answered. "Collected her pay and moved on. Something about family in LA or Frisco, I'm not sure."

"I see. And no way to contact her?"

Mr. Dahlquist shrugged.

"They come and go. Too many to keep track of. But, the other two are here. Now, if you'll excuse me."

The invitation to leave was clear and final. Dr. Nolan motioned Eileen and Mrs. Ramirez toward the door.

"Thanks for putting up with us," Dr. Nolan said before leaving. "This should be our last official visit."

Mr. Dahlquist did not respond. His focus had already returned to business.

They went into the heat, then walked toward the processing plant where the workers were fed. The meal had just been served. Dr. Nolan smiled and waved as they entered the building.

"Now we've got reverse climate change," he said under his breath. "It suddenly got a lot cooler around here."

"You believe that crap about the girl leaving?" Eileen asked.

"I think the scientific term is 'bullshit,'" Dr. Nolan said.

"She told me she had no family here," Mrs. Ramirez added. "No one at all."

Dr. Nolan nodded, trying to formulate a new plan. He surveyed the dining area. No one had been sent to keep an eye on them.

"Okay. Eileen and I will work the crowd," he explained. "Mrs. Ramirez, I want you to concentrate on the other young woman who works in the kitchen. See if she knows anything about the girl. Be a little pushy if it seems necessary. Ask her if she needs help."

Dr. Nolan and Eileen began walking between the rows of tables, smiling and asking if all was well. One worker after another, women, men, young, old, all nodded and answered, "Si, all was good." It was obliquely unanimous.

Mrs. Ramirez went directly to the kitchen, but she was back in less than five minutes. The expression on her face was easily readable.

"I am sorry," she said. "She had one answer for every question. No se. I don't know. When I asked if she needed our help, the answer was the same, she didn't know. She is like a witness that is coached. They don't think. Just answer."

Dr. Nolan nodded. Since the CDC had cleared the farm twice, why such a concerted effort to obstruct and restrict their access? What was the point of limiting their freedom to interview the workers?

"Well, I guess we're done," he said. They made their way back to the car, soaking wet with perspiration. The air conditioner was a relief, but almost too cold. Just as they were backing out, Mr. Dahlquist left his office, heading for his own car. Dr. Nolan rolled down his window.

"The girl. When did she quit?"

"Yesterday morning," the man answered.

"Somebody drive her somewhere?"

"Jesus, I don't know," Mr. Dahlquist said in disgust. "Probably got a ride to the bus station. Are you done?"

Dr. Nolan smiled.

"All finished. Have a nice day."

He rolled the window up and headed for the main road.

"He has the same answers as everyone else," Mrs. Ramirez observed. "No se."

"Just a coincidence, I'm sure," Dr. Nolan said. He piloted through the desert and shimmering heat. At Holtville, he pulled into the local grocery store and parked.

"Ice cream?" Eileen asked.

Dr. Nolan smiled, then looked at Mrs. Ramirez.

"I shouldn't," she said.

"I won't tell."

"Okay. Chocolate, please."

He nodded, went inside, pleased to find a decent assortment of Ben and Jerry's in the freezer case. Selecting two, he went to the counter.

"Where can I buy a bus ticket?" he asked the clerk.

"Here. You need one?"

"No, not today." Dr. Nolan smiled. "I'm with the Center for Disease Control. We're trying to track a young girl who might have left on yesterday's bus."

"Nope. Only one bus a day," the clerk said. "People wait in here, by the door. One woman with three kids. Five men, all Mexicans."

"No girl fifteen to eighteen?"

"Nope. I was here all day. Not much else to do but watch people."

"You've been very helpful." Dr. Nolan smiled. "Thanks a million."

He went back to the car and rewarded his two assistants.

"Wow, the good stuff," Eileen said. She looked in the plastic bag. "No spoons? I guess we can wait five minutes and drink them."

"Oh, shit," Dr. Nolan said.

"Not to worry." Mrs. Ramirez laughed. She dug through her large purse, producing a spoon and a fork. "I always take lunch to work to save money. Which one do you want?"

"The fork is good," Eileen said. "Gives me an excuse to eat faster."

"Mrs. Ramirez, you always save the day," Dr. Nolan told her. "Now, let's get you home before your daughter gets mad at me. I'm scared of lawyers."

16

AFTER DROPPING MRS. RAMIREZ OFF at her car, Eileen and Dr. Nolan ate an early dinner at a local Thai restaurant. They reviewed every shred of new information that five days had uncovered, but there were no connecting bridges.

"I hate to admit it," Dr. Nolan said, "but I'm out of ideas. I thought the girl would give us something, but now that's gone."

"You really think she quit?" Eileen asked.

"Hell, no, not for a second. And she wasn't on the bus leaving Holtville," Dr. Nolan said. "But we can't just barge in there and search the place, as much as I'd like to."

"So, what next?"

"More thinking," Dr. Nolan said.

Back at the hotel, he escorted Eileen to her suite, then sat reading through the red charts that he had packed away. The fatal cases had been mostly older, but some of the victims had been children, their lives taken away by an invisible enemy.

And, with each death, there were family members whose lives would be forever changed.

He fell asleep in the chair, startled awake by three muffled explosions from outside. He looked out the window, but only saw tail-lights through the tinted glass. Still fully dressed, he went down to the lobby, two hotel employees peering nervously out through the double glass doors.

"Someone was shooting. I think they drove away. Cops are on the way."

"Is anyone hurt?" Dr. Nolan asked.

"I'm not going out there to check," the night clerk said emphatically.

Dr. Nolan looked over the parking lot in both directions. He pushed the door open and went out, listening for any sounds. In the distance was the police car responding to the call, the siren still faint. He circled out about twenty feet, stopped, then advanced further. Nothing seemed out of place. Finally, at the sidewalk that bordered the street, there was no sign that anything unusual had happened.

It wasn't until he was walking back to the hotel that he heard the crunching of broken glass under his feet. It was spread out like glittering diamonds on the pavement, and it had all come from their rental car. Stepping closer, the entire length of the driver's side was shredded and peppered with holes. Every panel, tire, and window had been obliterated, the car now listing like a sinking ship.

More and more hotel guests and staff had come out of the building. When the police officer arrived, his beacon lights rhythmically illuminated the three dozen onlookers in alternating waves of red and blue. Standing nearest the scene, the patrolman came up beside Dr. Nolan.

"Holy hell," he said. "This yours?"

"Yeah. A rental," Dr. Nolan said. He had a huge grin on his face.

"Why are you smiling?" the officer asked him.

"Just struck me funny," Dr. Nolan answered. "I get to call the rental agency and tell them their car is shot."

"Boy, is it. Buckshot," the officer said. "You know why anybody would do this?"

Dr. Nolan's smile drew down, but did not totally disappear.

"No. Not really," he answered truthfully. Suspicions would not be seen as evidence.

"Maybe just kids playing with dad's shotgun," the patrolman said. "I'm going to need your personal information for my report. Let's go inside where there's better light."

He followed the officer into the hotel, Eileen waiting, also woken from sleep by the commotion. When he had finished all the paperwork and signed his name, he gave her a full accounting of what had happened. She listened, her face pale for once.

"Jesus, Sean, what the hell is this about?"

"Just a warning," he said, smiling again.

"And why are you amused?" she demanded.

"Because now I know what happens next," he explained. "A few hours ago, I was ready to give up. This just put everything into focus again."

"I don't see where getting our car shot to pieces is some divine revelation," she said.

"Come on," he said. "I need coffee."

He led her upstairs to his room and put the coffee maker back to work, then pulled the two chairs close together, face-to-face.

"You've been the perfect partner once again," he began. "But, I want you to call Southwest and take the first flight back to Portland. I want you out of here this morning."

"Wait a minute," she protested. "You haven't told me what you're thinking, what you're going to do. You're just ordering me to leave."

"That's right. You're fired," Dr. Nolan said. "If I get you out of here, you won't be in danger, and you won't be an accessory."

"An accessory to what!? What the hell are you talking about?"

"Just telling you makes you an accessory, so I'm not telling you. Please. Please go home. Go next door, book a plane, then call Mike and tell him when you get in. Yesterday I was frustrated, but now I'm pissed off, and the best way to help is to just go home."

She glared at him, the red blush coming back to her cheeks. Without another word, she left the room, slammed the door, leaving him alone. He could hear her voice on the phone a few minutes later.

He took out his wallet, fumbled through a dozen business cards taken from the hidden pocket, finally locating what he needed. He sat down on the bed, took a deep breath, then dialed the number, tempted to utter a silent prayer.

"Hello," the sleep-thickened voice answered.

"Kid, thank God you're home! What's your schedule?"

A moment passed.

"Doc? Doc, that you?" Jed Marcus was much more awake.

"You between assignments?" Dr. Nolan asked.

"Yeah. Just got back three weeks ago. This works out so I miss summer in Afghanistan." For nearly five years he had done private security work in the Middle East. His military experience and special talents had made him a valuable asset.

"You up for a little moonlighting?" Dr. Nolan asked.

Jed Marcus laughed out loud. His last interaction with Dr. Nolan had been entertaining and highly educational.

"Anything, anytime, Doc," he said. "Maybe you could start with the basics. What's going on, and what's the plan?"

Dr. Nolan explained the connection to the CDC and the search for the Legionnaires' source, the four cases at one farm, the suspected illegal workers, the changing response to their inquiry, then finished with a description of his mortally wounded rental car. Half a minute passed in agonizing silence.

"I'm putting you on speaker mode," Jed finally answered. Dr. Nolan could hear drawers open and close, then the sound of papers folding and unfolding. Chair legs scooted nearer on a wood floor.

"Okay, where the hell are you at?"

"Imperial, California. Almost to Mexico, and a long way from heaven," Dr. Nolan added.

"Okay. Here we go. Just a sec," the younger man said. "Hmmmm. Thirty, thirty two hours by car, if all goes well."

"Car? Why not just fly in?" Dr. Nolan asked.

Jed laughed again.

"Let's just say that what I'm bringing with me doesn't fit well with TSA guidelines. I already don't like this, and you haven't even gotten to the plan part."

Dr. Nolan hesitated. He checked his watch, calculating Jed's arrival time as late Thursday afternoon.

"One of the workers at the farm was a fifteen year old girl from Guatemala," he told Jed. "When we went back to interview her again, they said she had left. I checked the bus station, and they said no. No one fitting that description bought a ticket. I think she's still there, and they don't want her talking to us."

"And you think these are the guys that trashed your car?" Jed asked.

"Only thing that makes sense," Dr. Nolan answered. "And, even that makes no sense. We'd just about given up by then."

"You're sure on somebody's radar," Jed told him. "I take it you want to find this girl if you can? Maybe get her out of there?"

"Something like that," Dr. Nolan agreed. "The way I look at it, if someone isn't happy where they're at, and you kind of help them relocate somewhere else, that wouldn't really fit the definition of kidnapping. It would be like a moving company, more or less. Just helping someone move."

Jed laughed at his meandering justification.

"Or, like a repo job," he suggested. "Taking back property illegally obtained."

"That works, too," Dr. Nolan said. "But this is a fifteen year old kid who's scared to death. We're going to make sure she isn't property."

Jed was busy writing out a list.

"Farm is where? How big?" he asked.

"East of Holtville," Dr. Nolan explained. "Flat open land, two thousand acres of crops. Pretty isolated area. I've got good maps here."

"Okay. I need aerial, too. I'll look on Google," Jed told him. "And, I'm going to need help. I'm thinking two. Probably a thousand a day. That good with you?"

"No problem," Dr. Nolan said. "I've got an expense account. Anything else?"

Jed was tapping his pen.

"You said Eileen Carson was there, too?"

"Next room," Dr. Nolan said. "But, I'm sending her home."

"Good. Good. Reserve two rooms on your floor, one on each side of you. Is there a fire escape?"

"End of the hall," Dr. Nolan said.

"Perfect. Get the room closest to the door, the other one between you and the elevator. Got it? If they give you any static, move to a different hotel and call my cell."

"Okay. That it for now?" Dr. Nolan asked.

"One last thing, Doc," Jed added. "Stay close to home till we get there, okay? People with guns make me nervous."

Now it was Dr. Nolan who laughed.

"I don't like guns either," he told the young man, "but your mom scares me more. Don't say a word about this. She's still pissed about the last time."

"Oh, she still loves you, Doc. I'll just tell her I'm taking off for sunny California for a little R&R. She'll never know."

"God, I hope not," Dr. Nolan said. "And, kid, thanks for being available. I know what to do, just not how."

"It'll be a blast." Jed laughed. "No pun intended. Be there as quick as we can." The phone went silent.

Dr. Nolan sighed, refilled his coffee cup, then eased back into one of the lounge chairs. Just the knowledge that Jed Marcus was willing to help was an enormous relief. He could feel the tension ease along his upper back. For ten or fifteen minutes, he was able to doze off, still exhausted from the early morning excitement.

A hard knock on his door woke him. Eileen was back, still unhappy.

"You get a flight?"

"No. Sit down." She made it a command. He reclaimed the armchair, and she sat on the side of the bed. "I'm not leaving!"

"Look, Saint Eileen, I—"

"Shut up and just listen. We faced bad before, and this is no different. Mike agrees with me. He already booked a flight in later tonight. You're not doing this, whatever this is, without us. Is that clear enough?"

Dr. Nolan just sat and stared at her, not saying a word. He already knew there was nothing to be won by mounting a counter argument. They were going to stand with him, no matter what. It had been decided. He finally smiled and gave a single nod of his head, an acknowledged surrender.

"Well, okay then," he almost whispered. "I guess we better get busy. I've got Jed Marcus driving down with two other people to help, but they won't be here till late tomorrow. We need transportation. You want to see if you can get a replacement car? The cops towed the other one out a few hours ago."

"Easy," Eileen said. "Are the police even doing anything?"

"They got pictures of the guy on the security camera, but it's dark and grainy. No ID. He just walks up, pumps three shots into the car, and walks away. He knew it belonged to us."

Dr. Nolan sat at the small desk and opened his laptop. He scanned his e-mails, stopping to read the one sent just an hour ago by Dr. Pulliam from CDC headquarters in Atlanta. There was a request for a detailed report on how they were faring. He motioned for Eileen to take his seat, then went and looked out the window as she reviewed the text.

"How do you want to respond?" she asked.

"Four words," he said. "Doing well. Pressing on."

She looked at him and laughed.

"A little short on details though, don't you think?"

"Minor point," he said. "It's concise, accurate, positive in nature, and very witty. It may well be the best report I've ever written."

Eileen shook her head, typed in the message, then hit the "send" tab.

"What next?"

"Google Earth, or whatever it is," Dr. Nolan said. "See if you can get overhead pictures of the Dahlquist Farm. Jed may need them."

Eileen typed in Holtville, but on every series of photos, the Dahlquist property was a peripheral image. There was not enough detail to be useful.

"That sucks," Dr. Nolan said. "Okay. You arrange new wheels. I've got to book extra hotel rooms. I'll be back."

It took a great deal of explaining, then a second, more urgent tone of request, but Dr. Nolan was able to reserve rooms on the third floor wing that coincided with Jed's instructions. At some point in time he would have to explain his erratic and eccentric spending to the CDC, but that was a worry for another day.

Back upstairs, Eileen was just getting off the phone.

"We can take the shuttle back to the terminal and get another car," she said, "but…"

"Big but, or little but?" Dr. Nolan asked.

"There's a five hundred dollar deductible on the other car insurance," she explained.

"That's a little but. That's on the CDC." Dr. Nolan smiled. "Let's go."

Catching the first van out, they were in possession of a new, sparkling white Jeep Cherokee half an hour later. The car did not ride as smoothly, but the air conditioner was akin to a wind tunnel.

"Much better." Eileen smiled. "Where to now?"

"El Centro," Dr. Nolan said. "Find every big city park you can on the map."

Eileen had located three by the time they reached the city. Directed by the Garmin, Dr. Nolan located the first, surveyed the area from the street, then shook his head.

"Next."

The second recreation area featured a pool and tennis courts, the first filled with people seeking relief from the heat, the other deserted.

"Nope." He typed in the next address. The last park was an open expanse of baseball, football, and soccer fields. Dr. Nolan pulled into a shaded area at the curb. He left the engine running and told Eileen he would be back in a few minutes.

In the center of the football field, a man in his mid-thirties was practicing with his drone, executing aerobatic maneuvers, even flying between the goal-posts.

"You're pretty good with that." Dr. Nolan smiled, coming up to him. "I'm Dr. Nolan with the CDC. You interested in a little espionage work?"

The man brought the drone in for a landing.

"Espionage? Like spying?" he asked, his eyes wide.

Dr. Nolan laughed.

"Not really. My partner and I have to inspect a large farm near Holtville for any signs of open water. The place is too big, and it's too damn hot. We were wondering if you could do it with your drone. It has a camera, right?"

The man nodded.

"Pretty good one," he said with pride. "Holtville, huh? How much are we talking?"

Dr. Nolan took out his wallet and counted his cash reserves.

"How about two hundred dollars, and I get the video chip?"

"Deal. I've got a back-up battery," the man said. "But the lift in this hot air is limited. Maybe five, six hundred feet."

"Perfect," Dr. Nolan said. "The more detail, the better for us. I'll bring you right back when we're done."

"Cool." The man smiled. "So you guys are like agents?"

"We are indeed," said Dr. Nolan. "Just not secret or glamorous. We just do dirty, boring stuff. Wouldn't make a very good TV show."

"Well, it still sounds interesting," the man said, a little disappointed.

"At times," Dr. Nolan admitted. He introduced the young man to Eileen. "This is our new pilot and surveillance expert."

Eileen just smiled and shook hands, not sure why his services were needed. As the car headed toward Holtville, it began to dawn on her that a strategy was already in play, and she was officially a part of it.

Dr. Nolan passed the Dahlquist Farm, then pulled to the shoulder of the road about half a mile beyond the entry gate. Their new assistant set up his flight pad on the hood of the Jeep, almost too hot to touch. He checked the controls, engaged the miniature camera, then sent it skyward.

The low amplitude buzz of its rotor blades was barely audible. Dr. Nolan watched the screen, directing the young man to sweep the fields and building sites, then the property directly to the west. In fifteen minutes, they had a bird's-eye view of the entire area.

"You know, sometimes I catch people in pretty compromising positions," their pilot announced.

"Careful, son," Dr. Nolan said. "I'm a government official, remember? You don't want to be admitting to things like that." It was all he could do to maintain a serious expression.

"Oh, right. Right. I didn't mean anything. Filmed a house fire once," he said. He landed the drone in a cloud of dust near the road, retrieved it, then presented Dr. Nolan with the plastic video card.

"Your government thanks you," Dr. Nolan said. He paid the man's fee, then returned to El Centro, barely an hour after their first meeting. It had been a brief, but very productive partnership. They waved goodbye to him and headed back north.

"I suppose you're not going to explain this little adventure?" Eileen asked.

"Can't. You know the rules," Dr. Nolan reminded her. "No knowledge, no culpability. It has to stay that way."

"Okay, boss." She sighed. "You realize we haven't eaten all day."

"Jesus, sorry. Let's get cleaned up and grab something," Dr. Nolan said. "Then we can go back and wait for Uncle Mike."

After a quick change, they found a chain restaurant that served breakfast twenty four hours a day. The food was standard and plain, but it was savored as a banquet offering. It had been over a day since they had tasted food.

The waitress refilled their cups with steaming hot coffee and placed the bill on the table. Dr. Nolan noticed the man at the nearest booth to the right smiling at him. He politely nodded and offered a smile in return.

The stranger, a tan, lean fellow in jeans and a checked shirt, two days of gray speckled whiskers on his face, put his napkin down, stood, and approached them.

"You some kind of fairy?" he demanded. "What the hell you smiling at?"

"Oh, shit," Eileen whispered, not looking up.

Dr. Nolan regarded the man for a moment.

"I was just being courteous," he explained. "If you haven't encountered that word before, you should look it up in the dictionary."

"Oh, shit," Eileen said again.

The man moved forward until his thighs were touching the table. She could see his right hand clenching.

"So, you're a smart-ass fairy?"

Dr. Nolan recognized the intended threat, and he had no experience or interest in fighting with anyone. But, he also knew this was an orchestrated situation that was only going to play out in one direction.

He sat still, meeting the man's eyes, a faint smile showing.

"Are you making a derogatory reference to members of the LGBT community or comparing me to a seagoing vessel that transports people and cars over inland water-ways?"

"Fucking smart-ass," the man said. Eileen saw him turn slightly, his right hand now a fist. As he swung forward, she threw the scalding coffee into his face and eyes. At the same instant, Dr. Nolan instinctively raised his left arm to block the punch, only taking a partial blow to the side of his face. In the adrenaline rush of the moment, he felt absolutely no pain.

The same could not be said about their new dinner guest. Both corneas had been blistered by the hot liquid., and he had buckled to his knees, screaming in pain and unable to open his eyes.

Dr. Nolan and Eileen made a quick walk to the register. He tossed down two twenty dollar bills as they passed through the door, not waiting for change. A cab at the corner offered them a safe retreat and a much quicker ride back to the hotel.

"Jesus, I think you just saved my life." Dr. Nolan laughed, more anxious than amused.

"I figured you weren't much of a fighter," Eileen said. "Why did you keep needling him?"

"Wouldn't have mattered," Dr. Nolan told her. "He was sent there to start trouble. I think someone wants me out of commission."

He could now feel his left cheek beginning to sting. The cab was just pulling into the Courtyard entrance.

"Maybe we should stick to room service until Mike and Jed get here," Eileen suggested. They walked down the air-conditioned hallway toward their assigned suites. Eileen grabbed a pitcher of ice cubes from a machine in the alcove.

"I feel pretty safe with you as my body guard," Dr. Nolan said. "What would you have done without the coffee?"

Now Eileen laughed. It was not her first fight.

"Knee him in the groin, with as much force as possible," she answered. "That's usually a show-stopper."

Dr. Nolan nodded, wincing slightly at the thought. He slid the card key through the lock, went into his room, and looked at his face in the mirror. His left eye was filled with blood over the sclera, but the pupil region was clear. The upper cheek and eye socket were already swelling.

Eileen had filled a towel with ice.

"Lay back and keep this on," she instructed him, pointing to the bed.

"Yes, Doctor." He laughed, following her orders. She took a seat at the small desk, staring down at the floor.

"This just got more serious," she said in a low voice. "You have any idea what's going on?"

"It did, and I might," Dr. Nolan answered. "But, just like back home, this doesn't make me want to quit. Just makes me more determined to get answers. Somewhere along the line we made someone nervous enough to try and warn us off. Now I want to know who and why?"

Eileen had proven her resolve and resilience, but she was clearly uncomfortable.

"We're off our home turf here, Sean," she reminded him. "I'm serious about room service. Until we get some backup, I think it's best if we stick to phone and computer work. When do you think the second-string guys will show up?"

"Late tomorrow if they take turns driving," Dr. Nolan said. "But I agree. We'll just make follow-up calls for now. I don't want to get in any more fights."

Eileen laughed.

"You didn't get in a fight," she corrected him. "You punched a blind guy in the hand with your face."

"That's your version." Dr. Nolan laughed in response. "You ever see the movie with W. C. Fields where he plays the guard in the bank? He accidently stops a robbery, but each time he retells the story, it gets bigger and better. The way I remember it, there were at least three guys with baseball bats." He looked at her with his one undamaged eye.

She shook her head.

"That's the old fish story. The minnow becomes a whale," she said. "Women may exaggerate at times, but men just outright lie, and they do it with a straight face."

"It's a defect in the Y chromosome," Dr. Nolan explained. "Now, let me take a nap. We can review files later. Those four guys I tuned up wore me out."

Eileen rolled her eyes and moved to the door.

"Okay, Captain Avenger," she said. "I'll keep watch till Mike gets here. Next time there might be four guys."

Dr. Nolan did not answer. The same thought had crossed his mind. Their inquiry into the source of the Legionnaires' outbreak had now become something else, and he had no idea what.

17

DR. NOLAN SLEPT FOR NINE hours. Yawning himself awake, the dull ache in his left jaw reminded him of the evening's festivities. He went to the bathroom mirror expecting the worst, then was heartened by what looked back. His left eye was still red, but the lids were not swollen shut, and only a small area of bruising had developed over the high cheekbone. He did not appear too lopsided.

Still fully dressed, he went next door and knocked, very pleased when Mike answered. He gave the big man a hug.

"Damn, you look trampled on." Mike laughed.

"Four big guys and a midget," Dr. Nolan said. "Did Eileen tell you?"

"She left out the midget part." Mike laughed. "And some of the specifics got changed around."

"I'll tell you the real story later, when she's not around," Dr. Nolan promised. "Is that coffee I smell?"

Eileen vacated a chair, then poured him a cup from the room service tray.

"How do you feel?" she asked.

"I actually feel great," he said. "That's the best night's sleep I've had in a week. What time you get here, Mike?"

"About 10:00 p.m. We thought it best just to let you be," Mike said.

"We've got more back-up coming tonight," Dr. Nolan explained.

"I heard," Mike said. "Just like old times. Eileen said you won't explain what you're planning to do."

"For your own good. Just for a while," Dr. Nolan said. "This isn't like back home. I don't want you to have any legal exposure. Sheriff Dent isn't around to smooth out any ruffles."

Mike nodded slowly. He pointed to a large, nickel plated revolver lying on the bed.

"Brought a friend with me," he said. "Anyone shoots at us, it won't be a one sided conversation."

It was the largest pistol Dr. Nolan had ever seen. His thumb would have fit in the barrel.

"Jesus Christ, Mike, you fly in with Clint Eastwood?"

"No, but it's the same gun. Forty-four Magnum," he said proudly. "I might not hit anyone, but I'll sure as hell scare them to death."

"Hopefully, there's not going to be any need for guns, but I appreciate the extra precaution. That thing scares me just looking at it with one eye," Dr. Nolan said.

"You want to hold it?" Mike asked.

"No thanks. I've already got penis envy," Dr. Nolan said. "That will just make it worse. You ready for an errand?"

"Just say the word," Mike said anxiously. He was already suffering from cabin fever.

"We've got to get the Jeep back," Dr. Nolan explained. "Got left behind in all the excitement. It will give us an excuse to get out of here for a while."

"We all stay together, right?" Eileen said, not a question.

"Right. Give me a minute to wash up," Dr. Nolan said. He went back to his room, shaved with extra care, brushed his teeth, then found the video chip from the drone survey. Downstairs he asked the desk clerk if there was an Office Max in town.

"No," the man said, "but there's one in El Centro. Shopping mall on the left just as you get to the second light."

They called a cab for the short ride to their car, but Dr. Nolan had him drive down through the airport, into the parking garage, and out the exit, watching the side mirror to see if they were being followed.

"Saw that in a movie," he explained to Mike and Eileen. Reassured, he allowed the driver to take a more direct route back to the restaurant parking lot. The Jeep Cherokee was still waiting where they had left it. There were no bullet holes or blemishes.

The Office Max was easy to find, and there were only a few customers ahead of them. Eileen sat down at one of the computer terminals, getting instructions from the staff on how to print individual images from the video chip. With Dr. Nolan and Mike on each side, they ran the film over and over in slow motion, selecting wide angle views that showed every building and access road within a two mile radius. The clarity and detail were surprisingly good, and the printed copies were of equal quality.

"Now what?" Eileen asked.

"We go back to the hotel and wait," Dr. Nolan said. "I need to check in with my girls after missing yesterday, and it's too risky to be out and about right now. Watch TV, read, whatever. I hate it, too, but it's safe."

Mike and Eileen agreed. They returned to the hotel, parked as near to the main lobby doors as possible, and settled in. Dr. Nolan knew that tomorrow would be a different story.

18

Keenan Dahlquist was at home when the call came in from Dell Sprague. He excused himself from the dinner table and went to his study, closing the door behind him. Pouring a double serving of scotch, he sat down and redialed the number. The past few days had robbed him of sleep, and his mood was in fragile decay.

"It better be quiet there," he said, referring to the farm.

"Not a word from anyone," the foreman answered. "I don't think our visitors will be back. Too high a price."

"I don't pay you for your thoughts, Dell," Mr. Dahlquist informed him flatly. "How's your man doing?"

"Blistered his face and eyes is all. Week or so and he'll be okay," Dell explained.

"Word out he got bested by a woman?" Mr. Dahlquist asked, half laughing.

"Everyone heard. But he still got the job done. There won't be any more trouble."

Keenan Dahlquist learned forward on the desk, his forehead cradled in his left hand. A full minute passed before he spoke again.

"I still want the girl out of there," he said. "Tomorrow. I've made arrangements for her to go north. You can send anyone you like to drive her, but you stay close to home. At least for a few days. I want to make sure this all settles out."

"Okay," Dell answered. "You still want her guarded?"

"Like Fort Knox. Tomorrow she's somebody else's problem," Mr. Dahlquist said. "And, don't call me unless it's a goddamn emergency. We clear?"

"Yes, sir. Good night." Dell Sprague hung up. With one of his men out of commission, even he would have to pull sentry duty for part of the night. The thought rankled him. It would be quicker and easier to deal with the problem in a different manner, but he knew it wouldn't be a good business decision. With Mr. Dahlquist, business always came first.

19

Jed Marcus arrived at just past 7:00 p.m. Dr. Nolan gave him a bear hug in the hallway, then dragged him into his room, his two travel companions close behind.

"Goddamn, kid, you're a sight for sore eyes," Dr. Nolan beamed.

"You look like you've got sore eyes," Jed remarked. "What the hell happened?"

"Five guys and a fat woman with tattoos jumped me in an alley," he explained, then waited for the knowing laughter to ease away. "Guy punched me in a restaurant. Just another warning," he admitted.

"Great. Eileen okay?" Jed asked.

"Hell yes. She burned half the guy's face off with her coffee."

"Good for her. She still here?"

Dr. Nolan nodded. He motioned for everyone to sit.

"Wouldn't leave, bless her," Dr. Nolan explained. "Now, Mike showed up with an artillery piece. We've just been lying low as instructed." Dr. Nolan reached up and knocked on the wall. In half a minute, both Mike and Eileen joined them, relieved and thrilled they had extra support.

Jed was warmly greeted. The other two men, each about thirty, hung back. They were both tall, powerfully built, clean shaven, and neatly dressed.

"You want to do the honors?" Dr. Nolan asked Jed.

"Oh, sorry. Steve and Deuce. No last names. Served with both in Iraq," Jed explained. Everyone shook hands.

"Deuce? Is that your real name?" Dr. Nolan asked.

"It's how many times I've been wounded," the young man said. "Might change."

"Hopefully not on this trip," Dr. Nolan remarked. "You made good time getting here."

"Took turns driving and sleeping," Jed told them. "Could have been here sooner, but we didn't want to get pulled over for speeding and have someone look through the car." He smiled broadly.

Dr. Nolan nodded with a vague stare, not certain he wanted to know the details.

"Well, we're glad you're here," Dr. Nolan said. "I managed to get the extra rooms as requested. You're all now officially working for the CDC. Kind of. I've got the key cards here. You probably want to get settled and get some dinner."

Jed looked at his two team members, then tilted his head slightly toward Dr. Nolan.

"We talked this out on the way down," he said. "Best to start work tonight. Delaying lets other people make plans. They won't be expecting anything this soon."

Dr. Nolan just stared at him, his heart rate climbing. It was an effort to swallow.

"Tonight?"

"It's best. Element of surprise," Jed told him.

"Jesus, kid, give me second," Dr. Nolan said. He sat down and looked at the floor. It was crazy, but it actually did make sense. Always better to act than react, he thought. "Okay. I see your point. Good. Good. Tonight it is."

"Perfect." Jed smiled. "We've got some gear to bring up. Can you man the exit door for us? No reason to use the lobby."

Dr. Nolan nodded, waited for a minute after the three men left, then walked to the end of the hallway. He had Mike unlock the door to the last suite and hold it open. Three soft taps announced their return. Both of Jed's team carried in a large duffel bag made of green canvas. Jed brought a small travel case in one hand, and a long, narrow metal box in the other. They quickly ducked into the room. Steve and Deuce were already unpacking. Laid out on the bed were three assault rifles, three 9-millimeter semiautomatic Berettas, dozens of ammunition clips, and two grenades.

Dr. Nolan and Mike shared a look of growing concern.

"Don't worry." Jed laughed. "Defense only. We don't want trouble any more than you do. Just safer to be prepared, that's all."

From the small suitcase, Jed took out a box of enormous shells and placed them on the desk. There were some that were rounded, and others sharpened to a point, all with stamped patterns made of different metals.

"Are those what I think they are?" Mike asked.

"Ammo for the fifty," Jed nodded. "You never know." Next came half a dozen small radio units and night vision goggles.

"I can see why you didn't want to get stopped by the state patrol," Dr. Nolan said.

There was a knock on the door. Eileen came in with the folder holding the aerial maps.

"Thought you might need these," she said, staring at the arsenal of weapons neatly placed on the bedspread. She was not smiling.

"Thanks," Dr. Nolan said. He took the photos from her, but kept hold of her hand until she met his eyes. "This is the part where you and Mike have to bow out temporarily. I don't want you involved in this. Later, you can help, but not now. Please understand."

She did understand, but not knowing was an equal torment.

"Okay. I'm trusting you," she said, "but you better not get hurt. Your girls need their father."

"I think I'm in pretty good hands," he said. "I'll check in by cell phone when this is over. Promise."

Mike and Eileen went back to their room, not happy to be ostracized, but accepting the rationale.

"You've got intel? Good job, Doc," Jed complimented him. He laid out the overhead images of the farm and surrounding area, then checked the general location on the map, noting the roads, entry and exit points. Steve and Deuce leaned over his shoulders, studying the terrain. Dr. Nolan pointed out the old farmhouse, the processing plants, the office, and the workers' housing, even the electronic gate.

Deuce leaned closer and tapped his finger on one of the pictures. Jed held it up closer to the reading lamp.

"I bribed a guy with a drone to shoot them," Dr. Nolan said. "Not quite satellite technology, but it was all I could think of on short notice."

Steve found a folding magnifying glass in one of the duffel bags and brought it over to the desk.

"These are great," Jed told him. "What altitude?"

"Five hundred to a thousand feet," Dr. Nolan said. "Kind of up and down."

"Take a look here with the glass." Jed pointed. "We've got the Lone Ranger."

Dr. Nolan frowned at the remark, then sat down and examined the picture under the light. At the southernmost corner of the workers' compound, a pickup was parked in the shade of a tree. Next to it was a man sitting in a chair, a rifle lying across his lap.

"Jesus, I hadn't noticed that," Dr. Nolan admitted. "Good eye."

"We look at a lot of photos like that," Jed explained. "Shadows. Footprints. Changes in the dirt color along roads. You just pinpointed one target. This will make things a lot faster."

"What are you thinking?" Dr. Nolan asked.

They all moved closer to the desk. Jed reconfigured the aerial views into one cohesive picture.

"You, Steve, and I drive east of the farm," Jed began. "I want to stay away from the house and processing sheds. Steve will go in with me and cover from about seventy-five yards out. I'll locate the target, deal with any obstacles, then we're out. Deuce will park on the west side to monitor any activity coming or going. He's our last backup in case of trouble."

"And, I'm the getaway driver again, right?" Dr. Nolan smiled.

"Right." Jed nodded, smiling. "Just don't lock the door like last time."

Dr. Nolan remembered their first covert mission. There had been some minor flaws in execution.

"I was nervous," Dr. Nolan admitted.

"It's okay to be nervous," Steve said. "We are, too. Just focus on the job. It helps."

"How's your Spanish?" Dr. Nolan asked Jed. "You use the word 'target,' but this is a frightened teenage girl. It's going to scare the shit out of her when you come through that door."

Jed nodded.

"I know a little," he said, "But you're right. Got any ideas to help?"

Being dragged out of her room by a man with a gun could create havoc. Dr. Nolan considered options. He could try to have Mrs. Ramirez on the cell phone to speak with her, but even that would be noisy and potentially dangerous. Then he remembered the note Maya had written and secretly placed in his pocket. He went to his own room, found the slip of paper, and brought it back to Jed.

"She wrote this to us when we visited the farm," he explained. "Show it to her. She'll know you're with us."

Jed looked at the three scribbled words.

"Worth a try." He smiled. "Looks like we're back in business, Doc. Never a dull moment."

"It's not intentional," Dr. Nolan said. "It just seems to happen. Sheriff Dent said my nickname should be 'Shit Storm.'"

Jed, Steve, and Deuce all laughed.

"That's good. I like it," Jed told him. "Better than 'Shithead.' I think it was kind of a compliment."

"Maybe," Dr. Nolan said. "So, what time do we leave?"

"You said it was about a forty-five-minute drive? Say one thirty, just to be safe. We go in at three o'clock, out by three fifteen. That gives us time to eat, check equipment, and take a little rest."

"I don't think I can rest," Dr. Nolan said, standing and moving to the door.

"Try," Jed told him. "Remember, you're in charge of the most important job. The getaway."

"I hope so," Dr. Nolan said.

20

THE TWO CAR CONVOY HEADED out precisely on schedule. Dr. Nolan took the lead, Jed and Steve both dressed in desert camouflage fatigues. Deuce followed alone in the second car, still wearing casual clothes. If anyone questioned them, the cover story was a CDC field survey of local farms. Weapons were to be kept out of sight until needed.

They travelled south on 86, took the cut-off east to Holtville, then followed the narrow side roads leading to the Dahlquist Farm. Traffic was light at first, then became nonexistent as they moved further out into the rural countryside. Conversation was limited to radio checks and one final review of their plan.

Deuce pulled to the shoulder of the road about half a mile from the gated entry to the farm. He left his assault rifle covered with a towel on the floor of the back seat, but his sidearm was tucked behind his right lower back with the safety off.

"In place," he said over the radio.

Dr. Nolan continued past the farm, turning the Jeep around to face in a westerly direction at about the same distance. There was no moon-light, but the sky was a clear canopy of flashing stars. It was the perfect set of conditions. Jed and Steve checked their weapons, looked at the aerial photos one last time, then got out of the car.

"Well, Doc, see you around." Jed smiled. The two men switched on their night vision, radioed Deuce they were moving, then disappeared down the bank, swallowed by the darkness in just seconds. Dr. Nolan checked his watch. It was 2:56 a.m.

Jed and Steve crossed a shallow drainage ditch and moved onto the narrow access lane that bordered the entire farm. Fifty yards south was a crossing path that separated fields and gave passageway to farm vehicles. Spaced about ten feet apart, they walked at a good pace for over a quarter of a mile. The faint outline of the two houses was still a dark shape to the left. Jed made a hand motion, then crossed into a planted area of low growing vegetation. Stepping over the rows onto barren soil, they made no sound. About seventy-five yards out, Jed motioned Steve to take cover.

"Anyone follows us out, please discourage them," he whispered.

Steve nodded and smiled. He brought his assault rifle to a ready position.

Jed angled to the left again, a flanking maneuver to come in from the far side of the southernmost structure. He could already see a vehicle parked in the same general area where the day guard had been stationed. As he moved closer, he could see a figure in the front seat, the low melody of country music floating out of the open window. It was clear they were dealing with undisciplined amateurs.

From the side and right rear position, Jed was able to take cover behind a nearby shade tree, only eight to ten feet from the car. He slowed his breathing, then took two coins from his pocket. Tossing the first, it clanked off the right front fender.

The man behind the wheel got out, pulling a Winchester lever action rifle from the seat. One slow step at a time, he circled around the front of the vehicle, looking in all directions. When he turned away, Jed threw a second coin, this one bouncing on the hood. As the man turned back to the sound, Jed took two steps and slammed the butt of his rifle against his left cheek. His jaw broken, he fell without making a sound.

"Dumb ass," Jed muttered under his breath. He checked the man's pocket for keys, found what he was looking for, then dragged the body alongside the car and out of sight. He stood for a moment, the night sounds of insects and whispering breeze undisturbed. There were no other hot targets in his field of vision.

He went to the door of the last apartment, reassured when he found it secured with a chain and padlock. He tried each small key on the guard's ring, the third one turning with a loud click. He carefully removed the chain and laid it on the ground. Taking a flashlight from a shirt pocket, he opened the door and stepped into the room.

The two beds were empty, but the far one was rumpled, the covers thrown back, and the pillow dented at the center. He took another step forward and followed the beam of light. A figure in a white night-dress was huddled on the floor, her face toward the wall, only her dark hair showing.

"Amigo," Jed told her. He pulled the note Dr. Nolan had given him from his pocket and directed the light onto it. "Amigo," he said again.

The girl slowly turned to look in his direction, then saw her hand written message. She stood up and came closer.

"Silencio por favor." Jed smiled, putting a finger across his lips. He pointed to the girl's bare feet. Understanding, she put on a pair of open sandals, her only shoes. He motioned for her to follow, put the note in her hand, then paused at the door.

"Have target. Moving," he said into the radio.

He led her outside, retracing his approach path, swinging away from the building and out into the field. Holding her hand, the return was slow, her steps hesitant and unsure in the darkness, his brightly lit by the night vision goggles. It took ten minutes to make it back to where Steve was monitoring their progress.

"Any activity?" Jed asked.

"Ghost town," Steve answered.

"Okay. She can't see out here, and we need to move faster." He called Dr. Nolan. "Any traffic?"

"Nothing," Dr. Nolan said. He had been nervously waiting for them to make it back to the Jeep.

"Okay. Watch for our flashlight. When you see it, give us headlights," Jed instructed him.

"Okay. Roger," Dr. Nolan said. It was already three-thirty. Early farm workers would soon be on the road.

Jed was not happy, but there was no other option. They switched off their night vision, using the flashlight to guide them. They kept the girl between them, gently, but firmly urging her along by holding her elbows. They reached the crossroad, then the peripheral lane, then followed the headlights of the Jeep up and onto the road. With the girl in the back seat, Jed and Steve climbed in on each side of her, their assault rifles pointed down at the floor, but still handy.

"Okay, wheelman," Jed ordered. "Go, and go fast."

Dr. Nolan turned, gave Maya a big smile, then put the Jeep into drive. He did not burn rubber, but by the time they passed Deuce he was doing about sixty. He only slowed when they navigated through Holtville, most of the town still sound asleep.

"Bueno! Bueno!" Dr. Nolan said. "You have any trouble?"

"I didn't," Jed answered. "But one of their guys needs a little facial surgery. Consider it payback for your bloody eye."

"But alive, right?"

"Don't worry, Doc. He was still breathing. I know your rules."

Dr. Nolan nodded. He was elated that the girl was safe, relieved that Jed and his team were free from harm, but never eager or at ease with violence.

"Good," he said. "Nice job."

They were back on Highway 86, just nearing El Centro. The eastern sky was pinkish gray. Dr. Nolan saw a doughnut shop open on the right side of the road and pulled to a stop. He turned to Maya and held out his hand. She leaned forward, took his hand in both of hers, then bowed to touch it against her forehead. She was crying.

"No. No. Es beuno," he said again, wishing he knew a better way to tell her she was free and moving toward a better life.

"Coffee? Café? Leche? Aqua?" he asked. The girl just nodded.

"Be back in a minute," Dr. Nolan announced. He waved at Deuce in the chase car, then went into the bakery, purchased a dozen mixed pastries, four large coffees, and a cup of hot chocolate. On the way back he rewarded Deuce, then returned to the Jeep with a cake doughnut wedged in his mouth. He mumbled something inaudible and handed everything to Jed.

"Have to make a call," he repeated after swallowing.

"Make it quick, Doc," Jed suggested. "I don't want to be sitting out here in the open."

Dr. Nolan nodded and held up two fingers, then walked out away from the car. He dialed his cell phone by a street lamp and waited. It took eight ring cycles to wake Mrs. Ramirez from sleep.

"Yes? Hello?"

"Mrs. Ramirez. Dr. Nolan. I apologize for the early call, but I need your help. You remember the girl from the farm, Maya?"

"Yes. Oh, Dr. Nolan. What time is it?"

"Four thirty. I'm sorry," he said again. "Maya, the girl from Guatemala. I have her with me. In my car."

"What? How can that be?" Mrs. Ramirez asked, shock in her voice.

"Long story," Dr. Nolan explained," and one you shouldn't hear for now. I can't take her back to the hotel, and I can't take her to the authorities. They'll just ship her over to immigration. I was wondering…I was hoping I could bring her there, to your house? Just for a while."

He cringed, waiting for an answer, not certain what he would do if she refused.

"Yes. Yes. She is welcome here. Where are you now?"

"El Centro," Dr. Nolan said.

"The first light in Imperial, turn left and go about a mile to Copeland Street. Turn right. Four houses up is me. I will give you the address and turn the lights on."

Dr. Nolan sighed.

"Thank you for this," Dr. Nolan told the woman. "You might want to give Elena a call. I think we're going to need legal advice."

"I think that is a good idea," Mrs. Ramirez agreed. "I will make coffee for you."

"Mrs. Ramirez, this is why I fell in love with you," Dr. Nolan said. "But make lots of coffee. There's five of us." He hung up before Mrs. Ramirez could reconsider.

Dr. Nolan nodded to Deuce and climbed back into the Jeep. He grabbed another doughnut.

"Who was that?" Jed asked.

"My fiancée." Dr. Nolan smiled. "She just offered us a place to hide out. Those assholes know where we're staying and what the new car looks like. No way we can take the girl there."

"Agreed," Jed replied. "You trust this woman?"

"Completely," Dr. Nolan said, pulling out onto the main road, traffic now beginning to build with early commuters and transport trucks. "We've worked with her all week. She's an angel."

"I don't know too many angels," Steve offered from the back seat. "I'll try to watch my language."

"That'll be a first." Jed laughed. "So, what's the long view here, Doc? What's next?"

"Kind of loose at this point," he admitted. "I need to question Maya, but she was too scared at the farm to say anything. I'm hoping now that she's safe things will change. She's got answers that I need, and Mrs. Ramirez may get her to cooperate. That's the endgame."

"It's your dime, Doc." Jed nodded. "We'll just go with the tide. Beats watching daytime TV."

They had pulled into Copeland Street. It was a tidy, well-kept neighborhood, all single-level, small houses. The fourth one on the right was lit up like a Christmas tree. Dr. Nolan pulled in beside Mrs. Ramirez's Camry, and Deuce parked along the street.

"Can we keep the assault rifles out of sight?" Dr. Nolan asked.

Jed smiled. He and Steve laid their long weapons on the floor.

"Sidearms only." He smiled. "We'll rotate someone outside just to be careful."

Deuce was delegated with perimeter guard duty. He turned their car around to face the main entry point. The others, with

Maya and Dr. Nolan leading, went up to the house, just ready to knock when the door swung open. Mrs. Ramirez, dressed in a robe and slippers, her hair down, came rushing out and hugged Maya, stroking the back of her head. She was speaking in Spanish so rapidly that Dr. Nolan could only catch random words.

"Come in. Come in. Come in," she scolded them. She had Maya sit on the sofa, then noticing her nightgown, she went to a hall closet and brought back a light-weight blanket to wrap around her.

Mrs. Ramirez gave Dr. Nolan a warm hug next. She stepped back, smiling, then saw his eye and cheek. She put a hand on each side of his face.

"Oh, my, Dr. Nolan, what has happened to you?" she asked, her smile gone, replaced by genuine concern.

"Your daughter slapped me," he told her. "For a girl, she hits pretty hard."

Mrs. Ramirez stared, then started laughing. She hugged him again.

"Now, I know you are okay because you are lying to me," she said. "Sit. Everyone sit. I will get the coffee. Then breakfast." She disappeared into the kitchen.

"I see what you meant, Doc. She is an angel," Jed agreed. "This will be a good place for the girl, but if you come back, don't use your car. Can't risk being followed. My guys know how to lose tails."

Dr. Nolan nodded. Maya just sat on the couch, her head down. She was exhausted, and still fearful. Mrs. Ramirez came back with a tray filled with coffee cups, milk, and sugar, sat down beside the girl, and looped an arm around her shoulder, holding her close. It was instinctively maternal, and just what was needed.

Dr. Nolan introduced Jed and Steve to their hostess.

"So many handsome men." She smiled. "I will make bacon and eggs. Then I will take Maya shopping for some clothes. This will be good."

"And maybe a nap," Dr. Nolan suggested. "She had a busy night."

Mrs. Ramirez rolled her eyes.

"Being around you is always busy." Mrs. Ramirez laughed. "But I'm glad you found her. I don't care how."

"We did kind of find her," Dr. Nolan said. "That's a perfect analysis. Lost and found."

Jed and Steve nodded, both with serous expressions. A knock on the door had them instantly on their feet, one at the window and one at the door, both with guns drawn. Deuce gave them a thumbs-up from the car. It was Elena.

Jed opened the entrance just wide enough for her to come into the living room. Her expression was surprise mixed with disbelief. She had not expected to see her mother's home filled with armed strangers. She brushed past the men, went to her mother, and sat down beside her. She hugged the woman, then squeezed Maya's hand.

"Not to be rude," she said, looking at Dr. Nolan directly, "but what have you got my mother mixed up in!? And, where did you get this army?"

Dr. Nolan smiled and leaned forward in his chair.

"It's actually a very simple story, if I leave most of the first part out," he explained. "The second part goes something like this. We liberated Maya from a bad situation. She's illegal, scared, and may have information critical to my investigation. Since I don't trust immigration or the local police, the only person I could turn to was your mother."

Elena stared at him, processing the words.

"And, I'm glad he did," Mrs. Ramirez added. "This girl needs our help."

Elena dropped her eyes and started shaking her head from side to side. The tension in her face slowly eased, the beginnings of a resigned smile just showing. She turned and kissed her mother on the cheek.

"Okay, Madre," she said, then turned back toward Dr. Nolan, her dark eyes narrowing again. "And you, outside!"

Dr. Nolan nodded. He put down his coffee cup, stood up slowly, then shot a glance at Jed.

"Keep your gun ready, just in case," he joked, heading for the door. He let Elena go first, then they sat down next to each other on the front step of the porch. The sun was now fully entrenched above the eastern valley, but only beginning to warm.

"Okay," Elena said. "First, tell me what happened to your face?"

"Your mother did it," he said. "I asked about a dowry, and she punched me."

"Nice try." Elena laughed. "My mother was good with a wooden spoon, not pugilism. Real story, please."

Dr. Nolan sighed. It was time to deal with the truth.

"The farm where they were holding Maya," he began. "First, they shot up our car, then sent a guy to warn me off. No big deal."

"That explains the body guards," Elena said. "But, this is a big deal. You have any idea how many laws you've broken? Now you've got my mother involved, and she won't back down either. This is going to take some time and creative thinking."

Dr. Nolan could smell the scent of her, a softly mixed floral bouquet with a trace of vanilla just barely detectable.

"You're beautiful when you're angry," he said.

"Be serious," she answered.

"I am, and you are," he repeated. "You're beginning to interfere with my rational thought processes."

"I don't believe you have any." She laughed. "But thank you, I think."

He leaned just enough to touch against her shoulder. She did not pull away.

"I know I've created a mess here," he said. "But I wanted Maya safe, and I need her to answer some questions. It really is important. Then, maybe you can help figure out what's best for her. She's still just a kid."

Elena sighed.

"Dr. Sean Nolan," she said. "A week ago, I didn't know you existed, and my life was quiet and simple, and predictable, and my mother wasn't harboring a fugitive. You certainly have a talent for creating waves."

"Does that mean you'll help?"

"Yes, Sean," she said. "Give me some time. If I don't help now, my mom will probably get out the wooden spoon."

21

Keenan Dahlquist moaned, looked at the clock on his bed table, then picked up the ringing phone.

"The girl's gone," said Dell Sprague.

"What the fuck are you saying! Gone how?" Mr. Dahlquist demanded, now fully awake.

"They took her sometime last night. We found Pruett with his face busted up. Now I've got two guys out of commission."

"Goddamn it! No one saw or heard anything?"

"Nothing," Dell Sprague admitted. "They were in and out fast. Came in over the fields. It sure wasn't that damned doctor."

Mr. Dahlquist was staring at the wall.

"No. But you can bet he's behind it. He's obviously got people working for him, but he's the key player. We've got to get the girl back before she talks."

"You want him gone?" the foreman asked.

Keenan Dahlquist hesitated. His anger made it a tempting thought.

"Don't kill him," he said. "But you have permission to be as persuasive as necessary to find out where the girl is. I don't care what shape he's in later."

"Okay. I'm going to need some new people," Dell Sprague explained. "You okay with a little bonus money?"

"Not an issue. Just find the girl. That's all that matters. And her you can kill."

Dell Sprague hung up the phone.

22

AFTER BREAKFAST, DR. NOLAN AND two of his protectors returned to the hotel. They had decided to keep one person on duty with Mrs. Ramirez and Maya. Steve had volunteered for the first shift. Every twelve hours there was to be a switch in personnel, and it was a pleasant posting. Mrs. Ramirez supplied a constant supply line of food and beverages, and the house had excellent air-conditioning and a DISH satellite. It was heaven.

After updating Mike and Eileen on the merciful relocation of Maya, minus the details, Dr. Nolan, Jed, and Deuce headed for their rooms for some much needed rest. The emotional fatigue had now transformed to physical exhaustion, and they were beyond the point of productive action. The added sound proofing of the airport hotel offered a cocoon of silence, and the heavy drapery effectively blocked any incoming light.

Dr. Nolan floated in dreamless solitude. There were no voices, no questions, no demons of torment. It was a deep and honorably earned respite, and the musical incoming call modem on his cell phone could not reach to the distance he had travelled. It repeated its annoying prelude over and over again, and no one was home.

In mid-afternoon he stretched, rubbed the sleep from his eyes, then showered and scraped the whiskers off his face. With fresh clothing, he finally checked his messages. There were eight calls from the same local number, but nothing other than a long silence offered during the recording phase. On the last call, near the end, a frustrated voice said, "The fucker won't answer," just before it disconnected.

Dr. Nolan walked down the hall to Jed's room and handed him the phone. The younger man listened through the entire cycle.

"Someone seems anxious to talk to you." He smiled. "What a surprise." He called Deuce and asked him to join them.

"Should I call back?" Dr. Nolan asked.

"No. Let them sweat," Jed answered. "They may be under a little stress about now. Won't be long before they try again."

"Okay. I made coffee," Dr. Nolan said. "I'll go get it, and we'll wait them out."

He had not been back in Jed's room for over ten minutes when the next call came. He sat down at the desk and switched over to the speaker app.

"Dr. Nolan. How may I help?"

"You ever answer your goddamn phone?" the voice asked.

"I just did. Is there something else?"

The man's annoyance was etched sharply in his tone.

"Listen, smart ass. You've got something that belongs to us, and we want it back!"

"I don't follow," Dr. Nolan said, taking some enjoyment in toying with the caller. "I have property that belongs to you?"

"You know what I mean," the man said. "We want to meet and come to some arrangement."

"But I don't want to meet with you," Dr. Nolan explained. "Only your boss. That's the offer."

They could hear muffled background voices and then a pause.

"That can happen," the man finally said. "There's no reason for this to get out of hand."

"Agreed," Dr. Nolan stated. "What do you suggest?"

"There's an old factory off 111 about six miles south of El Centro," the man said. "Be there at ten tonight."

Jed was shaking his head. He grabbed a pen and jotted down a short list. Dr. Nolan read it and nodded.

"No. Out in the open," he said. "I'm not big on private meetings."

Again, there were background voices, but nothing clear.

"Okay. Near there is an old billboard on 111 for car insurance. The gecko guy. Park there at ten and wait."

Jed wrote out another change.

"No. Two AM," Dr. Nolan said. "I'm kind of a late night person."

More moments passed.

"Okay. Two AM at the sign. And just you," the voice said.

"And your employer," Dr. Nolan reminded him. "I'm looking forward to meeting him." He ended the call.

Jed was staring at him from across the desk.

"I don't like this," he said. "What's the upside? You got the girl out, so who cares?"

Dr. Nolan sat back and braced his hands on the arms of the chair. He was framing his response in a way that would make the risk acceptable.

"When Maya got her message out, it said, 'Please help us!' Not her, us. I think there are more people at risk. I don't know how, or why, or even who is behind this, but I can't let it go now. They shot my car, punched me, and now I'm getting crank calls on my personal phone. I can't take it anymore."

Jed nodded and smiled.

"I'd be pissed, too," he said. "But, what does this meeting get you? You know they're planning to force you into giving Maya back."

"That's their plan," Dr. Nolan said. "Right now, I've got nothing to take to the police. I'm going to shoot video tonight, get them talking, and see if the boss man actually shows up."

Jed looked at Deuce, but only got a shrug of the shoulders as a response. He pulled the map close to him and calculated travel time, then looked at his watch. They had over nine hours to prepare. He motioned Deuce over to join them.

"Okay, but my way only," he told Dr. Nolan. "You're wearing a vest tonight. No argument. Number two, Deuce is going to disable the cabin lights in the Jeep. He'll be on the floor in the back. Three, you get there early, say, one thirty. Pull off the road, set up your camera, then sit on the hood and wait. They'll drive past once or twice to check things over, then pull in facing you with their lights on to keep you blind."

"How do you know all this?" Dr. Nolan asked.

"Because, that's what I'd do," Jed told him. "Don't talk. Listen. You park directly under the sign facing south. This is critical. Under the sign, facing south. And, when they get there, I want you to hold your left hand up at shoulder level. If I see someone reach for a weapon or you lower your hand, I start shooting, and Deuce comes out of the car. Is that clear?"

Dr. Nolan met his gaze, and there was no room for negotiation. Those were the rules.

"And, where are you going to be?" Dr. Nolan asked.

Jed stood up. He took the long metal case from the closet, laid it on the bed, undid the latches, then placed the fifty-caliber sniper rifle on the covers.

"I'll be there," he said. "In fact, I'll be there about four hours before you. Deuce can drop me off, then come back and get you."

Dr. Nolan looked at the gun, half weapon, half computer.

"How will we know where you're at," he asked Jed.

Jed took the box of shells from the nightstand and began loading the clip.

"You won't," he said. "That's the whole point."

23

THEY WENT OVER THE PLAN a dozen more times in the next two hours until it was all reflex memory. Just after dark, Jed changed back into his camouflage fatigues, put three bottles of water into a pack, made certain there was a chambered bullet in his Beretta, checked the batteries in his night vision goggles, tested the radio, then smiled at Dr. Nolan.

"Wear the vest, and don't fuck up," he said. "I'll see you later."

He and Deuce checked the hallway, then went out the emergency exit to the car. A landscaping truck was parked near them, and Jed borrowed a shovel and placed it in the trunk alongside the metal case. They drove in silence down Highway 86 until a crossroad headed east that merged with 111. When they located the billboard, they continued north for about a mile, then pulled a U-turn and doubled back. There was still traffic, but the flat terrain allowed ample warning of any approaching headlights.

Parking near the roadside sign, Deuce and Jed walked north along the opposite lane, their flashlight beams cutting away the darkness. About fifty yards up the road was an elevated rise of dirt and sand held in place tenuously by tumbleweed roots. Jed checked the sight path to where their car was waiting.

"This'll do," he said.

While he cut away low branches in the dry vegetation, Deuce went back and retrieved the shovel and gun case. In the gap between passing vehicles they took turns digging out a foot deep hollow in the soft earth, the end to the south sloped and open. Satisfied, Jed drank one bottle of water, then covered himself in salvaged foliage from the trimmed bushes. He checked his watch.

"I guess I'll see you back here in about three hours," he told Deuce. They were forced to crouch down behind the mound of dirt as two cars went past.

"Makes me nervous working with rookies," Deuce commented.

Jed nodded.

"But give him credit, he's got hair. We just have to keep him from getting himself killed. My mom wouldn't forgive me."

Deuce stood up slowly, looking in both directions.

"How do you want to play this?" he asked.

Jed followed, then stretched out in the newly dug trench, struggling to find a comfortable position.

"Whoever is out front is my target," he said. "You work from right to left, and don't waste time wounding anybody. Any weapon is a death warrant."

Deuce opened the gun case and handed him the large-bore rifle. Then he laid out a small tarp just below the extended muzzle and covered it with a layer of branches.

"You look good," Deuce said. "Don't fall asleep."

"I won't," Jed answered.

They were done.

24

Dr. Nolan treated Mike and Eileen to dinner in the hotel restaurant. With the others occupied elsewhere, it was not wise to appear in public. They discussed the situation with Maya, and Dr. Nolan emphasized it was still a priority to interview the girl in the next day or two. It would all depend on how successful Mrs. Ramirez and Elena were in making her feel at ease. He did not mention any other planned ventures.

"So, we just sit and wait some more?" Eileen asked. "I don't feel like I'm helping."

"There is one fun job you could do." Dr. Nolan smiled. "You could start cataloging our expense account. We've got to turn in some kind of official accounting when this wraps up. Just to keep our boss happy."

Eileen gave him a knowing grin.

"Let's see. One wrecked car. Translator fees. Drone pilot. A three man army at a thousand each a day. Extra travel and hotel costs. What am I missing?"

"Well, we're not done yet," Dr. Nolan said. "Just get something on the computer. And don't use the word 'army.' It was necessary security. Be creative."

Mike was shaking his head.

"If she kept expense records on the farm like that, I'd fire her." He laughed.

"We're going to get fired pretty soon anyway." Dr. Nolan shrugged. "But, it might be prudent not to send anything in till the last minute."

"Oh, now we're prudent?" Eileen looked at him with raised eyebrows. "There are a lot of words I can think of to describe you, Sean, but that's a stretch. Most of them would be antonyms."

"If you're going to use slurs like that, this conversation is over," Dr. Nolan said, trying to sound serious, then shifted to another tack. "I'm doing the best I can here. I've sacrificed, suffered, given a hundred and ten percent. I just keep giving, and giving, and it's never enough."

Mike monitored his performance with the keen eye of a movie critic, then raised his hands and began to applaud.

"That was pure genius." Mike laughed. "I'm using that some day."

Eileen elbowed him.

"Won't work for you either," she informed him. "I live on a farm, remember. One thing I know is bullshit, and between the two of you, it's about knee deep."

Dr. Nolan bowed slightly and folded his napkin on the table, smiling broadly.

"I love you both," he said, "and I'm grateful for your help. Let's get some sleep, and maybe tomorrow we get lucky."

They shared the elevator up to the third floor. After waving good night, Dr. Nolan went into his room, took his cell phone off the charger, then made certain he remembered how to engage the video recorder. Satisfied, he turned on the television just loud enough to be noticed in the next room, quietly went back into the hall, and tapped on the door to Deuce's suite.

"How you feeling, Doc?" the young man greeted him.

"Like I want to throw up," Dr. Nolan answered.

"Good. That's normal." Deuce smiled. "Take your shirt off."

Dr. Nolan did as instructed, holding his arms out as Deuce fitted him with a flak jacket, pulling the Velcro straps as tight as possible.

"Like wearing thermal underwear in hell," Dr. Nolan joked.

"Long johns won't stop a bullet," Deuce corrected him. "Put your shirt back on, but don't tuck it in. Let it hang loose. Maybe they won't notice."

Dr. Nolan admired his new, bulkier image in the mirror.

"Too many doughnuts," he said.

Deuce put two extra ammunition clips in each front pocket, then looked at the clock.

"You ready?"

Dr. Nolan tried to think of something funny or witty to use as a response, but his throat was suddenly dry. Even in the air-conditioned room he was sweating, and all he could do was nod. They went out, walking as slowly as possible against the far wall, the carpet keeping secrets. Deuce opened and closed the exit door without making a sound, the thick, hot air greeting them back outside. It was still in the mid-eighties.

Dr. Nolan got into the Jeep behind the wheel, pleased the responsibility of driving offered some minor distraction. They headed south, retracing the same route Jed and Deuce had taken earlier. Traffic was light and widely spaced. Dr. Nolan could feel his heart beat rising as each mile of pavement fell behind them.

Deuce went over every detail one final time. As they drove, he snapped the covers off the indoor lights and removed the bulbs. He opened his door slightly to make certain they were all decommissioned, then squeezed into the rear seat and lay back, not wanting to take any unnecessary risks.

"I see the billboard," Dr. Nolan announced. It was 1:35 a.m.

"Good. Drive about a mile and check for parked cars," Deuce said. "If we're clear, turn around and pull off right under the sign. And, don't get too far off on the slope. I don't want to jump out on uneven ground."

Dr. Nolan nodded in the dark, but said nothing. He slowed, careful to leave flat ground to the right of the Jeep, then turned off the key.

Deuce unlatched the right rear door just far enough so he could kick it open. After putting the window down, he scooted lower behind the seats, chambered a live round, then concentrated on slowing his breathing cycle. The adrenaline rush was beginning to sweep through him, and he loved and hated it with equal measure.

"I've got to pee," Dr. Nolan whispered. It was not an urge to be ignored or postponed.

"Nerves do that," Deuce answered in a normal voice. "Just don't get over five feet from the car. It's about time to set up, anyway."

Dr. Nolan got out and relieved his stress on the back tire, glad that no one drove by. Out of danger, he went to the front of the Jeep, turned on his phone, then propped it inside the bumper, making a guess at the proper angle. His watch indicated one-forty-two. He took a deep breath, brushed the dust off the hood with his right hand, then heaved himself onto the warm metal. It was not hot enough to burn him, but it did nothing to offer comfort.

As each set of headlights became visible in the distance, he would hold his breath, watching them grow closer out of the darkness. Then would come the wave of heated, dust filled air as they passed, and he could breathe again. The lights growing brighter from behind were worse still, each one a torture until they became retreating taillights staring back at him in the night.

He brushed away perspiration from his forehead, actually wishing he had water to drink. He leaned back and looked at the stars, then refocused on another vehicle approaching. He recognized the silver Ram truck with the roll bar from his visit to the Dahlquist Farm. It slowed slightly, either two or three shadows in the cab, then sped up again and disappeared.

In two minutes it was back, another slow reconnaissance pass, speeding up for about half a mile, this time making a much quicker U-turn. As Jed had predicted, the truck pulled to a stop in front of him, the headlights on high beam, nearly blinding him. He held his left hand up at shoulder level, then shielded his eyes with his right hand. He heard both doors open and close, but could only see shadows.

"Dr. Nolan, you've become a problem," a voice said. "Where's the girl?"

"Safe now," Dr. Nolan answered.

The voice moved closer, just slightly to his left. Dr. Nolan recognized the figure surrounded by a halo of light.

"I was hoping to speak to the boss, Mr. Sprague," Dr. Nolan said. "I don't believe that's your title."

"I'm the boss here, Doctor," Sprague told him. "The girl. Where is she?"

"I believe in a late night meeting with her attorney," Dr. Nolan explained. "Seems like she has quite a story to tell." It was a risky gamble, but he wanted to test a theory.

Dell Sprague hesitated just long enough to show his uncertainty.

"What story? What did she say?"

"Just explained how you're running your farm with illegal workers. Almost like a slave plantation," Dr. Nolan guessed.

Dell Sprague hesitated again, but had not been moved to a defensive position.

"Everyone around here uses illegals. So what? I think you're full of shit," he said. "Where is she?"

Dr. Nolan sighed deeply.

"You know, you're the second person that's told me that in the last few hours," Dr. Nolan admitted. "I may develop some kind of a complex."

"You're going to have more than that," Dell Sprague informed him. "We're going to break both your arms, and then your legs if you don't give us the girl." He took another step closer. His right hand began to reach toward his rear waistband, and at the same instant, Dr. Nolan dropped his left hand.

As the armor-piercing bullet exploded the radiator and tore into the engine block of the pickup truck, it lifted off the ground, settling just as the thundering sound wave pushed past them. In the shower of near boiling coolant and deafening sound, Deuce had come to a standing position behind the open door of the Jeep. When the man on the right started to raise his hand, he fired twice in rapid succession, the first round shattering the windshield, the second striking the gunman in the right shoulder. He spun sideways and fell to the ground screaming. Deuce rotated left, the gun now aimed at Dell Sprague's head, only ten feet away.

"Don't do it!" Deuce warned him. He already had a half squeeze on the trigger.

Dell Sprague visibly slumped his head and shoulders. As he slowly raised his hands, so did the third man. Deuce just held his position.

"You okay, Doc?" he asked.

"Other than being deaf, yeah," Dr. Nolan said, his voice shaking. He scooted down from the hood, then leaned back against the car for support.

Footsteps approached from behind them. Jed, still covered with sagebrush branches and shedding clouds of dust, an apparition, appeared in the light. He walked up to Dell Sprague and pushed the muzzle of his rifle against the underside of his chin, forcing his head up at an angle.

"The only reason you're alive is because the Doc said no dead bodies." Jed reached behind him and took the pistol from his belt, then tossed it into the darkness. Then he motioned the other man to discard his weapon. "Two fingers," Jed told him. "Nice and slow."

Dr. Nolan went over to the wounded member of their team. The bullet had entered and exited the muscle layers beneath the shoulder joint, and he had a good arterial pulse at the wrist. Dr. Nolan took off his shirt and showed the injured man how to apply pressure to the wound, then helped him stand.

"What do we do with these guys?" Deuce asked.

Jed waved his rifle barrel at them.

"Take off your boots," he said.

"Jesus, man, there's snakes out here," the third man said.

"Then you best not step on any of them," Jed told him. "Take off your boots."

Both men sat down in the dirt and pulled off their footwear, then stood again.

"Start walking," Jed told them, pointing north. "Some idiot will probably stop and give you a ride sooner or later." They let the wounded man keep his shoes.

They watched as the three gingerly walked up the road and disappeared from sight. Jed took off his shirt, discarded the plant life, then shook off the remaining dust. He opened the tailgate of the Jeep and put away the sniper rifle, then helped Dr. Nolan get out of his vest.

"Jesus, what kind of bullet was that?" he asked, looking at the smoldering truck.

"Special order," Jed told him. "And very expensive."

"We'll put it on the expense account." Dr. Nolan smiled. He retrieved his phone from the bumper.

"No need," Jed told him. "I borrowed it from a rich uncle. It's all good. You ready to go home?"

"I got my phone," Dr. Nolan answered.

Jed and Deuce started laughing. Standing half naked in the desert at two-thirty in the morning, his left eye bruised and bloody, now Dr. Nolan was having trouble with his hearing.

Jed put a hand on his shoulder.

"You're priceless, Doc," he said in a loud voice." Let's get out of here."

Dr. Nolan was replaying the film from his camera. Not only was the picture poor, he could barely understand what was being said.

25

It was just like home, Dr. Nolan mused. Every time he tried to catch up on sleep, the phone would disregard his best intentions. After a three hour nap, it was the concierge desk calling with a message from Dr. Shriver at Memorial Hospital. They had confirmed a new case of Legionnaires' disease.

He went next door to wake Eileen, then showered away the early morning outdoor adventure, not bothering to shave. Dressed and ready in ten minutes, he collected Eileen, asked Mike to ride shotgun, then headed toward the large medical center in El Centro.

"What does this mean?" Eileen asked.

"It means the bug we thought was gone may be staging a comeback," he said. "They'll be able to confirm if it's the same serogroup. Kind of like a fingerprint."

"But, it's been what? Over two weeks. How can that happen?" she asked.

"Like a lot of this, it makes no sense," Dr. Nolan admitted. "But at least this will be fresh information, something new to go on."

They pulled into the parking lot, only half full on a Sunday morning. Mike was left in charge of the car. Dr. Nolan and Eileen went in through the ER and paged Dr. Shriver from the desk.

"Well, déjà vu," she said, coming out to greet them, but without humor. She led them back to the lounge area. Eileen took out a notebook to write down any information.

"What have you got so far?" Dr. Nolan asked. He spotted a pot of coffee, bringing two cups back to the table. Dr. Shriver was avoiding caffeine and alcohol for the duration of her pregnancy.

"Okay. Cecil Wynens," she began, reading from a three by five note card. "Seventy-two-year-old white male. COPD, heart disease. Fevers started yesterday. Nausea and vomiting last night, then rapid respiratory decline. Paramedics got him here with a PO2 of 74 on high flow oxygen. We had to tube him in the ER. Chest X-ray looks like a snowstorm. Gram stain showed nothing, so we already suspected Legionnaires'. RNA testing confirmed it about an hour ago. That's when I called."

Eileen had given up, not able to keep pace with the rapid dissertation.

"Can you translate that?" she asked, her eyes fixed on her brother-in-law.

Dr. Nolan nodded.

"It's a confirmed case of Legionnaires'," he said. "But he probably won't survive. He's already on a breathing machine."

"Which means he won't be answering any questions," Eileen noted.

"You get any information?" Dr. Nolan asked.

"Nothing, sorry," Dr. Shriver said. "He has a wife at home, but she's housebound with her own problems. RA, I think. We've got social services working on a care plan."

"Where does he live?" Dr. Nolan asked.

"Seeley. Small town about eight miles west. Just off the freeway."

Dr. Nolan finished his coffee, then nodded at Eileen.

"Well, we're still on the payroll. You feel like taking a drive?"

"Better than being stuck in the hotel," she said.

They thanked Dr. Shriver, wrote down the address of the latest victim, then went and rescued Mike from the heat. The freeway access was only a few miles away, and the exit to Seeley came into view in just minutes. The Garmin led them the rest of the way.

Dr. Nolan explained the rules of confidentiality to Mike, then stationed him on the front porch in a shaded chair. Still covered by the auspices of the CDC, Dr. Nolan knocked on the door, heard a voice give permission to enter, then led Eileen into the small living room.

Dark and cloistered behind thick drapery, it was almost like night. Mrs. Wynens was small, thin, and almost childlike, her physical presence dwarfed by the reclining chair that offered her comfort. A walker was on one side of her, a small end table covered with medication bottles on the other.

"Mrs. Wynens, I'm Dr. Nolan from the Center for Disease Control, and this is Eileen Carson. We're so very sorry about your husband's illness, but it's critical we ask you some questions. Do you feel up to speaking with us?"

"Talking is one of the few things I can still do," she answered, a polite smile given with her words. She offered her right hand, but could only lift her shoulder a few degrees, and her right elbow was frozen in partial flexion.

Dr. Nolan bent down on one knee and gently took her hand between both of his, careful not to apply pressure. Her skin was drawn tight and leathered, the tissues around her finger joints puffy and swollen. Her hand curled inward like a claw, the base of the thumb pulled out of its socket. At the wrist, the tendons had twisted and deformed, creating an outward angle from the forearm.

"When were you diagnosed?" he asked her, still holding her hand.

"Oh, twenty, twenty five years ago," she said. "Couldn't open a jar lid or hold a spoon. Finally went to the doctor. Said it was rheumatoid arthritis. Got worse fast after that. Arms, knees, even my neck doesn't turn much."

"What do they have you on?" he asked, a warm smile putting her at ease. She reminded him of an elderly patient in his own practice, horribly crippled and in constant pain, but never willing to surrender her life or independence.

"Methotrexate now," she answered. "Couldn't afford the other ones. Some were more than we get a month in Social Security."

Dr. Nolan nodded. It was a familiar problem.

"Are you taking pain meds?" he asked.

Mrs. Wynens nodded to the collected bottles next to her.

"Some," she said. "Try to stay at two a day. They make me sleepy."

Dr. Nolan lightly guided her hand to rest on her lap, then pulled a chair close to her and sat down.

"Can I get you anything, Mrs. Wynens?" Eileen offered.

"There's an Ensure in the refrigerator," the old woman said. "Get them free from home health. Chocolate, please. Strawberry ones taste like crap. Hard to carry anything with this walker."

Eileen went to the kitchen and returned with the requested drink. She had put it in an ice filled glass. Mrs. Wynens had to use both hands to hold it steady. Watching her, Dr. Nolan knew she could not remain in the house alone. Her future had just been rewritten, and would end in an assisted living facility or nursing home.

"You've fought this for a long time," Dr. Nolan told her. "Tells me you don't give up easy. The next few days are going to be pretty difficult. You still got some grit left?"

Mrs. Wynens nodded slowly, not meeting his eyes at first.

"He's not coming home again, is he?" she asked, referring to her husband.

Dr. Nolan had always hated issuing proclamations of time estimates, or odds, or likelihood of outcomes, but he also refused to avoid telling patients the truth. It was their right to be given honest answers.

"The type of pneumonia he has is frequently fatal," Dr. Nolan explained. "His lungs have been so seriously damaged that I think it is unlikely he can recover."

Mrs. Wynens nodded again.

"I saw it in his eyes," the old woman said. "When he couldn't breathe, he already knew. I kissed him goodbye when he was on the stretcher and told him to be strong. He was already going away."

"If it's any help," Dr. Nolan said, "he's not suffering now. There's no pain. The brain goes into a deep sleep, a peaceful place far away from where we are."

"I hope so," Mrs. Wynens almost whispered. "He deserves that much." There were no tears or sign of emotion, just a graceful resignation.

"Do you have any family?" Eileen asked after a moment.

"Kids are all grown and moved away," Mrs. Wynens said, then smiled. "All doing fine, all busy with their lives."

"Have you called them yet?" Eileen asked.

Mrs. Wynens shook her head.

"No. I've just been sitting here waiting," she explained. "Just waiting."

Eileen glanced at Dr. Nolan, just long enough to convey her decision.

"How about I stay here today and help with those phone calls?" she suggested. "Dr. Nolan can get along without me for a few hours. I bet you haven't eaten anything today either, have you?"

Mrs. Wynens smiled at her. She was now officially under the care of Saint Eileen, at least for the time being.

"We can make that work," Dr. Nolan said. "Are there neighbors we can contact that might lend a hand?"

"Thank you, yes," Mrs. Wynens said. "Mrs. Croft across the street. Blue house. She shops for me sometimes. Thank you both. But, you had questions for me you said. How can I help you?"

Dr. Nolan took her hand again.

"The pneumonia your husband has is the same illness that made so many people sick about a month ago. We thought it was over, but it isn't. Somewhere in the past week or so he was exposed to the source. Can you remember anywhere he went, anything he did? Was he around anyone who was ill?"

Mrs. Wynens sat forward in her chair, going over the days one at a time.

"The grocery store two, no, three times," she began. "He drove me to the doctor's office on Tuesday to have my blood drawn. Let's see. He had the oil changed in the car before getting his dentures fixed. Then…"

"He went to the dentist?" Dr. Nolan asked, suddenly more interested. Contaminated medical equipment was a frequent hiding place for bacteria and viruses.

"Algodones," the woman said. "Across the border. It's a lot cheaper to go there."

"When was that, Mrs. Wynens? What day did he drive there?"

"We stopped to change the oil after my appointment on Tuesday, so, Wednesday," she said. "He was gone most of the day."

"This is important, Mrs. Wynens. Do you know what route he took? If he stopped anywhere along the way?" Dr. Nolan asked.

Mrs. Wynens shook her head.

"I'm sorry, no. He was tired out. Came home, made dinner, and went to bed. He just told me his dentures fit better."

Dr. Nolan was frustrated and disappointed, but Mrs. Wynens was not to blame. She was as much a victim as her husband.

"Okay. Thank you." He smiled. "I need to go follow up on some other leads. I'm going to borrow Eileen for a minute, then she can stay with you today. All right?"

"Thank you for coming," she told him. "I didn't know what to do. You've been very kind."

"You've been the best part of my day," Dr. Nolan told her. "I'll see you again." He went back out to the front porch area with Eileen close behind.

"Does the visit to the dentist help?" she asked.

"No, goddamn it! Sorry," Dr. Nolan apologized. "It just points south again. He could have taken a half dozen different roads. Every time I think we may get somewhere, we end up with nothing."

"But, the time frame fits? Right?"

"It's perfect," Dr. Nolan said. "But where the hell did he run into this infection? And who's next?"

"Where are you headed?" Eileen asked.

"Back to the hotel. I better notify CDC that we're active again. Then, I'll get Jed or one of his team to drive me out to see Maya again. Too many people know the Jeep."

"You want Mike to go with you?"

"No. He stays with you." Dr. Nolan smiled at them both. "Work some kind of miracle and see if you can get someone to help out here. This is what you excel at. I'll call later."

Eileen and Mike were left to track down Mrs. Wynens' family members. The hospital services would not be very reliable on the weekend, and leaving the old woman alone could precipitate another disaster. It was a necessary detour.

Dr. Nolan drove back to Imperial. It was an anger-fueled commute. Back at the hotel he put the car in park, turned off the key, then slammed his fist against the steering wheel.

"Fucking moron!" he shouted to himself. The lack of sleep, the emotional turmoil, the failure to find any answers were all becoming one overriding monstrosity. He sat, working to control his breathing, to let the wave of emotions ebb away.

He checked his watch. Already early afternoon in Atlanta, he went to his room and placed the dreaded call to Dr. Pulliam. It went to voice mail, but the return call came halfway through his first cup of coffee.

"Sean. Good to hear from you," Dr. Pulliam said. "I read your report. At least it didn't take up much of my day."

Dr. Nolan cringed slightly with the rebuke.

"That's why I'm calling," he said. "Kind of a solemn addendum. We've had another confirmed case just this morning. Senior citizen with COPD. Probably not going to make it."

"Great. Any leads?" Dr. Pulliam asked.

"Nothing. We can't interview him. All I've been able to prove is that every patient travelled to the south, some into Mexico, some not, but still no common denominator."

There was a pause on the other end of the line.

"I originally gave you two weeks when this went quiet, but now it's hot again. I know you did your best, but I'll have to get a team back down there. Probably tomorrow," Dr. Pulliam explained.

"No. I understand. The two of us can't cover this large an area. Let me know how we can assist on this end. If you want us to stay, great. If not, we'll plan on packing up when your people come in."

"Okay, Sean. Thanks. I'm still stretched thin, but I should be able to arrange something by late tomorrow," Dr. Pulliam said. "And, don't feel bad. We couldn't find it either. Sometimes the bugs win."

"Yeah. Mother Nature's revenge," Dr. Nolan added. "Still pisses me off."

"Touch bases in the morning, Sean. And pray no new cases show up."

"That I can handle," Dr. Nolan said. He ended the call, then tossed his cell phone on the bed, leaned back, and stared at the ceiling. He had successfully accomplished nothing. Even his assumption about Dahlquist Farm had been wrong. Dell Sprague had basically laughed at him when he suggested they were covering up the use of illegal workers. It was just routine business. But, if it was such a normally accepted part of the local practice, why the threats? Why was the girl such a priority? Why were they so focused on getting her back?

26

DELL SPRAGUE WAS PACING NERVOUSLY up and down the parking lot of a Target store in Brawley. After walking for an hour, he and his two associates had given up and just sat on the shoulder of the road, thumbs out, swearing at passing vehicles, until a local worker gave them a ride to town.

His first call was to a local veterinarian who moonlighted on human patients, and for the appropriate fee asked only limited questions. His second call was to Keenan Dahlquist. He offered no details, but made it clear he needed to be picked up as soon as possible. While he waited, he purchased a pair of inexpensive tennis shoes that gave some relief to his blistered feet.

The Cadillac Escalade pulled up alongside him just before 10:00 a.m.

"Your fucking doctor has his own fucking army," he said, climbing in. "They blew my truck in half and shot Trevor, then took our boots and drove off. These guys are military, I'm telling you."

Keenan Dahlquist was not amused, but he almost laughed.

"Did you find anything? What about the girl?"

"I'm not sure they have her," Dell explained. "He didn't know anything. Just some bullshit about having illegals working on the farm. If they do have her, she sure as hell didn't tell them anything."

Mr. Dahlquist nodded. It was entirely possible the girl was so terrified, that she would never talk.

"That's all he said?"

"He's clueless," Dell repeated. "But the other two were pros. They would have killed us except for him stopping them. I think we should just back off here. Now I'm down three guys, and I don't want to be number four."

Keenan Dahlquist was considering options. There had been no contact with local authorities, and now it appeared that Dr. Nolan was a defensive player, and not an offensive threat. If there was any unusual activity, his sources in the police department would have given him a warning.

"We've got trucks scheduled tomorrow," he said. "Everything is already in place. People have been paid. We'll let this go through, and then we can ease off for a while."

"Jesus, I don't know," Dell protested. "Why take the risk?"

Keenan Dahlquist smiled for the first time.

"This one is special," he said.

27

Elena called at 10:40 a.m., the first good news of the day.

"Progress," she announced. "Yesterday, we just let Maya rest and settle in, went clothes shopping, sat and watched TV, just normal stuff. I was able to make some calls in between. There are safe houses in the San Francisco area that are willing to take her in. She can start school, work on her English. Then this morning, I was able to track her parents down in Guatemala. I explained what was going on, and I told them Maya could help us by talking about being on the farm. They were on the phone for half an hour, but Maya says she will talk to you now."

"Jesus, you have been busy," Dr. Nolan said. "How did you find her folks? That was brilliant."

"Called the local Catholic church," Elena explained. "They knew the family. Drove out and brought them to town. They were so happy and relieved to know she was in the U.S., they spent half the time crying."

"You might have just saved more than Maya," Dr. Nolan told her. "We got notified this morning about a new case of Legionnaires'."

"Oh, God, here? Where?" Elena asked.

"Patient is from Seeley, but we know he went to Algodones last week. We've got to find out where Maya was before, where she came from. She's the only possible lead I have left," Dr. Nolan said.

"I understand. How soon can you get here?"

Dr. Nolan thought for a moment. He couldn't drive the Jeep there and risk being followed. He was going to need guidance from Jed.

"I'll call when I'm on my way," he told her. "Just need to iron out some wrinkles."

Jed had managed to get a six hour break and was ready for the challenge. Deuce and Steve had traded watch duty at the home of Mrs. Ramirez, and Steve was feeling left out of the fun from the night before. He was anxious to be more of an active player.

"Grab two of the radios," Jed told him. "You head out in the Jeep and circle the area three times. I'll watch and see if there's a tail. If we're clear, the Doc and I will drive down to the airport in the car. You follow, park in the short term lot, enter the departure level, go down to the arrival floor, and we'll pick you up. All weapons stay in the car for now."

"Be nice if we had eyes in the sky," Steve commented.

"Our budget is a little tight for satellite surveillance." Jed laughed. "And, we're not exactly dealing with ISIS or the Taliban. This will be good enough on short notice."

Steve nodded, took the keys from Dr. Nolan, and went downstairs. Jed watched from the third floor window as he passed by the hotel on three slow circuits, each time following a different route. It did not appear they were stirring any unusual interest.

"Okay, Doc, our turn." Jed nodded to the door. They drove down airport way, pulled to the far end of the baggage claim area, and waited. Steve joined them five minutes later. He slid into the back seat and racked a live round into the chamber of his Beretta.

"This beats babysitting." He smiled. "But, man, that Mrs. Ramirez is a doll. She was waiting on me hand and foot. Tough duty."

"And, I was laying in the dirt with ants crawling up my ass," Jed reminded him. "You're not getting any sympathy from me."

"Yeah, but you got to shoot something. I was watching reruns of *Saturday Night Live*."

Jed just shook his head. He followed Highway 86 south, watching for the turnoff to Mrs. Ramirez's house. Making frequent checks of the rearview and side mirrors, he was convinced there were no extra travelling companions.

Dr. Nolan called Eileen on her cell phone to check in and get an update on any short term remedy for Mrs. Wynens.

"Saint Eileen, how goes the battle?" he asked.

"We got lucky," she said, clearly relieved. "A daughter in Fresno is flying in late this afternoon. At least that will hold things together in the short term. After that?" Her voice trailed off.

"Good work," Dr. Nolan said. "You just scored extra points to get into heaven. I may need to borrow some of them in the future."

Eileen laughed.

"I think you're in pretty good shape all on your own, Sean," she told him. "You sound more upbeat than this morning. What's up?"

"Long story for later," he said. "But, Elena and her mom called. They got Maya in touch with her parents, and she's willing to talk. I'm almost there now. Keep your fingers crossed."

"And my toes," Eileen said. "Call right away if you get something."

"You'll be the fifth or sixth person to know. I promise. Talk to you soon."

Jed parked three houses down from the Ramirez home on the opposite side of the street. He instructed Steve to walk around the block twice before joining them, just as an extra precaution. Elena was waiting at the door. Dr. Nolan hugged her.

"I owe you," he whispered.

"Do you ever." She smiled. "I could be the first person disbarred before passing the bar. And, you're ruining my work schedule."

"It's Sunday," Dr. Nolan reminded her. "Even you get a day off once in a while."

"Not with you in my life," she said. "Get in here and out of the heat."

Jed greeted Mrs. Ramirez, then took a position near the front window.

"I have coffee for you, Doctor," Mrs. Ramirez called from the kitchen. Dr. Nolan found her, kissed the back of her hand, and bowed graciously.

"You're spoiling me, and my assistants, so I hear," he told the woman.

"Oh, they are good boys," she said. "It is no trouble."

"Don't make them go soft on me," Dr. Nolan warned her. "We've still got bad guys out there."

She handed him a coffee cup, smiled, then nodded toward the table.

"Maya, hello, hola," he said. The young girl, dressed in jeans and a white blouse, did not even look like the child they had rescued two nights ago. Sitting on the far side of the dining set, she looked up for a half second, smiled, then looked down again. Mrs. Ramirez's calico cat was nestled in her lap, purring so loudly, it reminded him of an electric toothbrush. The girl was lightly stroking its fur.

"They're BFF's," Elena joked. "The cat even sleeps with her."

"That's a good thing." Dr. Nolan smiled. He looked at Elena with a question. "Have you spoken with her about the farm?"

"No. Waiting for you," Elena explained. "She's still afraid, and I thought one telling would be enough. Do you have five dollars?"

Dr. Nolan looked at her in surprise. He reached for his wallet and handed her the bill.

"No. For Maya," she said. "Give her the money."

Dr. Nolan put the note on the table and pushed it across in front of the girl. Elena sat down next to Maya, then explained in fluent Spanish what to do. The girl nodded, picked up the money, and gave it to Elena.

"There. I'm officially under retainer. Nothing said here is public information from this point on." Then she handed the five dollars to her mother. "Mom, you're now working as my translator. Are we all clear?"

"When do I get five dollars?" Dr. Nolan asked.

"When you earn it." Elena laughed. She sat down on one side of Maya, her mother at the girl's other shoulder. They were providing her a zone of comfort. Dr. Nolan sat opposite them, as far away as possible.

"You ask your questions, and we'll do our best to translate," Elena explained. "Sometimes the words vary from country to country, culture to culture, so be patient with the answers."

Dr. Nolan nodded. The girl was still keeping her eyes down and away from him.

"Maya, es usted muy valiente," he told her in a clumsy, stumbling accent. She gave a slight nod. "First, I need to know how long ago she came to work for the Dahlquists."

He waited for the question to navigate two languages.

"She thinks five or six weeks ago," Elena said. "She travelled for months to get here, so the days lose their value."

"And, how long after she arrived did she become ill?'

Again, he waited.

"One, two weeks," Elena said. "Many people got sick. They took her to a clinic, then the big hospital in the city, but she was allowed to go back to the farm with medicine."

Dr. Nolan nodded, taking notes on a small pad.

"Did she know the man who died?"

"No," was the answer. He needed no translation.

"Now, this is crucial, muy importante," he emphasized, leaning forward. "I need to know where she came from. Another farm? Was she working somewhere else? How did she end up at the farm where we met her?"

The rephrasing of this question was long and laborious, and Mrs. Ramirez assisted. The girl hesitated, but given some assurance and encouragement, she finally began a long narrative, none of which could be followed by Dr. Nolan. The rapid pace of her speech made it difficult for him to even identify random words. Finally, at a pause point, Elena looked back toward him.

"She left her village with a married couple who protected her from harm. Mostly on foot, sometimes on buses, sometimes by train, they got to the Mexican border. With no papers, she could not apply for asylum. Her parents had given her all their money. For two thousand dollars, a man told her he could get her into California. There would be work and a place to stay. It was her only hope."

Dr. Nolan nodded. It was a story repeated a hundred times a day along the border.

"And, how did they get her in? Car? By foot?" he asked.

Maya shook her head to both questions. Her response was much longer. Elena listened carefully.

"By truck," she finally explained. "They were taken in the night. Two big trucks with wooden boxes. Six people in each truck. They told them to lay down, then covered them with heavy tarps."

Dr. Nolan remembered the two double-bed semitrucks he had seen at the Dahlquist Farm. They were loaded with sugar beets and headed for a processing facility somewhere near Mexicali. It was beginning to make sense now, why there was such an aggressive reaction to his inquiry, and why the girl was a threat. They were not only profiting from an illegal work-force, they were the ones smuggling them into the country.

"Good. Good," he said. "Only one last question. Did the truck stop anywhere? Did Maya go anywhere besides the farm?" Dr. Nolan had to work to keep his voice and words steady and calm. His heart was racing as Elena spoke to the girl, her answer long and wandering.

"After hours of travel, the truck broke down. They walked in the dark to a cantina and waited. When the people came, they fed them and had them sit in the grotto with the Virgin Mary. She prayed for hours. Then a van came and took them to the farm."

"The cantina? Was there a name? A sign? Anything?" Dr. Nolan almost pleaded.

Elena relayed the question. The girl could not read English.

"She says it was the Red Horse Cantina," Elena told him.

Dr. Nolan pressed both hands down on the table, trying to remember the CDC list of test sites. He and Eileen had spent an entire day duplicating their route through the southern valley. There were no cafes or restaurants that even had a similar name. Was it in Mexico? Was it further east or west? Then, no, the other victims did not fit that scenario. It would provide no common point of contact. Many of the patients interviewed had denied ever crossing the border.

"Is there another word that sounds like horse?" he asked, desperately trying to find a connection. "Mule? Donkey? Is she positive it was the Red Horse Cantina?"

Elena asked again, but the answer was the same. It was not going to change.

"Damn it." Dr. Nolan sighed. He had them thank Maya over and over again, then he went outside and called Eileen.

"The list from the CDC that documented all the businesses they tested. Where is it?"

"In my room," she said. "Did you find out something?"

"Yes. No. I don't know," Dr. Nolan said. "We're coming to get you! See if the neighbor can keep tabs on Mrs. Wynens. Be there in half an hour." He sat on the porch, his thoughts jumping from one problem to the next. Nothing was simple or straightforward.

Elena tracked him down.

"Quite a story," she said, sitting next to him. "Can you imagine living like that as a teenager?"

"Not at any age," Dr. Nolan answered. "Just the luck of being born in one country versus another. It doesn't even seem real."

"Maya did great, don't you think?" Elena said.

"She was great. You were great. Your mom was great. I'm the one that isn't doing well."

"Don't pout," Elena said. "You got Maya out of a bad situation, and you got more answers. That's pretty good for a weekend's work."

Dr. Nolan pulled out his wallet. He looked through his cards, finally locating the phone number of Ted Neely, the Border Patrol agent that was an old friend of Sheriff Dent.

"If Maya was a witness in a criminal case, would it help to keep her here?" he asked.

"During the case, yes," Elena said. "But then she would get deported. It wouldn't get her a green card. And sending her home would be a death sentence. She already had one brother killed by gangs. There's no future for her there."

Dr. Nolan nodded. He had suspected the answer. After the risks taken to free her, he had no intention of losing her in the court system. He took out another five dollar bill and handed it to Elena.

"What's this for?"

"My retainer," Dr. Nolan said. "I may need your services."

"Do you think I'm cheap." She laughed.

He handed her another five dollars.

"I think you're priceless," he said.

28

THEY WERE ON THE ROAD again. Steve had stayed behind at the house, and Jed and Dr. Nolan were on their way to Seeley to collect Mike and Eileen. It was early afternoon.

"Sergeant Ted Neely, please," Dr. Nolan said, trying one ear, and then the other. His hearing was still in recovery mode, a high-pitched tone rising and falling at random intervals. "How come you're not deaf from shooting that fucking cannon?"

Jed laughed.

"Because I wear earplugs," he said. "Doc, you should know better."

"I am better," Dr. Nolan answered. "Next time, instead of holding my hand up, I'm plugging my ears."

"This is Ted Neely."

"Mr. Neely. Sergeant Neely. This is Dr. Nolan with the CDC. I believe Sheriff Dent is our mutual friend. He told me you were someone I could trust."

"That's good to hear. I've known Bob for a long time," Sergeant Neely said. "He warned me you were headed down this way."

"Good warning, or bad?" Dr. Nolan asked.

"Just said you had a talent for finding trouble, that's all. You find some?"

"Quite a bit," Dr. Nolan admitted. "I was wondering if we could meet. Dinner on me."

"You realize it's Sunday. Can this wait?"

"No," Dr. Nolan said. "It's waited too long already."

He could hear the phone being covered, then muffled voices.

"Okay. I'm out in Ocotillo. Big Ed's Barbeque at five o'clock. You like ribs?"

"No."

"Perfect." Sergeant Neely laughed. "See you there."

Dr. Nolan hung up just as they pulled into the driveway of the Wynens home. Eileen and Mike were waiting. Jed was already moving again before their seat belts were buckled.

"Neighbor offer to help?" Dr. Nolan asked.

"Widow across the street. Nice lady," Eileen said. "She'll stay until the daughter arrives."

"You're a nice lady," Dr. Nolan added. "Thanks for doing that."

"It was a pleasure," Eileen said. "Now, fill me in."

Dr. Nolan recited Maya's account of her journey north, the border crossing, the truck breaking down, and their accidental confinement at the Red Horse Cantina.

Eileen was equally confused.

"There was a Black Stallion Roadhouse," she said. "Somewhere near Calexico. And, a Red Robin in El Centro. I don't remember anything else like that."

"And a grotto. She prayed to the Virgin Mary," Dr. Nolan added. "We're going over that list again, and every goddamn local phone book you can pull up on the computer. Even Mexicali. Something has to match up."

"Looks like room service again," Eileen said.

"Not for me," Dr. Nolan told her. "I've got a date later."

"Mrs. Ramirez or her daughter?" Eileen asked, more than a little on the coy side.

"Ex-Army guy working Border Patrol," Dr. Nolan said. "Hairy legs. Tattoos. Not really my type."

"Sounds good to me," Mike said. "That's what I'm used to." Eileen elbowed him hard.

"You'll be sleeping in Jed's room for that." She laughed.

"No, ma'am," Jed countered. "I can hear him snoring through the soundproof wall. If he was in my room, I'd have to shoot him."

They were all laughing. It was a momentary reprieve, an escape to the sublimely ridiculous. By the time they reached the hotel, Mike and Eileen were holding hands.

"How touching and romantic," Dr. Nolan quipped. "Now, quit screwing around and get to work." They stopped at the reception desk and borrowed every phone book available, then went to Eileen's room to get the CDC files. A make-shift office was set up in Dr. Nolan's room, the coffee pot was started, and the review session began.

Jed and Steve left them alone and went to ransom the Jeep from the airport parking lot. Mike read through both the white and yellow pages of the phone books while Dr. Nolan and Eileen reviewed the CDC tally sheet line by line. There was absolutely nothing that even faintly approximated a Red Horse Cantina. The only glimmer of hope was a Red Canyon Café down Highway 86 near Calexico.

With the paper trail at an end, Eileen entered the Internet and worked her way through each town and community to the south, even into Mexicali state. There was a Spotted Mule Bar near Calexico, and it was begrudgingly added to their list, but it was a poor return on the invested time.

Dr. Nolan leaned back and stretched, then rubbed his eyes.

"According to Maya, there were eleven other illegals on that truck. At least one of them knows English," Dr. Nolan said. "If we can get access to them, guarantee their safety, there's a chance we can get better information. We know they stopped somewhere."

"Great. I don't think we're getting back on that farm," Eileen said. She and Mike were still in the dark about the early morning confrontation with the Dahlquist foreman.

"No. But, we can get the workers out if there's an immigration raid."

Eileen raised her eyebrows.

"And just how do we arrange that?" she asked.

Dr. Nolan smiled and checked his watch.

"We bribe a government official, lie, and file a false police report."

Mike starting laughing.

"That's what I was thinking," he said. "Isn't that a saying, 'Great minds think alike'?"

"More like 'Two idiots don't make a right,'" Eileen offered. "Are you serious?"

"I am indeed," Dr. Nolan assured her. "And, this is why I don't let you in on some things until after they happen. You keep looking and see if any lights come on. Jed and I have an appointment."

"You have bail money?" Eileen called after him.

"No." He smiled. "But I've got a lawyer on standby."

29

Big Ed's Barbeque was exactly as he imagined. There was country music overhead, sawdust on the floor, Western motif displayed on every wall, and an electronic bull ride in one corner of the dining area, surrounded on all sides by thick cushions. Dr. Nolan and Jed stood just inside the doorway, looking from table to booth until they spotted a solitary diner at the last cubbyhole, his back to the wall.

The man was stocky, hair cropped short, built like a boxer, and appeared close to Sheriff Dent's age. Dr. Nolan approached close enough for his voice to be heard.

"Sergeant Neely?"

"Jesus. No rank. Ted. Just Ted." He smiled, extending his hand.

"Then I'm Sean, and this is Jed," Dr. Nolan said. They sat down across from the man, who was studying them both.

"You're military, for sure." He nodded to Jed.

"Two tours in Iraq, one in Afghanistan," Jed told him. "Now I do private work."

Ted Neely nodded.

"It's in the blood," he commented. Then he turned his eyes toward Dr. Nolan, just the hint of a smile beginning to show. "And, you're the big troublemaker. Glad to meet you both. Order something fast. I'm starving."

Dr. Nolan liked him immediately. He was all business, but easily amused. His analytical skills were constantly in play, but he remained open and friendly, without any prejudgment outwardly showing.

Jed, swept up in the ambiance, ordered an enormous platter of barbecue delicacies that included beef, chicken, and pork. Dr. Nolan, wishing to avoid late night repercussions, chose safety first and settled for a burger and fries. When the waitress had left, Ted Neely wasted no time in commandeering the conversation.

"So, what is this about?" he asked. "Bob told me you were working for the CDC."

"We are," Dr. Nolan began, "but we ran into a secondary problem that's stalling our investigation, kind of a roadblock keeping us from getting answers."

"You're federal," Sergeant Neely reminded him. "Why not have the locals kick the door down? Why call me?"

Dr. Nolan scooted closer to the table and met his eyes for a long moment.

"If I present this as a hypothetical, say, a work of fiction, there wouldn't be any legal ramifications from us just talking, would there?"

Ted Neely smiled at him.

"You sound more like a lawyer than a doctor," he said. "But no, not from me. I love a good story. Have at it."

Dr. Nolan placed his cell phone on the table, then folded his hands in front of him.

"First off, our make-believe investigators found three cases, no, four cases of Legionnaires' at one farm. That in itself made no sense. When they went there to do follow-up interviews, one of the victims, a young illegal, asked for help, said she was being held against her will. Then, somehow, these investigators were able to get her out. Okay so far?"

Sergeant Neely leaned back, his eyes glittering, shooting a quick, knowing glance toward Jed. He was laughing, but it was a staccato, hoarse sound that was just above a whisper.

"This is good so far. Keep going."

"Well, the lead investigator then gets his car shot up, punched in the face, then the farm foreman requests a meeting and threatens to break my, his, legs and arms if the girl isn't returned. In the meantime, we, I mean they, the investigative team, learns that the girl was smuggled in by truck to the farm with a bunch of other illegals. Kind of like a side business. The girl is too afraid to talk to the authorities, and she won't risk being deported, so that brings us here."

Sergeant Neely was staring at him, but no longer laughing.

"That's one hell of a story," he said. "Do these other investigators have any hard evidence?"

Dr. Nolan turned on his phone, keyed up the video, then handed it to him. The headlight glare made any visual recognition impossible, but the dialogue was clear, including the threat. Then came the loud report of gunfire.

"Holy fuck! What was that!?" Sergeant Neely half jumped from his seat. He had heard the first shot echoing, quickly followed by the two rapid pistol discharges.

"Thunder, I think," Dr. Nolan offered.

Sergeant Neely looked at Jed again.

"Three oh eight?" he asked.

Jed shook his head.

"Fifty."

"You aiming at anybody?" Sergeant Neely asked.

"Just killed their truck," Jed told him.

"No bloodshed?" the sergeant asked.

Jed squirmed in his seat just a tiny bit. His expression remained stoic and steady.

"Nothing to speak of," he said. He did not add that a few inches of side pull in the excitement of the moment had saved them from digging a grave in the desert.

Sergeant Neely nodded. He turned back to Dr. Nolan, pointing to his bruised face and bloody eye.

"So, this guy in the story got punched in the face. What happened to you?"

"Organ grinder in an Italian restaurant thought my tip was too small." Dr. Nolan smiled. "The monkey smacked me when I wasn't looking."

"Dangerous world," Sergeant Neely remarked. "This story of yours has a little bit of everything. This girl you mentioned won't testify?"

Dr. Nolan was adamant.

"No. But, if an anonymous tip isn't enough, I will. An illegal smuggling cartel exposed four workers to Legionnaires', and one of them died. Not to mention the slave labor side of it."

Their food arrived, and for twenty minutes there was no conversation. Dr. Nolan knew the sergeant was thinking over options, a glance here and there with unanswered questions still to settle. Finally, he pushed his plate back, wiped his hands and mouth, then took the last drink of his beer.

"What do you need out of this?" he asked Dr. Nolan.

"A little justice would be a start," Dr. Nolan told him. "But most of all, I need to talk to the other people that were on the truck with the girl. They stopped somewhere, and that's the key to everything. I don't know if you heard, but we've got a new case at Memorial. This could all blow up again in a hurry."

Sergeant Neely nodded. He took a notepad from his shirt pocket, then pulled the cap of his pen off with his teeth.

"You said Dahlquist Farm? I've seen that name before. Twelve people at two thousand dollars a head. Not exactly a high profit enterprise. You figure in bribes, drivers, maybe security. Pretty thin margin." He was taking notes.

Dr. Nolan was momentarily taken aback as Sergeant Neely reviewed the known details of what they had uncovered. Keenan Dahlquist was sitting on a multimillion-dollar business, and his father was not in good health. His full inheritance and ownership of the family farm was not that distant a reality. Why would he be involved in such a scheme? Why assume the risk-reward being put in play for maybe a million, a million and a half dollars a year minus expenses? Maybe he didn't know about it. Was it possible that Dell Sprague actually was at the center of everything?

"What? I'm sorry," Dr. Nolan said. "My left ear is still ringing."

"I'll bet it is." Sergeant Neely smiled. "You need to talk to these workers ASAP, right?"

"Yes. Every minute matters," Dr. Nolan said. "It sounds like a cliché, but this actually is a life-and-death situation."

Sergeant Neely put his note pad away.

"I'm going to check a few things out," he said. "If I can put something together, it will have to be federal. Too many leaks on the local level. You want to be involved?"

"I want access to those workers on the spot," Dr. Nolan said. "I've got a translator that works for the court system, and we've been to the farm twice. They know us. I think, if they know it's safe for them, someone will talk."

Sergeant Neely nodded, then looked at Jed.

"I could use you." He smiled. "But, I have a feeling our methods might be a little at odds. You ever think about backing down a notch, give me a call. We're always looking for talent."

"You sound like Doc," Jed told him. "He's always trying to get me back in school."

Sergeant Neely stood up and shook hands.

"Thanks for the story, Dr. Nolan," he said. "Bob will get a kick out of this. He promised you wouldn't be boring. You'll hear from me by noon tomorrow."

Dr. Nolan gave him a card with the hotel number and his cell.

"Thank you for being a good audience," Dr. Nolan said. "I'll be waiting."

He left a tip on the table, paid their bill at the front counter, then he and Jed headed back north.

"Reminds me of a drill instructor I had," Jed remarked. "I think he's a stand-up guy."

"Sheriff Dent vouched for him," Dr. Nolan said. "That's good enough for me."

They drove in silence for a time, a broken dish of moon guiding their path. It was now just cool enough to let the air conditioner rest.

"What if they can't get something in the works fast enough?" Jed asked at length.

Dr. Nolan had been bothered by the same thought.

"Then, maybe we go back on graveyard shift," Dr. Nolan told him. "I wonder how many spare bedrooms Mrs. Ramirez has?"

30

Dr. Nolan could not turn off the questions. After a quick call home, he propped up in bed and went over the CDC test site list one more time, almost praying a name or address would magically appear that had been missed, overlooked in all the previous reviews. Maya had been so certain it was the Red Horse Cantina. Finally with a name to identify its existence, there was nowhere to place it.

Sleep was gentle when it finally came. His physical body, overly fatigued and drained by the emotional toll of the past few days, relaxed and gladly accepted a floating retreat to weightless reserve. But his mind would not follow. Not yet at the point of exhaustion, there were dendrites and axons making new connections, a search engine of triggered neurons exploring the archives of memory, electrical and chemical messengers combing through catalogued files, like dusty books on the lower shelves of a library.

His first dream was a treasured vision from his childhood. On a day trip to the eastern plains of Oregon, he had seen a herd of wild horses running free. Descendants of old Spanish stock, they were small, sturdy animals with long flowing tails and manes, their bloodlines linked to the conquistadors and the pages of history. Then came other fragments, pictures, photographs salvaged from time. Roy Rogers and Trigger. *My Friend Flicka*. Elizabeth Taylor in *National Velvet*. Faster now, a flickering newsreel of moving images, blurred, blended, one superimposed on another. *Mister Ed*. The drunken horse in *Cat Ballou*. The Four Horseman of the Apocalypse. Winged Pegasus...

He lurched awake, drenched in sweat and chilled. Turning on the light, he dialed the home of Mrs. Ramirez, each ring unanswered an agony.

"Yes. Hello?"

"Mrs. Ramirez. Wake Maya. Ask her if the horse had wings?! Did it have wings?!"

"It is early. Now?"

"Yes. Now. Please," Dr. Nolan urged her on. He waited, minutes passing, his feet tapping the floor.

"Si. Yes," Mrs. Ramirez finally answered. "El rojo cabello con alas. With wings."

"I love you both," Dr. Nolan shouted as he hung up. He pulled on his jeans and went to the next room, pounding on the door, Mike and Eileen still blinking awake when they answered.

"Con alas," Dr. Nolan shouted, almost laughing. "Wings. Red horse with wings. She wasn't reading a name! It was a sign! The Exxon Mobile sign! We're looking for a service station that sells food. Ten minutes! We're leaving in ten minutes!"

He ran back to his room, soaped up and rinsed off in seconds, dressed, then grabbed his files and laptop. Jed had heard the noise. He was waiting in the hall.

"I'm coming, too," he said.

"Gladly. You and Mike both. All the old team," Dr. Nolan said.

It was not fully daylight when they piled into the Jeep. Eileen rode up front with Dr. Nolan. He handed her the CDC outline.

"How do you want to do this?" Eileen asked.

"Down 86, then back on 111. If we come up empty, then 115. We check every Mobil station south of where we are right now. I don't care how long it takes. Start going over the list, and then double check Mobil dealers on your computer."

Eileen began her duties in less than a mile. The first station was just outside Imperial. It was not a match. Between their starting point and ending point, there were twenty three more stations to visit. As each was revisited and removed from contention, it was a relief and a renewed anxiety. In just over two hours, they had covered Highway 86 to the merger point with 111.

They were nearly to the outer fringes of the Calexico suburbs when Dr. Nolan suddenly sped up, took a sharp left turn, then slammed on the brakes in the parking lot of the same gas station and convenience store they had stopped at earlier in the week. But, he was not looking at the Mobil outlet. The old derelict, seemingly abandoned building next to it was open for business. The plywood had been taken off the windows, and near the road was a hand painted sign advertising homemade tamales and tacos.

Dr. Nolan leaned his head against the steering wheel and closed his eyes.

"Son of a bitch," he said. "CDC didn't miss anything and neither did we. It was closed down when they checked this area. There was nothing to test. No reason to look."

Eileen started to open her door.

"No. No one but me," Dr. Nolan said. "This is a potential contamination site. Just wait here for now."

He got out of the car, collected his medical bag from the rear compartment, then went in through the single front door. A Hispanic woman with a bright smile welcomed him from behind the counter. Beyond her, through an open window, he could see people working in the kitchen. The dining area itself was small, only five tables. Against the far wall was a refrigerator unit filled with water and soft drinks. There was no drinking fountain or restroom facilities visible.

"Hello. I'm Dr. Nolan from the Center for Disease Control," he told the woman. "We came by here five or six days ago, and the building was all boarded up. When did you open again?"

"Miercoles. Wednesday," the woman explained. "We had been away for a while. My husband was sick, so we went home to Jalisco."

Dr. Nolan could see a legal business license on the wall behind the counter.

"When did your husband get sick?" he asked.

The woman was beginning to sense that something was not right.

"Five, six weeks ago," she said. "But he is fine now. Is something wrong?"

Dr. Nolan smiled and shook his head.

"You did nothing wrong," he assured her. "But, the sickness your husband had may have been the same one that made other people ill as well. You remember?"

The woman nodded. She called to her husband through the opening in the wall. He came out from the kitchen with the same open smile his wife had worn, wiping his hands on a towel.

"Dr. Nolan. I'm glad you're feeling better."

The man shook his hand, bowing slightly.

"Carlito Borreas," he said. "Thank you. Thank you. I am much better. No cough now."

"Good." Dr. Nolan smiled. "I was explaining to your wife that the sickness you had comes from bad water. When so many people became ill, the CDC was sent here to do tests. But, your café was closed. They never knew about it. We were sent to check everything again, but last week, when we travelled this road, you were still closed."

The woman looked at her husband, her eyes wide, then made the sign of the cross. He did not need her words.

"Oh, Dios," he whispered. "Out back there is a waterfall. People sometimes go there to sit in the shade."

"I need to go there. Can you show me?"

Mr. Borreas led him to a door that opened into the back of the building. It was a grassy area covered by the spreading canopy of a paloverde tree, only the last of its bright yellow flowers still clinging to life. There were three more small tables with chairs, and in the far corner was a three tiered fountain. Next to it was a stark white statue of the Virgin Mary.

"How does the fountain run?" Dr. Nolan asked.

"Just by pump," Mr. Borreas answered. "We have to add water when it gets low."

Dr. Nolan nodded. He set his medical bag on one of the tables, opened it, took out a surgical mask, and a sterile sample container.

"Do you have a bottle of bleach?" he asked the couple. Mrs. Borreas went inside, returning quickly with a gallon of Clorox.

With his mask fitted snugly, Dr. Nolan crossed to the fountain, found the small motor at the base, and unplugged it.

He took an equal amount of water from each of the three collecting pools, then poured the bleach into the remaining water. Capping the sample bottle, he sat down on the bench next to the Virgin Mother. It was where Maya had waited and prayed as she began her new life in America.

The small grotto was actually quite beautiful, the shade a welcome retreat, the landscaping meticulously kept, a place for travelers to spend a few quiet moments before moving on. And, by nothing more than the mischief of nature, it had probably caused the deaths of nearly fifty people.

Dr. Nolan stood, took one last look, then rejoined Mr. and Mrs. Borreas near the door.

"I will have this tested," he explained. "Don't let any customers into this area, and do not turn the fountain back on."

Mr. and Mrs. Borreas nodded, still obviously upset.

"We didn't know it could cause trouble to anyone," Mr. Borreas said. "It was to honor the Virgin Mother."

Dr. Nolan put a hand on his shoulder.

"This is just a bad accident, Mr. Borreas. It happens in many places all over the country when warm weather comes. What's important now is that we stop it. Okay?"

Mr. Borreas and his wife nodded.

"Is it safe to be open?" Mrs. Borreas asked.

"Yes. In fact, show me where I can wash my hands, and I'll take four tamales to go." Dr. Nolan smiled. He knew no other way to lessen their worry.

He packed the sample bottle away, paid Mrs. Borreas, even after she tried twice to give him the food as a gift, then left, telling them he would call them later. If this was ground zero, the infection window would remain open for ten more days, but that would be the end of it. The threat of any new cases would be over.

Dr. Nolan put the water sample in the Jeep, handed the food to Mike in the back seat, then buckled into the driver's position. He sat for a moment looking at the old building, the faded company sign just visible above the door and the side wall. Most of the words had peeled into fragments, but the red winged Pegasus was still clear. It was the only identification marker that Maya had seen.

"Well? You're killing me," Eileen told him, her hand on his arm.

"I believe we're done," Dr. Nolan said. He gave an account of what he had found, the reason the cantina had been closed, the stagnant water in the fountain, the heartfelt dismay and regret now plaguing Mr. and Mrs. Borreas. It was the telling of a tale that had no champions, no victory celebration. There were only victims and survivors.

"We can skip the other sites," Dr. Nolan said, pulling out into traffic and heading north. "The hospital can run this in about an hour. If we get a positive match, this part of our job is done."

"You've got to be happy about this, Sean." Eileen was smiling, thrilled they had accomplished their assigned mission. In just nine days they had identified the source of the outbreak. She had no way of knowing that only a single frame of the puzzle had been completed.

"I'm mostly tired," he explained. "Deep, down tired. If this proves out, we can get you and Mike back home. Maybe tonight."

"Mike and I? What about you?"

"Oh, probably need a day or two to finish up some details, write a report, fill in the gaps in our expense account. You know," he lied. Eileen turned and gave Jed a quick glance, but he avoided her eyes and looked out the window.

"Why do I smell a rat all of a sudden?" she asked, her suspicions rapidly escalating.

"That's your husband in the back seat eating all the tamales," Dr. Nolan informed her.

"Hey! These are great," Mike defended himself. "You want one?"

"Is there one left?" Dr. Nolan laughed. The intended diversion was a dismal failure. Eileen's unleashed curiosity now had an edge of annoyance.

"Not funny," she announced. "All this sneaking around stuff the last few days. Maybe you should fill in the details."

Dr. Nolan concentrated on the road, but he could feel her stare scorching the side of his face. He considered another fabricated response, then abandoned the attempt. Since the more legally precarious activities had already been accomplished without any knowledge or assistance on their part, Mike and Eileen were in the clear. If there were any consequences, they were both insulated.

"Uh, let's see. In the short version, we snuck onto the Dahlquist Farm and got Maya out. Actually, Jed did. I was the getaway driver. Then, the foreman and two of his henchmen threatened to rearrange my bone structure. Since they probably shot up our car, Jed shot up their car with a bigger gun. Then, just to be thorough, after Steve kind of wounded one of the bad guys a little, we sent them off down the road without their boots."

"Shit! Where was I when all this was going on?" Mike asked.

"Sleeping," Dr. Nolan said. "Then, after Maya told us about the smuggling operation, Jed and I made a report to the Border Patrol agent that Sheriff Dent gave us. An old Army buddy. We're waiting to hear what they want to do next."

Eileen sat back in her seat, then gave a single long sigh.

"So, the other night when you said you 'relocated' Maya, it was just your way of describing a kidnapping at gunpoint? That about right?"

"People keep using that word," Dr. Nolan protested. "She wasn't there by choice anymore. We facilitated her departure, that's all. Besides, that was all Jed's idea."

Eileen looked to the back seat again. Jed had a wide grin on his face, but said nothing in defense or denial.

"If you're not done, neither am I," Eileen said sternly. "What about you, Mike? You ready to go home?"

"No. Maybe in a couple of days," he said. "This is an interesting place."

Dr. Nolan gave Eileen a brief look, then just nodded. They were staying until there was nothing left undone.

"A fistfight and a gunfight in one week," Eileen noted. "What's next on your to-do list?"

"Well, I was going to eat one of those tamales," Dr. Nolan said. "But, Mike seems to have taken that option off the table, so to speak."

"Mike! You ate all four?" Eileen asked.

"He gave them to me." Mike smiled. "I thought they were mine."

On the verge of further verbal assault, Mike was spared by their arrival at the hospital. Dr. Nolan noticed two television news vehicles parked near the emergency room entrance. Word of the Legionnaires' case had gotten out, and the leading edge of a renewed panic in the community was threatening to spread.

"Okay. We're going in the front," Dr. Nolan explained. "I'll take the sample to the lab. You go find the cafeteria and wait there. Lunch is on the CDC. Except Mike. He just gets to watch."

Dr. Nolan found laboratory services on the third floor. He showed his ID and logged in the test sample. Giving his cell phone number, he explained that he did not want his name paged over the intercom system. When the results were final, they were to call him directly. Before he joined the others, he used the lab phone to call down to the ER and check in, asking that the physician on duty call when he was available. The last thing he wanted was to be dragged into the public eye.

Asking permission, Dr. Nolan waited in the lab where privacy was assured. Dr. Torrence, head of ER staff, phoned back within ten minutes.

"Dr. Nolan from CDC. We think we found the Legionella source. The lab's running tests now. Should be done in less than an hour," he explained. "If this is it, the press is going to expect an interview. I'm going to dump that on you or the hospital PR people. Refer to me as the CDC investigator. No name. Nothing else. Anything beyond that gets referred to the main office in Atlanta."

"I don't understand," Dr. Torrence said. "You deserve to take a bow on this."

"The first team in did 99 percent of the work," Dr. Nolan told him. "We just got lucky. It's kind of complicated, but I don't want any press coverage. Sorry."

"Well, okay," Dr. Torrence said. "I'll give the administration office a heads-up. Where did you find it? The source?"

"Family run restaurant near Calexico. They'd set up a religious display with a fountain and a statue of the Virgin Mary. They didn't know the water needed to be chlorinated."

"That's pretty fucking ironic," Dr. Torrence observed. "I can just see the headlines already. About an hour, you said?"

Dr. Nolan looked at the wall clock.

"Less now," Dr. Nolan said. "You'll be my first call. Thanks."

"No. Thank you," Dr. Torrence said. "Nice job."

Dr. Nolan hung up, told the lab techs he would be downstairs, then took the elevator to the main floor. The cafeteria was brightly lit by a wall-length bank of windows that faced a landscaped courtyard. His team had commandeered the corner table in the rear. They were already attacking trays of food.

Dr. Nolan grabbed coffee and a bagel, too anxious to take on more of a challenge. He checked his watch as he sat down. There was still half an hour to go.

"This is the worst part," Eileen said. "There's nothing to do except sit."

"Reminds me of when Cienna was born," Dr. Nolan told her. "I couldn't help with the delivery, so I was stuck being a passive observer."

"If you think that's bad, you should try the labor part of it," Eileen said. "That really sucks. If men had to give birth, there wouldn't be any overpopulation problems anywhere on earth."

Dr. Nolan raised his coffee cup in a mock salute.

"That we can agree on." He laughed.

"Hey, let's have another baby," Mike suggested, putting his arm around Eileen's shoulder.

"The only kids you're getting are grandkids, old man." She laughed. "Then we get to spoil them rotten and send them home. It's perfect."

Mike kissed her on the cheek.

"Okay. I can live with that," he said.

Dr. Nolan looked at Jed.

"How about you, kid? You're on the shady side of thirty now. Any plans?" Dr. Nolan asked.

Jed shrugged.

"I've got a girl. Just been too hectic going overseas and back all the time. I meant to tell you, but I signed up for some business classes at Clark College. Supposed to start next month."

Dr. Nolan clapped his hands.

"Goddamn! An early Christmas present," he said. "What happened?"

"Got tired of you and my mom always busting my chops." He laughed. "Besides, I get more active duty just keeping you out of trouble."

"A good day just got better." Dr. Nolan smiled. "You tell your—?" His cell phone rang.

"Dr. Nolan here."

"Hi. Sergeant Neely. Glad I caught you."

"Oh, shit," Dr. Nolan said. "Sorry. It's not you. I thought it was something else. What did you find out?"

"Dahlquist Farm," Sergeant Neely began, reading from his notes. "Big operation. Sends two semis through the border every week. Monday and Thursday. Always pass through just after midnight, come back at three o'clock to three-thirty. And get this. Always the same guard on duty. I love coincidences. Doesn't happen often, but it looks like we have an officer on two payrolls. We're going to get a court order to look at his banking records."

"Jesus, sorry," Dr. Nolan said. "How long will that take?"

"Doesn't matter," Sergeant Neely said. "I touched bases with an agent at ICE. They'd heard rumors before, but not enough to move on. Your information stirred up a little interest."

"And?"

"And, I explained the urgency," Sergeant Neely went on. "They want the locals kept out of the loop to prevent any leaks. Feds only, which includes you. Any interest in joining in on an immigration raid?"

"It would be a pleasure," Dr. Nolan said. "What are we talking about?"

Sergeant Neely gave the same hoarse laugh as the night before.

"This is Monday," he said. "They're going to tag the trucks at the border with tracking devices and follow them home. You can meet up with me at the federal building in El Centro at 2:00 a.m."

"Jesus. Perfect," Dr. Nolan said, then had a second thought. "My translator. She's been there twice with me. She's like a grandmother. They're more likely to talk to her than someone in uniform. Is that doable?"

"It's a stretch," Sergeant Neely said slowly. "She has to stay in a locked vehicle until we clear and secure the area. But, yeah, I see your point. We'll let you interview people on the spot."

"Thank you, Sergeant. This should tie up our side of things. We may have found the cause of the Legionnaires' outbreak, but getting corroboration from anyone else that was on the truck with our first contact is still critical."

"Glad to help," Sergeant Neely said. "And thank you for the case. Try to get some rest. It's going to be a long night."

"I'm getting used to that," Dr. Nolan told him. "See you at two o'clock."

Jed had been listening with interest.

"Good news?" he asked.

"On for tonight, but feds only. I get to go as a ride-along. Sorry."

Jed nodded and smiled.

"Looks like my team is out of a job," he said. "I'm glad this is working out. Would have been more fun the other way though." He was referring to the suggestion of a possible follow-up visit to the Dahlquist Farm.

Eileen gave him the raised eyebrow look again, but it was another forbidden topic that she and Mike were better off not knowing about. Dr. Nolan just shook his head, then looked at his watch.

"Goddamn it," he said. "Let's go." He jumped up and headed to the elevators with the others following. At the lab, he knocked on the door with an added emphasis. The tech running the water sample let Dr. Nolan and Eileen into the room, but Mike and Jed were left in the hallway.

"Sorry for the delay. We wanted to be sure," the tech explained. "Ran the sample twice. It's the same serogroup. You've got your bug." He was smiling.

"Wow! Just like that," Eileen said. "We actually did it."

Dr. Nolan was already on the phone to the ER. He notified Dr. Torrence, reviewed the ten day exposure parameters again, then sarcastically wished him well with the coming media storm.

"I'm getting off easy, too," Dr. Torrence told him. "The administrator and head of Infectious Disease are waiting for confirmation. There's a press briefing being set up for 5:00 p.m. Sure you don't want to be there?"

"It would interfere with my nap time," Dr. Nolan said. "I'm just glad it's nearly over."

"So's everybody. Someday I'd like to hear how you put this together," Dr. Torrence said.

Dr. Nolan thought for a moment. That day was not going to be anytime in the near future.

"Like I said earlier, just got lucky," Dr. Nolan explained. "Thank you for your help."

He clicked off his phone, scrolled through the file index, then dialed Dr. Pulliam's private number.

"Dr. Nolan," he answered. "We've been trying to reach you. We have an eight-man team heading to the airport as we speak. Should be there before midnight."

"You can save the airfare," Dr. Nolan said. "We found the source this morning. The lab ran the sample twice to be sure, but it's an RNA match."

There was silence on the other end of the line.

"I'll be damned," Dr. Pulliam said. "What did we miss?"

"Absolutely nothing," Dr. Nolan answered. "We found ground zero in a Mexican restaurant along Highway 111. There was a water fountain in the back dining area. The owners got ill just over a month ago and boarded the place up and went back to Mexico. Just re-opened last Wednesday."

"That explains the stop-and-start pattern," Dr. Pulliam said. "Still a ways to go until the risk factor vanishes, but well done. I'm truly impressed. Now, I owe Arthur even more money. He guaranteed you would have an answer before the two weeks were up."

"Wasn't it a two-part bet?"

Dr. Pulliam laughed.

"That's still confidential," he said. "How soon can you wrap up and submit a report? Hopefully, with a little more information than the last one?"

"It will be at least twice as long," Dr. Nolan promised. "I still need a few days. Just some loose ends."

"No problem. Relax a little. You can give me a full run-down later in the week. And, thank your partner for me. This may not qualify as a miracle, but it's in the same neighborhood."

Not really, Dr. Nolan thought to himself. It was merely a part of an ugly secret that was still only now being dragged into the light of day.

"Okay. I'll be in touch," Dr. Nolan said. He smiled at Eileen, then passed on the compliment from Dr. Pulliam.

"So, we're still on the payroll?" she asked.

"Still making the big money," he joked. Out in the hallway, they tracked down Mike and Jed, then took the elevator down to the lobby. The vaulted reception area was alive with activity. Chairs were being set up to accommodate a fairly large audience, a microphone and podium were being placed, and dozens of reporters and news outlets were doing preliminary updates for the briefing. For the local region, it was a huge story.

Dr. Nolan walked toward the entrance doors with his head down. Their casual dress only garnered a few dismissive glances from the media personnel. They looked like average, uninteresting relatives visiting a sick friend or loved one. As they passed the assembled press corps, one clear question filtered out above the low level murmurs.

"Anyone know what this CDC investigator character looks like?"

Eileen smiled and gave him a subtle nudge with her hand, but said nothing. They felt like schoolchildren sneaking out of class, and it created a feeling of mischievous exhilaration. Just through the sliding glass doors, they wanted to run and shout in a show of giddy liberation, but bridled their emotions and maintained a steady, deliberate pace. They weaved through a growing maze of satellite vans, climbed into the Jeep, then completed their escape. They were successfully anonymous.

"Bravisimo!" Dr. Nolan exclaimed. "Like we were never there."

"Why so shy, Doc?" Jed asked. "You don't usually turn and run so easy."

"'Fame is a fickle food on a shifting plate.'" Dr. Nolan quoted. "Emily Dickinson. Posing for pictures isn't in my job description. Besides, we've still got unfinished business. I need a break before we meet up with Sergeant Neely."

"I'm going, right?" Eileen asked, more as a statement.

"You, me, and Mrs. Ramirez, with a very large escort service. Jed, you and Mike have to sit this out."

Jed nodded.

"Sounds like we can pack up tonight and head home in the morning," he remarked. "Might cut over to San Diego and go up the coast. No big rush getting back. Kind of sad in a way though. Hanging out with you is always an interesting experience. Makes me wonder what's next?"

Dr. Nolan smiled at him in the rearview mirror.

"In four days, I get fired by the CDC and go back to being a small-town doctor. I'm not looking for a next time," Dr. Nolan said.

"'Things are where things are, and as fate has willed, so shall they be fulfilled.' Robert Browning. Not bad, huh?" the younger man responded.

"Jed! Poetry! I'm impressed," Dr. Nolan said, a wide grin on his face.

"Lot of time to read in a war zone," Jed explained. "It's not all comic books and video games."

"And more reason to be back in school, kid. You're too smart for what you've been doing." Dr. Nolan replied.

"We'll see," Jed answered. "Anyway, keep my number handy."

"I've got it memorized now." Dr. Nolan laughed.

They pulled into the Courtyard parking lot, now late afternoon, the sweltering heat nearly at it's apex point. Dr. Nolan stopped at the reception desk.

"Dr. Sean Nolan. I want to check out, then check in again. Same room. Register under the name William Osler." The clerk looked momentarily confused, but took his credit card and did as requested. He was officially off the radar screen if any industrious reporter attempted to track him down.

"Who's William Osler?" Eileen asked, watching as he filled out the new registration card.

"One of the father's of modern medicine. Started the concept of specialty training, helped found John Hopkins University, promoted bedside education, believed in patients' rights, and had a devilish sense of humor. Sometimes his big mouth got him in trouble."

"Must have been a relative of yours," Eileen suggested.

Dr. Nolan laughed out loud.

"Probably not," he answered. "But, I would have liked him."

Upstairs, he urged Eileen to try and sleep, then retreated to his own room. He sat on the bed for a time, then took down the map on the wall and spread it on the desk. With a red marker, he drew a circle along Highway 111 in the general location of the cantina. It was nothing more than an unnamed pinpoint in the galaxy, a travel detour in the journey of a life, a momentary pause to find food, a cold drink, to use the restroom. And, in a random, ever expanding universe, it was the place where death had chosen to sit and wait.

Dr. Nolan folded the map neatly, placed it back in the suitcase, buried it beneath all the medical charts supplied by the CDC, zipped the top closed, then placed it in the corner. He pushed his bed back into position, removed all the sticky notes from the wall and drapes, crumpled them up, then discarded them in the trash bin by the desk. This part of their job was completed.

He wrote out a check to Jed for twenty thousand dollars, took it to his room, gave his deepest thanks to Steve and Deuce, and hoped his gratitude was adequate for what they had done. It seemed odd saying goodbye to them, but their role had reached its ending place. The drama had moved to a new chapter.

Nearly done, he returned to his suite, undressed, set the alarm for 1:00 a.m., then dialed Mrs. Ramirez.

"Mrs. Ramirez. Estelle, my love. Do you know what today is?"

"Oh, Doctor, yes. Lunes. It is Monday," she answered.

"Close, but no. It's date night," he informed her. "I'm taking you out tonight."

"Oh, Dr. Nolan, it is already night," she said, laughing.

"I'm serious. You, me, Eileen. It's a secret, but we're going to be part of a raid on the Dahlquist Farm. I need you there. We've been given special permission to interview any illegal detainees before they take them away."

There was a pause.

"Those poor people," Mrs. Ramirez almost whispered, her words soft and floating.

"I understand what you're thinking," Dr. Nolan said, "but I think these workers are being treated badly. It's not a normal work situation. I think they're being taken advantage of, and it's a worse life than they left behind."

"I see. Like Maya being locked up," she said.

"Exactly," Dr. Nolan told her. "And, since we have to protect Maya, I need testimony from other workers that were smuggled in with her. Anyone else that waited in the grotto when the truck broke down."

"I understand. When would this be?" Mrs. Ramirez asked.

"Late. I will pick you up at one thirty. We meet with the authorities at two o'clock."

Mrs. Ramirez was willing to help, but clearly nervous about her participation. There was also the issue of Maya.

"I can call Elena and have her stay tonight," Mrs. Ramirez told him. "She can't be alone."

"Good. Perfect. But Elena can't know about the raid. Tell her you and I are eloping. Heading out to Las Vegas to find an Elvis chapel."

Mrs. Ramirez was laughing now.

"You are still too crazy for me," Mrs. Ramirez protested.

"When this is finished, things won't be so crazy anymore," Dr. Nolan promised. "Do we have a date?"

"We have a date," Mrs. Ramirez said. "But next time, maybe you take my daughter on a date. When it's not crazy."

"That would make me very happy," Dr. Nolan told her. "And, thank you for all the help you've given us. I'll see you at one thirty."

Dr. Nolan hung up the phone, turned the light out, and scooted down in bed. He tried to sift through the convoluted, twisted pathway that had led to this point. For all they had managed to accomplish, none of it would have happened without the support and guidance from so many others. They were all actors in a script being constantly written, and rewritten in an instant of time, the plot always changing.

He looked at the clock. In six hours, it would probably change again.

31

KEENAN DAHLQUIST LISTENED TO THE voice on the phone, his grip tightening around the receiver. It was not a conversation. The message was short and to the point, and there was no need for any questions. He replaced the phone quietly, then looked to make certain his wife was still asleep.

In the walk-in closet, he dressed, grabbed a hurried assortment of clothes, gathered a few personal items from the bathroom, then selected one suitcase. On silent feet, he went out, slowly walked to his office through the dark hallway, then finally turned on a light. Kneeling down, he dialed in the combination to the safe, then removed ten bundles of one-hundred-dollar bills and his passport.

He poured a double shot of scotch and sat down, his breathing labored. It was just after 2:00 a.m. His mind raced through a dozen different options, but there was only one that offered any means of security.

He dialed the office number at the farm.

"Hello?" Dell Sprague answered, not fully awake. He had been dozing on the sofa against the wall.

"Dell. Just listen. A federal warrant was just issued to ICE for the farm. They're already on their way, and they know about the trucks. It's too late to do anything now but let it play out. You understand?"

"Fuck! They're coming here?! Now?!"

"Dell. You need to hear what I'm saying," Mr. Dahlquist tried to calm him. "It's just an immigration warrant to round up illegals. If the transport issue comes up, deny any knowledge. Blame it on the drivers. You've got no record. This will probably go away with a fine, but worst case, I make it worth your while to keep me out of this."

Dell Sprague was looking out the window at the darkness, but he was listening.

"How worthwhile?" he asked.

"Half a million," Mr. Dahlquist said. "And, I'll supply the best lawyer money can buy. There isn't a farm in this valley that's not using illegal laborers. No one really cares."

Dell sat down at the desk. It sounded like a reasonable plan. Running wouldn't help at this point. It was better to openly admit to poor record keeping and being too busy with the harvest to check on documentation. It was simple, and even if he spent a few months in a federal detention center, he could take tennis lessons or enroll in college classes. The trade-off for half a million dollars was an attractive offer.

"So, admit to the illegal workers, deny any knowledge about moving people over the border, and tell them you knew nothing about it. None of it."

"That earns the half million," Mr. Dahlquist repeated. "And, I'll have you out on bail by this afternoon. Are we good?"

Dell Sprague felt a chill go through him, but he could not think of a different strategy. Either way he was going to be arrested. Better to be well compensated for his trouble.

"I guess that works," he said. "So, just sit here and wait?"

"That's right. Act surprised. Be helpful. Put on a show for them," Mr. Dahlquist said. "It will be over in a few hours."

"Okay. What about you?"

"They'll call me at home, ask me to come down. I'll be shocked, of course, and very disappointed in my foreman. A terrible thing. Then it starts to go away."

"All right," Dell said. "But, don't forget the lawyer. I don't want to sit in jail."

"Calling one now," Mr. Dahlquist said. "Just stick to the story."

Keenan Dahlquist hung up. He would get Dell a lawyer, but that would have to wait. Finishing his drink, he picked up his suitcase, left the house through the garage entrance, started his Escalade, and headed for the Mexican border.

32

AT THE BORDER CROSSING IN Mexicali, agents had managed to attach tracking devices to both trucks belonging to Dahlquist Farm. The vehicles had been waved through with little scrutiny to begin their scheduled return trip. Five positions in line behind them was a well-worn van stenciled with the advertising logo of a landscaping company. Eight ICE agents were inside, all heavily armed and wearing full body armor.

The truck drivers wasted no time with varied routes. It was all routine. They drove straight up 111, turned right toward Holtville, then entered the gates of the farm at 3:23 a.m. There was no notice given to the Pacific Gas and Electric truck they passed along the way. It carried an additional six agents. Sergeant Neely, with Dr. Nolan, Eileen, and Mrs. Ramirez as passengers, parked and waited behind the elementary school in Holtville. Next to them were three large vans to transport prisoners.

The actual raid turned out to be a low key event. Both ICE vehicles entered directly behind the semi-trucks, arrested the drivers, then handcuffed Dell Sprague when he came out of the main office building. After searching the processing plants, the agents on scene moved to the worker housing units. Sixty two surprised and fearful illegal employees of the farm were peacefully rounded up and moved to the large building with the kitchen unit. Each worker was bound with heavy nylon wrist restraints.

"All clear," came over the radio, and Sergeant Neely and the prisoner transport vans entered the property. Dr. Nolan saw Dell Sprague sitting in the rear of the landscaping truck as they passed. He was speaking freely to one of the ICE agents.

Now in the light of the yard, officers climbed onto the bed of each semi. In Spanish, they announced they were with immigration and ordered the trafficking victims to stand up with their hands in the air. Slowly, resigned to the inevitable, twelve people emerged from beneath tarps in the open transport bins. There were no weapons, no protests, and no opposition. In all, there were eight adult males, two teenage boys, and two girls that also appeared to be young. They were helped down, searched, restrained, then led to the same building as the other prisoners.

"Okay, Dr. Nolan, it's your show. We'll process people up front, then send them down to you," Sergeant Neely said. "Mike Simmons is in charge of ICE on scene. Any questions, ask for him or track me down."

"Thank you," Dr. Nolan said. "I was wondering. These people are scared. Would it be possible to let the kitchen workers make coffee, get water, maybe some food? They won't try to run. There's nowhere to go."

Sergeant Neely smiled.

"We'll ask and see. If we clear the kitchen of knives or potential weapons, I don't see the harm." He went off to find Agent Simmons.

Dr. Nolan, Eileen, and Mrs. Ramirez seated themselves at the last table nearest the kitchen area. Keeping the greatest distance from the official law enforcement activity provided at least a psychological separation between them. It did not ensure total privacy, but the barrier was enough that their conversations could not be overheard.

Sergeant Neely had managed to locate two women that worked as cooks. One was the young lady they had interviewed before. After Mrs. Ramirez did her best to reassure and offer them consolation, she ran through a list of questions that Dr. Nolan and Eileen had put together. Neither one had arrived with Maya, but both had virtually been imprisoned on the farm property. They were afraid of the immigration authorities, but almost felt as if they'd been rescued. Dr. Nolan cleared them to try to provide some refreshments for the other detainees.

"They have had a bad life here," Mrs. Ramirez said. "Even the pay was low. But, who could they complain to?"

"New kind of slavery," Dr. Nolan commented. "Why didn't the legal workers here tell someone?"

Mrs. Ramirez shook her head.

"They were probably afraid to lose their jobs," she explained. "It is easy to be replaced here."

"We never treated anyone like this back home." Eileen said, disgusted by what she had heard.

"There are good people and bad people everywhere," Mrs. Ramirez said.

The next worker was a young man from Venezuela. He had been there for five months, being paid twenty dollars a day. Allowed to mail money home to his family, he, too, had never left the property. Now he was facing deportation from one dismal situation to another. The look in his eyes was pleading. Dr. Nolan asked if he had attempted to work through the asylum process. The young man shrugged. The weeks and months needed to navigate the system would not help his family. It was that terrible, and that simple.

The women from the kitchen brought out coffee, water, juice, cans of soda, cheese, fruit, and cookies. Each interview was taking ten to fifteen minutes, but at least they could offer some human comfort. By the first lightening of the sky to the east, they had worked their way through a quarter of those being held. One ICE van had already left for the federal building in El Centro.

The next prisoner was a thin man near forty from El Salvador. His expression was fixed and stoic, but two or three times he glanced up at Dr. Nolan to make eye contact, almost as if he were trying to reach some decision. Mrs. Ramirez began the list of questions. When she asked about Maya, the man hesitated, then nodded. He had arrived at the same time as the girl, on the same truck.

Dr. Nolan scooted closer to the table.

"Ask if he would like something to drink?"

Mrs. Ramirez relayed the question, and Dr. Nolan understood the words. He poured the coffee, handed it to the man, then put his palm over the man's forearm for a moment.

"Muy importante," he said to him, then asked Mrs. Ramirez to repeat his words. "The sickness that made so many people ill came from the cantina where you all waited that night. It was an accident, but the waterfall was poison, filled with a dangerous bacteria. Peligroso. Muy peligroso. Did you become ill?"

The man listened, looked at him, then nodded.

"Por cinco dias," he said. They had brought him medicine from the doctor, but it was almost a week before he could work again. Looking down, a single tear ran down his cheek, then another, then another. Dr. Nolan gave him a napkin from the food tray, waiting for him to let the emotional tide run its course. When the tears finally stopped, he said something to Mrs. Ramirez, his voice still shaky.

"Lo siento mucho," she whispered, then leaned forward and grasped his hand. She asked two or three more questions, then turned to Eileen and Dr. Nolan. "The man who died was his brother. His real name was Arturo Guitierez. They were both ill, but his brother kept getting worse. They took him to the hospital, but he never came back."

Dr. Nolan wanted to ask why he had not spoken up before when they came to the farm, but the answer was obvious. They had all been told not to talk with anyone.

"Tell him how sorry we are," Dr. Nolan said. "Tell him the sickness took the lives of nearly fifty people before we could stop it. He was lucky not to be one of them."

Mrs. Ramirez translated the words. The man nodded as she spoke, then looked at Dr. Nolan again, adding a single sentence.

"Que?!" Mrs. Ramirez asked, stunned by his remark. Her face contorted in a look of disbelief, not certain she understood.

"What is it? What did he say?" Dr. Nolan asked.

"He says…He told me other people died here after his brother. All people that came with them," she said, still struggling to accept the reality of it.

"No! Wait! There were four cases reported," Dr. Nolan said. "His brother, Arturo, Maya, and two others. Now three others. What is he saying?" He looked at the worker and opened his hands in front of him to plead the question.

Slower now, Mrs. Ramirez asked him to repeat his story, to give more detail. The man hesitated, finally nodded, and began to speak. Mrs. Ramirez tried to write down every word that seemed a reference point. It was a full two minutes until he fell silent.

Even in the dim light of morning, Mrs. Ramirez appeared drawn and pale. The fatigue of the long night had been swept away and overcome with a deepening sadness.

"He tells me…," she began, then faltered, the words not easily offered. "He says…after the first workers became ill, they stopped taking people to the hospital. They brought medicine, but two days later, a man in the next room died. He saw them take his body away in the darkness. After that was a woman or a girl, he wasn't sure. They put them in the gray truck of Senor Sprague and drove away."

"None of this was ever reported," Dr. Nolan said, desperate for more information. He knew their informant had not been in a position to see where they went after leaving the farm, but he wanted to know every possible fact he could exercise possession of.

"Does he know how long they were gone? Did he see the truck come back?"

Mrs. Ramirez relayed the question, but the man seemed confused. He shook his head slowly from side to side. They did not leave, he told Mrs. Ramirez, just drove away into the fields, maybe two hours.

"Jesus Christ!" Dr. Nolan said, disgusted by what he was hearing. "They just disposed of the trash, then went back to work, like it was nothing. Like they never existed."

"So, they're just buried out there somewhere?" Eileen was incredulous.

"Or worse," Dr. Nolan sighed. "Burned. Left to the animals." He crossed to the other side of the table and sat next to the worker, putting a hand on his shoulder.

"Mucho gusto," he told him, then asked Mrs. Ramirez for more help. Would the man be willing to testify in court if it helped his immigration status? As a witness in a federal crime, there might be a way to protect him and allow him to stay in the country, to work and be free from worry?

The worker nodded to Mrs. Ramirez, and then to Dr. Nolan.

"Okay. Good. I wish Elena was here to offer some guidance, but we're going to have to trust Sergeant Neely. We can't let this go."

"This is a nightmare," Eileen told him. "This just turned into something a lot bigger, and a lot more terrible. It's like a made-up story."

Dr. Nolan stood up and motioned to the ICE agent nearest them.

"You know where Sergeant Neely or Agent Simmons are?"

The officer called over his radio.

"Up at the office cleaning out files and computer records," he said.

Dr. Nolan thanked him, then turned to Eileen and Mrs. Ramirez.

"I've got to fill them in and see if they'll protect our witness. If this works out, we don't need any more interviews. Take a break and keep our friend company."

It was just after 10:00 a.m., and the heat in the metal roofed building was oppressive. They had been speaking to detained workers for over six hours.

Dr. Nolan grabbed a bottle of water and went to find the supervising officers. Sergeant Neely and Agent Simmons were each at a desk in the main office. Dr. Nolan knocked on the open door.

"Dr. Nolan. You making progress? We're about finished here." Ted Neely smiled, waving him into the room. Dr. Nolan closed the door behind him, then sat down heavily on the sofa along the wall.

"I'm getting a lot of practice lately speaking in hypotheticals, but if an illegal had evidence of a capital crime, could he stay in the country? Work out some kind of deal?"

Both officers stopped what they were doing, their attention secured and undivided.

"There are exceptions for certain types of cases," Agent Simmons told him. "We'd have to talk to the district attorney, but yes, there are ways to protect witnesses. Why? What's this about?"

Dr. Nolan met Sergeant Neely's eyes. He trusted Sheriff Dent, and now he had to extend that same confidence to his old friend.

"The worker we've been speaking to is Ramos Guitierez. His lawyer will be Elena Cantrell in Imperial. He told us there are two dead bodies buried on the farm. Maybe more. He's your eye-witness."

Sergeant Neely leaned forward, then gave a quick glance toward Agent Simmons.

"Fucking A, Doc." He smiled. "You've been a busy boy. I guess we're not just about finished after all."

"What the hell is this about?" Agent Simmons asked him. Both men listened intently as Dr. Nolan repeated the account of the Legionnaires' victims, the withholding of medical care, their deaths, the disposal of their bodies, the erasing of their lives.

"And your guy can testify it was the foreman?" Agent Simmons asked.

Dr. Nolan nodded.

"He saw Dell Sprague, his truck, and the victims. He doesn't know where they took the bodies, but it was out toward the fields."

"We questioned that smug little prick for half an hour before carting him off to jail," Sergeant Neely told him. "He's innocent as a newborn. Doesn't understand how any of this happened. And, he bent over backward protecting his boss. Offered to take full blame for hiring the illegal workers."

"What about Dahlquist?" Dr. Nolan asked.

"He's in the wind," Agent Simmons answered. "Wife says he left early this morning. Won't answer his phone. Doesn't know where he is?"

"Could he have known about the raid?" Dr. Nolan asked.

"It's possible," Sergeant Neely admitted. "We try to keep a tight ship, but there's always the chance of a leak. We'll find him sooner or later."

Agent Simmons looked at his watch. His men had been on-site for almost nine hours.

"It's too late to do this justice today," he announced. "We'll come back in the morning with cadaver dogs and set up a search grid. Since you started all this, Dr. Nolan, I suppose you'd like to be around for the finish?"

"I would. Thank you. Just tell me what time," Dr. Nolan answered.

"Six AM to beat the heat," Agent Simmons quipped. "Neely, you free?"

"I'll arrange it." The man smiled. "I wouldn't miss this for anything. You want to keep this quiet for now?"

"Absolute silence," Agent Simmons said. He looked at his notes. "You said your guy's lawyer is Elena Cantrell? We can reach out and start working on some kind of agreement?"

"Perfect," Dr. Nolan said. "But give me about an hour to tell her about her new client. She doesn't know yet."

Sergeant Neely broke out in his rapid, raspy laugh.

"You're a piece of work, Doc," he said. "You keep friends very long?"

"No. Not really," Dr. Nolan admitted. "I just have a circle of people who put up with me. Most of the time."

"Well, that's something, anyway," Sergeant Neely commented, then he turned to Agent Simmons. "You want to take a run at this Dell Sprague asshole and see how he holds up?"

Agent Simmons thought for a moment, then shook his head.

"Let's talk to the DA about all this. If we find DBs, we can come at him with negligent homicide or second-degree murder. My guess is he won't be smiling anymore."

"Okay. Sounds good. Doc, you look beat," Sergeant Neely said. "Why don't you collect your staff, and I'll give you a ride back to your car."

Dr. Nolan stood up, stretched, then went to find Eileen and Mrs. Ramirez.

"We're done," he told them, both deeply relieved at the news.

"Do we get paid overtime, or hazard pay, or combat pay?" Eileen laughed.

"Only Mrs. Ramirez," Dr. Nolan said. "We signed up for this. I'm going to have you drop us off, then you head back to the hotel. Elena can give me a ride later. I need to explain what I've gotten her into. I kind of volunteered her services to help our friend."

Eileen gave an exaggerated smile that was much more of a grimace.

"I think it is lucky for you my daughter likes you." Mrs. Ramirez smiled. "You are a lot of management."

Eileen laughed.

"I think the word is 'mismanagement,'" she said. "Maybe I should have a talk with your daughter and explain a few things to her. She seems like a warm and caring person. It would be tragic if a lapse in judgment led her astray."

"That would be kind of you." Mrs. Ramirez laughed. "A mother always worries about her children getting mixed up with the wrong people."

"Jeez," Dr. Nolan protested, opening the back door to Sergeant Neely's patrol car and allowing the two women to be seated. "I'm not that bad. Really, I'm telling you." He climbed into the passenger seat next to Sergeant Neely, but received no verbal support or words of understanding. The two women were still laughing as they began to drive away from the farm.

"Sergeant Neely. Can I borrow your gun?" Dr. Nolan asked.

"No," said the sergeant. Now he was laughing too.

33

Elena was working at the kitchen table when her mother and Dr. Nolan arrived at the house. She was not laughing. Looking up at him from behind her computer screen, her eyes were a gathering of storm clouds. She stood up and gave her mother a long hug.

"You've had my mother out all night and half the day," she informed him. "Do you have any idea how old she is?"

"She told me thirty-nine," Dr. Nolan said. "Is that not right? She fibs to me all the time."

His humor was not working, at least with Elena. Mrs. Ramirez laughed out loud.

"I am not the fibber," she informed him. "You want more coffee? I'll put some on and check on Maya. Then you two can talk. I may need a nap."

"I'd love to hear some kind of an explanation for this," Elena said. "You've got my mother running around like a secret agent. This has to stop."

Dr. Nolan sat down at the table. Mrs. Ramirez set the coffee maker on, took her daughter by the hand, then made her sit as well. She kissed her on the forehead.

"Elena, you are my heart," she said. "This is a good man. Last night we did a wonderful thing to help people, to make things right. I have never felt so important in my life, except when I brought you to this earth. We helped free people who were being kept as prisoners, and we brought honor to the dead. I am blessed to be a part of this."

Elena held a tear back, then kissed her mother's hand. Her anger could not withstand the words just spoken. She smiled and nodded.

"Okay. Okay," she whispered. "I just worry, that's all. This has been so crazy."

"And fun," her mother said. "This doctor makes me laugh, even when we see terrible truth. If it was not so, my heart would break."

Mrs. Ramirez brought them each a cup of coffee, then went to visit Maya. Dr. Nolan kept his head down, not saying anything, only looking up every few seconds to test the weather. The clouds were beginning to lighten.

"All right, knock it off," Elena finally said. "You're out of the dog-house for now. But, I still want to know what you were up to."

Dr. Nolan sipped his coffee, nodded, took out his wallet, then handed her a ten dollar bill.

"This is a retainer for your newest client," he said, then spent half an hour going over the details of the immigration raid, the long interview process, and last, the stark revelation given by Mr. Guitierez about the other victims, and the apparent attempt to conceal their bodies.

She did not speak when he finished. Staring at the floor, she gave one deep sigh, went to place her cup in the sink, then turned to face him with her back against the counter. In her career working with immigrants, she had heard horrible, heart rending stories a thousand times, none worse than this.

"I will do whatever I can for Mr. Guitierez," she said at last. "And you? You're going back out there tomorrow?"

"I am. I can't stop until this is finished," he said. "The good news is, your mother can go back to harboring fugitives and stay at home. She's been a godsend, but we won't need her to translate anymore. The only people left to find are dead."

Elena looked at him for a long minute, but he could not read her expression.

"We found a home for Maya," she said finally. "A family with two teenagers is coming to meet her on Thursday. A whole new life."

"That's a good ending," Dr. Nolan said. "And, that's your doing. Thank you for that."

He stood and moved closer to her. His right arm circled around her as he placed his cup in the sink, lightly pressing up against her. Bringing his hands up, he brushed his fingers through her hair, then slowly leaned close and kissed her, long enough to know it was accepted and returned with equal passion.

"Wow, what brought that on?" She smiled.

"I've thought about it since the first moment I saw you," he said. "I had a breath mint handy, so I decided this was perfect timing."

She pushed him back slightly, but kept hold of him.

"You have a very predictable habit of trying to hide behind humor when serious moments arrive. Why is that?" she asked.

He kept focused on her eyes.

"I haven't wanted to want someone for a very long time," he told her. "When I feel like I'm drowning in the ocean, I tend to start looking for a life raft."

She smiled up at him.

"You could just take my hand," she told him. "I won't let go."

He leaned his forehead against hers, the scent of her almost making him feel dizzy.

"I'm almost afraid to ask another favor, but could you drive me back to my hotel?"

"It would be my pleasure," she said. "But, one last question."

"Yes?"

"Do you have any more of those breath mints?" she asked.

"Yes," he answered.

She hugged him tightly.

"Good," was all she said.

34

BEFORE SUNRISE THE NEXT MORNING, Dr. Nolan joined a convoy of vehicles at the federal building. There were three SUV's carrying personnel, a forensic unit, and a civilian pick-up with four search dogs. They arrived at the Dahlquist Farm with just enough daylight to begin work. Sergeant Neely was waiting, having made the drive from home in his Border Patrol unit.

"Long time no see." He nodded to Dr. Nolan, then handed him a government issue baseball cap with 'Border Patrol' stitched across the crown. "Souvenir. It'll make Bob jealous."

Dr. Nolan smiled, tried it on, adjusted the band, then placed it on his head, giving the brim a slightly curved squeeze.

"How do I look?" he asked.

"Like a doctor trying to impersonate a police officer." Sergeant Neely laughed. "You ready to get dirty?"

Dr. Nolan looked up at the haze of sun now fully visible to the east. At 7:10 a.m., it was already in the low eighties.

"I'm just ready to have this over," he said.

A tent with a long table and chairs had been set up by some of the officers just beyond the processing sheds. Since their only eye-witness account described Dell Sprague leaving to the eastern fields, they would have to cover those areas, as well as the open quadrants to the south. A map with grid lines was unfolded on the table.

"This will be slow and hot," Agent Simmons told them. "Stay hydrated. We'll start in the center road and let each dog work south and north at about fifty foot intervals. We break every hour to get the dogs water and a little rest. Questions?"

"We have anything more specific?" one officer asked.

"Nothing. Bodies left, and they didn't come back. That's all we know," Agent Simmons said. "Let's go find them."

The men divided into two teams. Beginning on the main cross-road, they began a slow march through the fields, some planted with crops, and some barren dust. The dog assigned to each group worked out ahead in a zigzag pattern, half a mile out to the perimeter, and then back, each circuit taking half an hour. There was an occasional dead mole or bird, but nothing to pique their interest.

The immediate excitement and anticipation of the search dissolved quickly in the stark drudgery and repetition of the work itself. The men walked with their eyes down, looking for any disturbance or unusual pattern in the soil. The dogs panted with tongues out, weaved back and forth, growing smaller as they moved away, growing larger as they made the return sweep. It was worse than slow. It was painfully tedious.

Dr. Nolan walked some of the early grids, but was soon under the tent with Sergeant Neely, water bottle in hand. He poured half of it over his head and down his neck, the salty sweat burning his eyes.

"This is pleasant," he remarked.

"Be over a hundred later," Sergeant Neely assured him. "This is the easy part."

"Sheriff Dent made a joke about this being close to hell," Dr. Nolan said. "How do these dogs keep going?"

"Desert dogs," Sergeant Nelly explained. "They're used to it. They get a lot of work along the border looking for people who didn't make it. The handlers will switch these two out about noon. Got a back-up team in the truck."

Dr. Nolan just shook his head. He was soaking wet with perspiration, his face streaked with dust.

"Pretty glamorous job," he said. "I think I'll stick to practicing medicine in a nice, climate controlled office. Less chance I'll die from a heat stroke."

Sergeant Neely laughed his agreement.

"Bob said you were pretty sharp," Sergeant Neely said.

"How many years have you known him?" Dr. Nolan asked.

Sergeant Neely did the math, seemingly surprised by his own answer.

"Forty-four years," he said. "We met up as kids in Vietnam."

"How long were you there?" Dr. Nolan asked.

"Long enough not to be a kid anymore," Sergeant Neely said. "Don't talk about it much."

Dr. Nolan knew it was not a subject open to further discussion.

"You sound like Sheriff Dent," Dr. Nolan told him. "I don't think he's ever talked about it. I'm sorry you had to go through that. And after? You have the usual PTSD issues readjusting?"

"Then, and now, Doc." Sergeant Neely forced a smile. "This some kind of free therapy session?"

"Jesus, no. Sorry," Dr. Nolan explained. "It's just that we're learning more and more about the after effects of active duty. A large percentage of these young people coming back from Iraq and Afghanistan are all screwed up. Sometimes it's easier to get over the physical wounds than the emotional ones."

Sergeant Neely stared out past him toward the agents in the fields.

"I think they should just learn there's no fucking winners in war," he said. "Just some people lose more than others. That's all."

Dr. Nolan nodded, then let any further questions slide away. The philosophical wisdom delivered by Sergeant Neely needed no further comment.

At around 11:00 a.m., the officers on search duty broke for lunch and a rest period in the shade. The enthusiasm level had gone down as the temperature continued to climb. Over half of the farm acreage had been cleared, but fatigue made the remaining terrain a daunting challenge.

Dr. Nolan approached Agent Simmons at the head of the table, reviewing a map of the farm.

"Any news on Dahlquist?" he asked.

"Crossed into Mexico through Arizona before we got word out," he answered. "Since then, nothing."

"How about Ben Dahlquist?"

Agent Simmons scooted his chair back, wiping a sweat trail from his temple.

"The old man? We talked to him yesterday. He hasn't been active in the business for years. More of an ambassador. He was pretty honest about having illegal workers over the years, but he didn't know what was going on here. He seemed genuinely upset about it."

Dr. Nolan agreed.

"I read him as a decent guy, too," he said. "Just a hardworking man who was proud of what he had built. Old-school type."

"Our money's on the son," Agent Simmons told him. "Innocent people don't usually try to disappear."

"The Mexican authorities," Dr. Nolan began, "are they usually willing to cooperate?"

"Yes, and no," Agent Simmons said with the hint of a smile. "Cash is king south of the border. You can bribe a lot of people, but not everybody. Mr. Dahlquist will show up on the radar at some point."

"And Sprague?"

"Out on bond, and still suffering from amnesia," Agent Simmons explained. "The only thing he keeps telling us is that his boss knew nothing. Got a good lawyer, too."

Dr. Nolan sighed. The process tested his limited patience.

"Okay, ladies," Agent Simmons was clapping his hands. "Round two. You've got fresh dogs. Find something."

There was some low frequency grumbling, but the search party loaded up with water bottles and headed out again. Only the golden retriever and yellow lab seemed energized. Dr. Nolan and Sergeant Neely stayed with the group to the north, but the afternoon was equally unproductive. All they managed was to eliminate possible areas of interest. They were just finishing the final grid section when a radio call requested Agent Simmons to meet the searchers at the far southeast corner of the property. As his SUV came down the perimeter road, Dr. Nolan and Sergeant Neely thumbed a ride. The air-conditioned vehicle was a brief visit to paradise.

Half a mile down the dust choked road was the south side team and their dog, most of the men sitting or kneeling, no shaded area to offer relief.

"What've you got?" Agent Simmons asked, jumping out of the car.

"Multiple sets of tire tracks up and down this bank." One officer pointed. The tracks were wide with a deep patterned tread, clearly visible in some areas, then disappearing in others where wind had erased them.

"You said Dell Sprague had a jacked-up Ram truck, right? We should be able to match these treads pretty easy," Agent Simmons said.

"Yeah, but his truck's either in the junk-yard or a repair shop," Dr. Nolan informed him.

"How the hell you know that?" Agent Simmons asked.

Sergeant Neely was already laughing, his distinctive, almost whispered anticipation of the coming answer.

Dr. Nolan kept a straight face.

"I think his engine blew up," he explained.

Agent Simmons looked at him suspiciously, then glanced at Sergeant Neely.

"Well, we can find it, one way or another," he said. "That will be enough for another warrant."

"What?! What the fuck are you talking about?" Dr. Nolan said. "Just follow the tracks!"

Agent Simmons shook his head.

"We will," he explained. "Just not today. We're at the end of Dahlquist land. Our warrant is only for this property. Period."

"You've got to be kidding?! You can see where the truck went!"

"Yeah, on someone else's property." Agent Simmons emphasized the point. "We need another warrant. Any evidence seized illegally could get thrown out of court."

"This is like telling a heart attack patient to come back tomorrow," Dr. Nolan said. "Do you see how insane this is?!"

"We live with it every day," Agent Simmons said. "But we have to do it by the book."

"Then you need a new book," Dr. Nolan said in disgust. He walked away a few steps and took a deep breath, then another. Spinning around, he went to where the handler was giving water to the golden lab. He knelt down and stroked the animal along her head.

"What's her name?" he asked.

"Mika," the man said.

"You mind if I take Mika for a walk?" he asked.

The man did not hesitate for an instant.

"It's okay with me," he said.

"And what happens if she finds something?" Dr. Nolan asked.

"She'll tell you." The man smiled. "She's a pro."

Dr. Nolan went to the command SUV, opened the back compartment, and took out a shovel.

"What the hell are you doing, Dr. Nolan?" Agent Simmons asked. "We're not authorized to go any further here."

"That's you," Dr. Nolan informed him. "I don't work for you. I'm a civilian, going out for a walk with his dog."

"But you've got no official status here," Agent Simmons said again.

Dr. Nolan forced a water bottle into his front pocket. He was smiling.

"You ever see *The Treasure of the Sierra Madre* with Humphrey Bogart?" he asked.

"What does that have to do with anything?" Agent Simmons demanded.

"In the movie, bandits come to rob them, claiming to be Federales. Bogart asks to see their badges." He hesitated for a few seconds, his smile growing with the memory. "The leader of the bad guys says, 'Badges! We don't need no stinking badges!'"

Sergeant Neely was laughing again, and so were some of the other agents.

Mike Simmons stood with his hands on his hips, glaring at him.

"He's just walking his dog, Mike," Sergeant Neely said. "And he doesn't need no stinking badge."

Agent Simmons dropped his head in an exaggerated expression of capitulation.

"I've got to write a report," he announced. "You've got twenty minutes, or I'll leave you in the fucking desert." He turned and went to his vehicle.

Dr. Nolan winked at Sergeant Neely, took the leash from the handler, then he and Mika headed down the dirt slope leading east. The sandy soil was loose, his footing so unsure that he had to walk sideways. The downgrade was not severe, but broken fragments of metamorphic rock skidded out from under his shoes, once causing him to fall and slide on the seat of his pants. Dr. Nolan could see that Mika was amused by her smile.

"Go ahead and laugh," Dr. Nolan told her, using the shovel like a cane. "You've got more legs than me."

At the bottom of the grade, the tire tracks turned south. The flat zone appeared to be the remnants of an old arroyo, worn into the earth before irrigation canals diverted all the water to more usable land. It was easy walking, and he and Mika covered a quarter mile in just a few minutes. As they neared a blind turn to the right, Mika began barking, pulling against her leash.

"Good girl," Dr. Nolan said. "Show me."

The golden lab was straining, almost dragging him. Coming around the wall of the narrow gorge, the focus of her interest was immediately clear. A partially chewed work boot was lying on the ground, and just beyond it an excavated depression. Dr. Nolan used the shovel handle to right the boot, the gleaming white ankle bones visible inside it.

"Good girl, Mika," he whispered. They moved to the disturbed area of dirt. The shovel blade brushed aside just enough soil to identify denim cloth and what remained of a thigh. Dr. Nolan stood to the side of the grave and pushed the shovel into the ground to mark the location. The coyotes had saved him from digging.

He led Mika to a shaded area along the bank, poured water in his hand for her to drink, then finished the bottle. The pressure from an early headache was warning him that his fluid status was not keeping pace with the heat. He petted the dog to reward a job well done. There was no time to grieve for the victims they had found. In all, he could see two other slightly mounded shapes in the dirt that did not match the surrounding topography. He hoped there were no others.

"Come on, girl," he told Mika. "I think we're done here."

The walk back was slow. Dr. Nolan knew they had been gone longer than twenty minutes, but after struggling up the final slope, the agents were still waiting. It took a moment before he could catch his breath.

"I'd like to report a crime," he told Agent Simmons. "Three graves about a quarter mile down the ravine."

"I'll be damned! Good job." He smiled, then turned to his men. "'Get forensics out here and set up a tent. I'll call in for a second team. Looks like another long night."

Nearly exhausted, four of the agents headed out to retrace Dr. Nolan's path. There was now an official crime scene, and hours of work still ahead.

Sergeant Neely slapped Dr. Nolan on the shoulder.

"You know what?" he asked, not waiting for a reply. "I'm beginning to like you."

"I'm glad to hear it," Dr. Nolan said. "But, I need to lie down in the car, I need at least three bottles of cold water, and I need two Aleve, please."

Sergeant Neely helped him into the back seat and turned the air conditioner on high. The pounding in his temples was nauseatingly painful. He could hear the sound of his own heartbeat, the rate near one hundred. After two full bottles of water, the anti-inflammatory medication slowly began to work. As the sick feeling in his stomach eased, Dr. Nolan fell asleep.

"You eat today?" Sergeant Neely asked, peering down at him from the front seat. It was pitch black outside.

"Goddamn! What time is it?" Dr. Nolan asked, sitting up slowly. His headache was mercifully gone.

Sergeant Neely looked at his watch.

"Almost nine," he said. "We ordered KFC. You want some?"

"Jesus, yes," Dr. Nolan said. "A whole bucket with mashed potatoes, gravy, and biscuits."

"We've only got the chicken," Sergeant Neely informed him.

"Good enough," Dr. Nolan said. He climbed out of the car, tested his legs, then stretched to loosen the kink in his neck. "How long was I out?"

"About five hours, give or take," the sergeant answered.

An open tent had been erected nearby. The advertised food was on the table, and to Dr. Nolan, it was the most sensually rewarding meal he had ever eaten. After two drumsticks and three thighs, washed down with stale coffee, he felt rejuvenated.

"What did I miss?" he finally asked.

"Three Hispanics. Two men and a woman. No ID. Probably won't have any dental records on file wherever they came from. We may get lucky from a missing person report, but more likely, two Johns and one Jane Doe."

But, at least they were not lost, and would not be forgotten, Dr. Nolan thought.

Agent Simmons came up the embankment following the beam of a flashlight. He grabbed a can of lemonade and sat down heavily.

"The insubordinate civilian is back among us." He smiled, nodding to Dr. Nolan.

"You can't talk to me like that," Dr. Nolan said. "I work for Border Patrol. I have a hat to prove it."

"Excuse me, Officer Nolan," he corrected himself. "I don't usually make offers like this, but we all owe you more than we can ever repay. Now that we've got all this, we're going to pull in Mr. Sprague tomorrow and have a little chat. If you'd like to watch him come apart like a cheap suit, be at the courthouse about noon. We'll let you see the show from the observation room."

"I'd be honored," Dr. Nolan told him. "Another option would be to bring him out here and bury him in one of those holes. I know where I can find a shovel."

Agent Simmons nodded his approval.

"Old West style," Sergeant Neely offered.

"But, not by the book," Agent Simmons reminded them. He stood up and offered his hand to Dr. Nolan. "It's been a good day, Dr. Nolan. Let's get you home."

35

After a long eight hours of sleep, Dr. Nolan took Eileen and Mike to breakfast at the Sheraton. It was not typical breakfast conversation, but he gave them an account of what had been found at the Dahlquist Farm. The final act of an overly drawn-out play was coming to an end. Given the successful completion of their assigned goal, the overall mood was somber.

Over coffee, Dr. Nolan produced a tangled mess of folded papers, receipts, and scribbled notes from his pocket, pushing them across the table to Eileen.

"Expenses." He smiled. "And, add breakfast today. My rough estimate is over fifty thousand."

"Shit! In twelve days!?" she exclaimed.

Dr. Nolan shrugged away the grand total.

"Well, there's the car, travel, extra rooms, meals, gas, security, drone operator, Mrs. Ramirez, Maya, legal fees, laundry, Mike's airfare both ways, and eye drops," he said, pointing to his left cheek. The bruising and hemorrhage in his eye were nearly gone.

Eileen laughed out loud.

"I'm not calling this in," she informed him. "I'll type it out and send it as an e-mail to the CDC."

"And then, don't answer their calls," Dr. Nolan suggested. "We were only contracted for two weeks. I'm resigning as of tomorrow so I don't get fired. You better book our flights out before you send that. The thought of being stranded here is a vision of purgatory."

"They ought to give you medals," Mike said.

"Never expected any, Mickey." Dr. Nolan smiled. "I'm just glad we were able to help. And, the best news of all, you don't have to walk around with that .44 Magnum pistol stuck down in your underwear anymore."

Mike affected a devilish expression.

"Comes in handy for scratching itches though." He winked.

"Oh, jeez. You're lucky you didn't shoot something off," Eileen told him.

"No, you're lucky." Mike laughed, giving her a hug.

Eileen just shook her head.

"So, tomorrow, huh?"

"Earlier, the better," Dr. Nolan said. "We've met some remarkable people, but it's time to go home."

Eileen was studying his face with an inquisitive look in her eye.

"Speaking of remarkable people, anything you want to share?" she asked. "You know, the hotel rooms aren't as soundproof as you might think."

Dr. Nolan could feel the heat in his cheeks rising to a blush.

"I…It's the first time…" He let the words trail off, not wanting to follow, not knowing how to respond.

"I think she's great," Eileen said. "And way too good for you."

Mike nodded.

"About time," he offered. "You can't hide up on that hill like a hermit all your life."

"Oh, I've got my girls to raise," Dr. Nolan said, trying to deflect their interest.

"That job's almost done," Eileen said. "Anyway, I think it's great. Now doesn't have anything to do with then."

Dr. Nolan nodded.

"You sound like Cienna," he said softly, remembering their conversation before he left.

"She's a smart girl," Eileen said. "And, just like you worry about them, they worry about you. I think—"

"Too much," Mike interjected. "You like playing matchmaker. He'll figure it out. I'm just amazed he ran into someone who can actually put up with him. He ain't much of a bargain."

Eileen smiled, but gave ground for the moment.

"Okay. Okay, I'll behave," she promised. "I guess we go start packing."

"And expenses, and airline tickets," Dr. Nolan reminded her. He checked the time. "I get to watch the feds interrogate Dell Sprague. Should be quite an event."

He paid the bill, dropped Eileen and Mike back at the hotel, then drove south to El Centro. The federal and state offices shared space in the same looming, six story stone building. Dr. Nolan read the directory, then checked in at the desk. A security badge and visitor pass were waiting, and after clearance through a metal detector and check-point, the elevator took him to the fifth floor.

"Dr. Nolan to see Agent Simmons," he told the receptionist. She nodded, dialed her phone, then had him wait in a small anteroom at the end of the hall. He had not finished the first article in *Time* magazine before Mike Simmons found him, a woman in a business suit with glasses and tightly bound hair at his side.

"Dr. Nolan, you look better than the last time I saw you," Mike Simmons greeted him with a welcome handshake, then turned to his counterpart. "This is Assistant DA Mary Kenner. If you think I'm a hard-ass, wait till you see her in action."

The woman smiled at the compliment, extending her hand, holding on to Dr. Nolan as she spoke.

"I've heard a lot about you over the past few days. It's a pleasure to finally meet you," she began. "You've been the key factor in bringing this case to light. If the stories are even close to the truth, I must say, your approach has been…unusual at times. You don't seem to like the word 'no.'"

"I believe Agent Simmons called me insubordinate," Dr. Nolan said.

"Well, in this instance it proved useful. You just shut down an illegal trafficking operation and uncovered three suspicious deaths. You ever watch a suspect interview before?"

"Only on TV shows," Dr. Nolan admitted.

She smiled at his answer.

"Not quite so dramatic," she explained. "But we do play good cop, bad cop. Dell Sprague is knee-deep in shit, and we're going to bring it up to his chin. The people he's hurt deserve a little justice."

"Any chance you could go higher?" Dr. Nolan asked.

Mary Kenner laughed for the first time, finally letting go of his hand.

"We'll see," she said. "In case there's any question later, Mike's the good cop."

"This will be fun," Dr. Nolan said. "Is Sergeant Neely here?"

"Already waiting," Agent Simmons told him. "Come with us, and we'll get you situated."

They led him down two corridors, stopping at a solid door with a key-pad entry. Mike Simmons typed in the code, allowing Dr. Nolan to enter. The room was small, only eight feet in depth and six feet wide. One wall was a see-through mirror into the adjacent room, only a little larger. There was a small corner table with a coffee pot, and four cushioned chairs. Ted Neely was sitting closest to the glass.

"I want to watch the little fucker sweat." He smiled. "How you doing?"

"Never better," Dr. Nolan responded. He mixed a cup of coffee and sat down one chair away.

The door of the interview room opened, and Dell Sprague came in and took a chair at the wooden table. Taking the seat next to him was an older man in a vested suit, his round face half hidden behind large bifocals. Obviously Dell's attorney, the man placed his briefcase on the table.

"Our guys will just let them sit and wait for a while," Sergeant Neely explained. "Helps set the tone." Dr. Nolan noted the clock on the wall. As the second hand made its slow arc, even he felt more nervous. A full five minutes passed before Agent Simmons and Assistant DA Mary Kenner came in, sitting opposite the two men. There were polite introductions, but no handshakes.

Agent Simmons activated the microphone bolted to the center of the table. He recited the date and time.

"Assistant DA Mary Kenner and Agent Mike Simmons are present to interview defendant Dell A. Sprague. Mr. Arlin Tooley is also present, acting as defense counselor," he said flatly, then leaned back in his chair, hands folded in his lap. Mary Kenner appeared uninterested in the proceedings. She only looked down, reading documents arranged in front of her.

"Dell," he finally spoke, "you've been busy. How long have you been smuggling illegal workers?"

"I told you already, I didn't know about the people in the truck. Those go out and come back when I'm off duty. I owned up to the illegal workers. I do the hiring. That's on me, but not the rest of it."

"That's odd," Mike Simmons answered. "The truck drivers say you gave the orders and were the one paying them. Let's see. A thousand per delivery, I believe."

Dell shook his head, still smiling.

"They're lying. Their word against mine," he said. "There's no proof I gave them any money."

Mike Simmons turned a page in the file open in front of him.

"We've also got bank records on a border guard that just happened to be working every night a shipment came through. He tells us you sent an envelope every week with five thousand dollars in it. That just another lie?"

"Damn right," Dell said. "I never handed anyone money. Those drivers are just making things up to get out of trouble."

Agent Simmons sat back again.

"And Keenan Dahlquist, your boss. He had no knowledge of this little side business?"

Dell Sprague was still smiling, and still on script. "Just like me, he knew nothing about this. All happened when we were off the property."

Agent Simmons nodded and closed his file. "Well, that about does it for me," he said, turning to the assistant DA. "You have anything further?"

Mary Kenner kept reading, almost as if she had not heard the question. After a full minute, she took one piece of paper and handed it to Dell Sprague's lawyer. His face reddened as he read the warrant.

"Dell Sprague," she said, finally looking at him. "You're under arrest on three counts of second-degree murder. We have a witness that saw you remove bodies from the farm and place them in your truck. We have tire marks that match your vehicle leading to the grave sites, and we have three dead victims. Have a nice fucking day." She gathered her papers, placed them in her briefcase, stood, crossed to the door, and knocked twice. As she left, another agent entered, handcuffed Dell Sprague, then secured his shackles to a ring on the floor. He wasn't smiling any longer. Panic was setting in.

"Murder!? What the hell are they talking about!? I didn't kill anybody! What the hell is this!?"

Dell's attorney put a hand on his shoulder to calm him.

"I need time with my client," he said. "I want the microphone off, and anyone in the next room out."

Mike Simmons nodded. He leaned forward and looked at Dell Sprague.

"It might interest you to know that your boss took off over the border, just about the time you were being arrested. Isn't that one hell of a coincidence?" He switched off the microphone, smiled, then left the room.

"C'mon, Doc," Sergeant Neely said. "We've got to give the little weasel his privacy." He led Dr. Nolan out into the hallway. Mary Kenner and Mike Simmons were nearby.

"Jesus, you are a hard-ass," Dr. Nolan said.

"I'm just a grandmother who doesn't like scum in my community." The woman smiled. "We were just betting on how long before they call us back in. Mike says fifteen minutes. I say less than ten."

"I'm not betting against you," Sergeant Neely told her.

Mary Kenner and Mike Simmons discussed their strategy. Dr. Nolan and Sergeant Neely ambled up and down the hall.

In eight minutes the guard heard a knock on the door. Agent Simmons re-entered the interview cubicle. Mary Kenner joined Dr. Nolan and Sergeant Neely in the observation room.

The microphone was activated again.

"This second-degree murder charge is ridiculous," the attorney stated. "He had no active part in the death of these victims."

Mike Simmons shrugged.

"I'm not the DA," he said. "I'm just the guy who helped dig three bodies out of the desert where Dell buried them. Withholding medical care from critically ill patients that leads to their death sounds like murder to me. It probably wasn't intentional, but the end result was the same. Ten to fifteen on each count, time off for good behavior, maybe you're out in seven or eight years. But, you are going to prison for this, Dell."

Dell just blinked at him.

"Jesus fucking Christ," he said. "All I did was follow orders! This wasn't my decision!"

Mike Simmons nodded.

"I believe you, Dell, but the witness saw you. As much as I sympathize, you're looking at a list of felonies a mile long. I know this doesn't seem fair, but you're the one on the hot seat. Remember? Your boss went on vacation."

"No. Fuck this," Dell said. He laid his head on the table for a moment. "This is all wrong. All wrong. I'm not the guy you want."

"Meaning what, Dell?" Agent Simmons asked. "I'd like to help you here, but you've got to meet me halfway. All the evidence points at you for this."

Dell Sprague was rocking his forehead back and forth on the table.

"What if I give you something?" he asked, even more desperate.

His attorney put a hand on his shoulder again.

"Let's not get carried away here," he said. "I think it would be wise to talk this over in private and let things calm down."

Dell snapped his head up and glared at the man.

"And fuck you, too!" he said. "I know who your work for, and it's not me! I don't want you near me!"

"Now, Dell…"

"Fuck you! You're fired! You're going to get me hung," Dell said.

"I believe you've been dismissed, Counselor," Agent Simmons said.

"You're making a mistake, Dell," the attorney said, moving to the door.

"I've been suckered the whole time," Dell told him. "First, Dahlquist. Then you. Not anymore."

Arlin Tooley knocked on the door, then left without another word.

Dell Sprague slumped his shoulders forward. Any resistance had been over-ruled by the future he was facing.

"Can we make some kind of a deal here?" he asked, almost pleading.

"I don't know," Agent Simmons told him. "We've got an air-tight case on the three dead workers. It would have to be something pretty big. Something we don't already know."

Dell Sprague nodded slowly, licking his bottom lip.

"Those people," he began, "Dahlquist didn't want any more investigators coming around. After the first few got sick, he said no more. No one else was going to the hospital. Too much attention. We just got medicine from Mexico. It was supposed to work, but it didn't."

Agent Simmons poured him a glass of water.

"Dell, that's mostly old news," he said. "We figured out that part of it, and we probably have enough to arrest Dahlquist already. You're not giving me a reason to go out on a limb here. Believe me, I want to help you on this."

Dell Sprague leaned back in his chair and closed his eyes.

"Okay. Okay," he said. "If I give you something even bigger, what do I get? I need to know up front?"

"I can try to get the DA back in here, Dell, but this better be worth her time. She just wants to clear cases, and you're already a slam dunk."

"No! Get her! Get her back here! I promise this is bigger," Dell repeated.

"Man, I hope so," Agent Simmons said. "I'm going to read you your rights again, just to be clear this is voluntary. Okay? This will show the judge you're cooperating. Then I'll go find the DA."

Dell listened to his Miranda rights again, then stated he was willing to testify in court to any information being offered.

"Good," Agent Simmons said. "I'll be back as soon as I can." He got up, left Dell alone, and joined the others.

Sergeant Neely clapped his hands.

"Nicely done," he told Agent Simmons. "Five more minutes and he'll confess to killing Jimmy Hoffa."

"I don't care about Jimmy Hoffa," the DA said. "Not my jurisdiction. What do you suppose he has?" she asked Mike Simmons.

"Hell if I know, but he's got my interest. He's at least convinced himself it's more important."

Mary Kenner nodded. She had to decide if it was worth the gamble.

"How do you read him, Dr. Nolan?" she asked.

"Scared. Betrayed. Desperate. Whatever it is, he believes it's worth selling," Dr. Nolan answered.

"Okay. Let's play this out. After you, Agent Simmons." She made a sweeping motion toward the door. Together they went back to where Dell Sprague was waiting, his feet tapping the floor. Dr. Nolan and Sergeant Neely scooted closer to the mirrored window and turned the volume higher on the speaker.

Mary Kenner took a seat directly across from their prisoner. She met his eyes, then took out a blank piece of paper.

"You've got five minutes of my time and one offer. You plead to manslaughter in the three deaths. All the other charges go away. That's three to five. If your story's as good as you say, I recommend leniency. You serve maybe eighteen months, and you're out. Done. Do you understand?"

Dell Sprague moaned, but nodded slowly.

"You can't just nod, Dell," Agent Simmons explained calmly. "You have to say it out loud. Is it clear what the DA is offering?"

"I understand," he said. "I still go to jail."

"But, you won't be an old man when you get out," the DA reminded him. "Speed it up, Mr. Sprague. Make a decision."

"Here we go, Doc." Sergeant Neely was smiling. "Ninth inning, two outs, bases loaded, full count. Nothing like it," he whispered.

Dell Sprague leaned forward and looked down at the floor. Dr. Nolan and Sergeant Neely had to strain to hear him when he spoke, his voice tired and distant.

"The illegals," he began, "it wasn't just about workers for the farm." He paused, knowing what the next words meant, what they implied, what they revealed. "Every week, we were ordered to find at least two girls. The younger, the better. Even more so if they were attractive. He wanted them to look good, you see. They were worth more. There was always a bonus for pretty ones."

"He? Meaning Mr. Dahlquist? Keenan Dahlquist?" Agent Simmons asked.

"Yeah, Dahlquist," Dell said. "He would come down early on shipment days. You know, inspect the merchandise, make a choice. He would keep one for two, three weeks, then get rid of them, pick a replacement. Some of them were just kids."

"When you say 'kids,' what are we talking about?" Mary Kenner asked, barely able to hold her emotions in check.

"Teenagers mostly," Dell Sprague said. "Some were younger. One said she was twelve, but who knows? Too young, anyway."

"And, when you stated that Mr. Dahlquist 'got rid of them,' what did you mean?" the DA asked.

Dell Sprague looked up at her, not with shame or an apology, just a simple answer.

"He sold them at auction," he said. "On the computer. They were worth a fortune."

Dr. Nolan fought to control his breathing. He felt the first wave of nausea, then a surge of heat followed.

"Restroom?" he asked Sergeant Neely, only able to speak the one word.

"Two doors left," Sergeant Neely answered, transfixed by what he was watching through the glass.

Dr. Nolan went out, his legs shaking. In the vacant bathroom, he made it into one of the stalls, managed to bolt the door, then collapsed to his knees. He laid his head on the seat of the toilet, a drenching sweat soaking his clothes. He recognized it as a vasovagal drop in blood pressure, just near the fainting point, but there was nothing to do but let it run its course. There was no controlling it.

He retched twice, his stomach muscles cramping in pain. Trying to slow and deepen each breath, the cooling perspiration began to quell the flaming rage and disgust, the hatred he felt. As he listened to Dell Sprague, all he could see were his own daughters, the same ages as the victimized girls being described. Then he thought of Maya, what she had endured. Fleeing a hopeless life of abuse and mistreatment, she had journeyed a thousand miles to find the same fate.

Dr. Nolan heard the door open. Sergeant Neely had come looking for him. He reached up and slipped the latch on the door, then sat up and scooted into the back corner of the stall.

"This is becoming a pattern." Sergeant Neely smiled down at him. He came in and sat down on the commode next to Dr. Nolan. "You better, now?"

"Some. I kept seeing the faces of my own daughters," Dr. Nolan explained.

Sergeant Neely nodded.

"I found a young mother and her baby in the desert years ago," Sergeant Neely told him. "She just crawled under some bushes when she couldn't go any further, and they both went to sleep. Baby was still cradled in her arms. Same thing happened to me that happened to you."

"Well, thanks for cheering me up, you bastard," Dr. Nolan said, forcing a smile.

Sergeant Neely gave a single, silent laugh.

"I just meant there's a limit. All the ugly, senseless things we deal with, there's a point where you can't stand anymore."

"No. I get it. Thanks," Dr. Nolan said. "Help me up, will you?"

Sergeant Neely gave him his hand, making sure he could safely navigate on his own. Dr. Nolan went to the sink and bathed his face and neck in cold water, then nodded to the sergeant that his faculties were again trustworthy.

"You're a good babysitter," Dr. Nolan told him. "I don't know what I'll do without you."

They went out into the hallway, just as the DA and Agent Simmons exited the interview with Dell Sprague.

"I'll have a warrant for the Dahlquist home in thirty minutes," Mary Kenner said as they approached. "I want every scrap of paper, pictures, videos, computers, anything not nailed down. Let's make sure this man never hurts anyone again."

"I'll get a team ready," Agent Simmons told her. "Maybe Dr. Nolan wants to ride along?"

"No. No thanks," Dr. Nolan said. "I think I'm off duty finally. I'm grateful you're here to do this work, but I'm going home to my family."

He shook hands with the district attorney and Agent Simmons, then watched until they disappeared from sight. Sergeant Neely held out his hand, but Dr. Nolan hugged him instead.

"No kissing," the sergeant warned him.

"Been an interesting few days," Dr. Nolan noted. "Sheriff Dent picks his friends wisely. Thank you for everything. Maybe someday you'll come up for a visit. We have rib joints in our part of the country, too."

"Might just do that." Sergeant Neely smiled. "And, Doc, try to stay out of trouble, okay?"

Dr. Nolan pushed the elevator button.

"I always try," he said. "Just doesn't always work out."

He waved as the doors closed, turned in his visitor pass at the lobby, then walked out into the open, clean air, a balmy 103 degrees. For once he didn't mind.

36

IT WAS JUST BEFORE 2:00 p.m. Dr. Nolan sat in the parking lot of the federal building, trying to force the immediate emotional reaction to Dell Sprague's confession to burn lower. Without allowing it to move into memory, it threatened to dominate his thoughts. It was a fog that obscured all other vision.

So much of Maya's affected behavior suddenly made more sense. It was not just fear and insecurity that coerced her withdrawal. It was the absolute terror and degradation she suffered. Her American dream, the anticipation of a new life, all of it had ended in hopeless despair.

He dialed Elena at the legal aid office.

"Sorry to bother you at work, but what time is the family coming to meet Maya?"

"You bother me all the time, Sean," Elena told him. "They're on their way. The plan was to stay overnight at the house, let everything settle a little, then head back to Marin early tomorrow. Why?"

Dr. Nolan hesitated briefly.

"I need to tell her something, and I don't want your mother there. This is important, or I wouldn't ask. Can you meet me there and help translate? We'll figure out some excuse to get your mom away from the house for a while."

Elena was unsettled by his request, but recognized it was something urgent. Any further explanation could wait.

"Thirty minutes," she told him, looking at her watch. "I'll send my mom out to buy some more clothes for her."

"Perfect. Thank you," Dr. Nolan said. "You like Mexican food?"

Elena laughed.

"On occasion," she said. "Is this an occasion?"

"Later…later this evening, I need to take a drive, and you need to be with me," he told her. "I know this quaint mom-and-pop cantina south of here. Nice people. They could use the business."

"Sounds intriguing," Elena said. "I'll see you soon."

Dr. Nolan hung up, then dialed Eileen. She was anxious to know how the interrogation had gone.

"I'll tell you later face to face," he said. "You get our flights booked?"

"Leave at one twenty-five to San Diego," she told him. "Two hour layover. Should get to Portland by dinnertime. Seems like we've been gone a long time."

"An eon," he agreed. "And the CDC business?"

"I'm sending it at close of business hours." She laughed. "Thought it might be safer."

"Good thinking. I've had enough angst for one day already. Oh, I almost forgot. In the morning, can you and Mike take the car back? I'll call a cab. Last minute errand came up."

"Involve anyone special?" Eileen quizzed him.

"As a matter of fact, yes, but it's none of your beeswax, buddy. It's on a need-to-know basis only."

"Is she beautiful, with dark hair?" Eileen laughed.

"Yes, and yes. Happy?"

"Ecstatic," Eileen exclaimed.

"Okay, enough," Dr. Nolan said. "I'll fill you in on the day's events when I get back."

"Yes, boss," Eileen said, her tone mocking.

Dr. Nolan hung up, then drove toward Imperial, taking the turn off to the Ramirez house. He arrived before Elena, then received a crushing hug from his ex-interpreter. Maya was sitting on the sofa with the calico cat curled at her side. She glanced up briefly, but said nothing.

"It is good to see you, Dr. Nolan." Mrs. Ramirez beamed. "I slept for a whole day after our last business. You still look tired."

"I'm just low on coffee," he told her. "Any chance you could help me out again?"

"Oh, always, anything," Mrs. Ramirez answered, already at work. "You heard Maya is leaving tomorrow morning?"

"Yes, I did," Dr. Nolan said. "And, we are, too. End of a long voyage. One that would have been impossible without you, Mrs. Ramirez. I'll never be able to thank you enough."

The older woman turned the coffee maker on and came to sit with him at the table.

"So much of a life is not so important," she said, smiling at him. "I think this was a very good thing."

"It was," he agreed. "A very good thing."

"And, now you just disappear," she said, a touch of sadness in her tone.

"Maybe not," he said. "I was thinking. You and I could open a detective agency, and then refer all the legal work to Elena. It would be perfect."

Mrs. Ramirez looked at him wide-eyed, then erupted into laughter, slapping her hand on the table.

"Now you are crazy again," she managed to say. "I will start missing you before you leave."

"You may not have a chance to miss me," he said. "I think Elena and I are going to stay in touch. Would that meet with your approval?"

She looked at him, her eyes shining. She put her right hand over her chest.

"It would honor my house and my heart," she told him. "And, I would get to laugh all the time."

"Who's laughing at what?" Elena asked, coming in from the living room, just hearing the last words spoken. She kissed her mother on the cheek, then squeezed Dr. Nolan's hand.

"Your mother was making fun of me again," he explained. "Every time I make a serious proposal, she just laughs. It's a constant test of my resolve."

Elena poured coffee and sat down.

"I think you already passed the test." Elena smiled. "My mother doesn't ever think anyone is good enough for me. With you, the jury is still in deliberation."

Dr. Nolan raised his cup in a salute to Mrs. Ramirez.

"To hope," he toasted. "Shakespeare said it was the only medicine left to the miserable." As he repeated the quote, he was suddenly reminded of Maya. The smile faded from his face. Elena saw the change in him.

"Mama," she said. "Sean needs to talk to Maya, to say goodbye. Maybe you could go pick up a few more outfits for her? Just for a little while."

Mrs. Ramirez nodded. She leaned closer to Elena and Dr. Nolan.

"The new family," she said. "When I told them about Maya and the cat, they thought it was a good thing. They are bringing a kitten for her as a surprise."

Dr. Nolan nodded his approval.

"That's a very good idea," he said. He took two hundred dollars from his wallet and gave it to Mrs. Ramirez. "You pick whatever seems best. My daughters won't allow me to be in the same store with them when we go shopping. It's a rule of some kind."

"That is a rule." Elena laughed.

"This is very generous," Mrs. Ramirez said, getting up and looking for her purse. "This will make Maya feel special."

"Thank you, Mrs. Ramirez," Dr. Nolan said. "If you could give us one hour."

"That is good. One hour," she repeated. She hugged Elena and headed out on her mission.

When her mother had gone, Elena could wait no longer.

"What is this about? Why the big secret?" she asked.

He took her hand.

"I don't ever want your mother to know about this, the details of it. I'll explain everything to you later, but for now you have to act the part of Maya's attorney. As hard as this is, it has to be like business. Otherwise, I can't do this."

Elena slowly nodded. She did not understand his request, but knew there was a reason.

He stood up and led her into the living room, then had her sit next to Maya. Dr. Nolan sat on the sofa table directly in front of the girl. Her eyes still down, he reached over and petted the cat napping next to her, then held his hand out to her.

"Hola, Maya," he said, smiling at her. The girl looked up once, then glanced at Elena. With her head still held low, she slowly reached up and placed her hand in his. He tightened his grip ever so slightly.

"Tell her my heart is broken, but I know what happened to her on the farm," he began, never taking his eyes away from Maya.

"What…?" Elena was startled, then remembered her promise. She repeated his words in an even voice. As she spoke, he could feel the young girl try to draw her hand away. He kept hold of her.

"It is the greatest sadness of my life, but there are terrible people in the world, in all places. But, they are the few. The good people in the world are what matter the most," he told her, then waited for Elena to translate.

"What happened was not your fault. There is no blame or guilt. This will be hard to remember for a long time, but the only shame here is for the bad people, not you. It will take years to heal from this, but it must become the past. Not to forget, but to not remember it as often. Do you understand?"

Again, Elena spoke the words in Spanish. Maya was no longer pulling her hand away, but he could see the first tears on her cheek. What he did not see were the tears in Elena's eyes. It was painfully obvious what had happened to the young girl.

"God has given you the chance for a new life that is beginning now. If you do not accept this gift, it would be the saddest thing of all. You have had a part of your childhood stolen from you, but the rest of your life belongs to you again. The bad people cannot win if we refuse to let them. Can you see that?"

Maya was crying harder now. She leaned forward as Elena spoke, resting her head against Dr. Nolan's chest. He put his arms around her and let the minutes pass. It was not the end of anything, not a resolution, not even the first moment of healing. But, it was a beginning.

After a time, Maya said something in a whisper, then leaned back enough to look at Dr. Nolan.

"She said, until you came there was no one. You were her prayer from the Virgin Mary."

He smiled and brushed the hair away from her eyes.

"I'm not sure I'm the answer to anyone's prayers," he said. "But tell her I'm glad we found her."

Maya nodded. The old cat stretched, climbed into the girl's lap, and rubbed it's head under her chin. Maya laughed and rubbed away the tickle. It was the first sound of joy Dr. Nolan had ever heard from her. The cat was clearly the better therapist.

"Tell Maya that I have to go home tomorrow to take care of my two daughters," Dr. Nolan said. "But, I will keep her in my thoughts forever, wherever she goes in this world. I will not forget her."

When Elena was finished, Maya spoke again.

"Que Dios te proteja," she said.

"May God protect you," Elena repeated.

Dr. Nolan smiled, gave her a last hug, then stood up, his first glimpse of Elena's reddened eyes. They went back to the kitchen.

"That was brutal," Elena told him. "You just found out about this today?"

Dr. Nolan looked at her and nodded.

"Turned out Dahlquist was running his smuggling operation to procure young girls. After raping them until he got bored, there would be a new victim. He sold the others."

"It's not talked about enough, but sex slaves number in the thousands," Elena told him. "Every state, most big cities. One of the oldest businesses on earth."

"Jesus, but here? The land of the free? My country? It's so ugly," Dr. Nolan said.

Elena gave him a long hug.

"Thanks for protecting my mother," she whispered. "This would have killed her. It almost killed me. Is this why you said we'd need a long drive later?"

"This, and just to have you to myself," he said. "I thought we might discuss the possibility of a commuter romance? See what the future holds."

"Could be fun." Elena smiled.

"Could be dangerous," Dr. Nolan added. "Brings a new dimension to the old line, 'My place or yours.'"

Elena laughed, then placed her hands along the sides of his face, kissing him over and over.

"In about three weeks, I find out if I passed the bar exam," she said. "How about I come for a visit? You think your daughters are ready to share you?"

"I do," he said.

She hugged him tightly.

"Then promise me," she asked. "When tonight ends, there are no goodbyes. Just say, I'll see you soon."

37

Dr. Nolan arrived back at the hotel just before 11:00 p.m. After the first agonizing recount of Dell Sprague's interview earlier with Elena, the second telling was less of an ordeal for him, but chillingly horrific for Eileen and Mike. It was not part of a world they knew or recognized.

The only consolation was that Maya had been rescued, and there would be no new victims at Dahlquist Farm. One link in a chain of human degradation had been broken.

Dr. Nolan left them trying to make sense of something that had no redemptive character, no plausible worth. He packed his bag, then tried to sleep, but was still wide awake when his cell phone rang at 2:00 a.m. It was Mike Simmons.

"Sorry it's so late, or early, but I thought you'd want to know," he said. "Keenan Dahlquist was just arrested in Costa Rica. Take three to four weeks to extradite him, but it's over. When we raided his home, he had volumes of child pornography, films, pretty raw stuff. Also found sixteen customers on his computer. The ripples just keep going."

"That's good news," Dr. Nolan said. "What do you think he's looking at for prison time?"

"Oh, Doc, it won't matter," Agent Simmons told him. "Even bad guys have rules. When the other prisoners find out he was abusing children, he won't live long."

"And they'll know? The other inmates?" Dr. Nolan asked.

Agent Simmons laughed.

"We'll make sure they know," he said. "Have a safe flight home."

Dr. Nolan stared at the ceiling. The thought of Dahlquist being murdered in prison was not a pleasing reality, but it did not bother him either. In all they had encountered in the past two weeks, there was nothing that fit the definition of justice. There were now officially fifty one victims of the Legionella outbreak, and hundreds of other lives twisted and damaged by human trafficking. There was no scale that he knew of that would ever balance any of it.

When the first fingers of daylight reached into the valley, he showered and shaved, called for a cab, then left the hotel for the last time. He paid for a messenger service to deliver the CDC files to Memorial Hospital, not wanting to risk a personal appearance. As he waited at the curb, he checked his phone. There were already nine messages from Dr. Pulliam at the CDC office in Atlanta. He had no intention of answering them. At least not today.

His errand was a brief drive north, and Eileen and Mike were waiting inside the airline terminal when he arrived. With one hand, he pulled his suitcase. In the other, he carried a medium sized canvas bag.

"Oh, shit, you've got to be kidding," Eileen said. "Attractive? Dark hair? You're terrible!" She was laughing.

Mike looked through the webbed opening.

"Jesus! What is that?"

Dr. Nolan looked offended.

"The dog we rescued in Westmorland," he explained. "No one adopted her."

"If that's a dog, it's the ugliest one I've ever seen," Mike told him. "No wonder nobody adopted her. She looks like that guy in *Star Wars*."

"She have a name?" Eileen asked.

"Mrs. Miniver." Dr. Nolan smiled. "And don't worry. She got a bath and a health check at the vet. They charge more to see patients than I do!" He gave Mrs. Miniver a rub under the chin with one finger.

"You're one of a kind, Sean," Eileen said.

"I assume that was a compliment," he said.

"Hmmmm…The girls know?" she asked.

"I'm calling when we get checked through. It was too late last night."

Clearing the TSA line, they reached their gate with thirty minutes to spare. Dr. Nolan found a vacant corner and dialed home. It was Cienna who answered.

"Dad! We were worried! We were just listening to a story about you on TV."

"Hi, baby. Put me on speakerphone. Is Aubriel there?"

"Yes! Yes! Where are you!?"

"On my way home," he said. "I miss you horribly. And what about the TV?"

"The news! They said you broke up some kind of human smuggling operation! You're famous!" Cienna shouted.

"Great," Dr. Nolan moaned. He glanced at his message list. There were now fourteen calls from Atlanta. "It's not that big a deal. I'll be home tonight, and I've got presents."

"Cool! What is it?" Cienna asked.

"Aubriel, for you, I picked up the newest CD from that singer, Billie Eyelash," he announced.

"*Eilish!*" Aubriel yelled back. "Not Eyelash! Eilish!"

"Whatever." Dr. Nolan laughed. "And, Cienna, this pained me deeply, but I picked up a driver's ed manual. I guess it's time."

"Yeaaaah!" Cienna shouted. "What else?"

"One special present, but you have to wait," Dr. Nolan said. "I'll see you in a few hours."

"Hurry! We want to hear all about your trip! We can't wait!"

Dr. Nolan closed his eyes. He would have to tell them some version of what happened, but they would never know the real story. Not ever.

"Okay! I love you both. See you tonight."

They were both still shouting when he hung up.

"Goddamn! Look at this!" Mike said, holding up the morning paper. The entire front page was devoted to the illegal trafficking ring and sex trade story. It was already a national headline.

"Shit! Good time to be leaving," Dr. Nolan said.

"Listen to this, 'According to District Attorney Mary Kenner, critical evidence uncovered by Dr. Sean Nolan, the regional CDC director, led investigators to Dahlquist Farm!' Pretty cool," Mike exclaimed.

"Evidently, I got promoted just before being fired." Dr. Nolan pointed out. "What a world."

"Man, this is good." Mike laughed, thoroughly enjoying the article. "You're like Dick Tracey."

Their flight was announced over the loud-speakers. Dr. Nolan picked up Mrs. Miniver, nothing but an enormous smile looking back at him.

"Hey, Eileen. Remind me to call Arthur Campbell next week. He made some kind of bet with Dr. Pulliam. I'm dying to know what it was."

"Do your own dirty work." Eileen laughed. "I don't work for you anymore."

"Ingrate," Dr. Nolan whispered. They found their seats, Dr. Nolan at the window, Eileen in the middle. The flight attendant reminded him to place the dog under the seat.

"Yes, ma'am," Dr. Nolan responded. He buckled in, then made certain no one was watching. Unzipping the dog carrier, he lifted Mrs. Miniver into his lap and covered her with a blanket, then leaned against the bulkhead, already feeling sleepy.

"You do realize you're breaking the rules?" Eileen reminded him.

Dr. Nolan smiled and closed his eyes.

"So, sue me," he dared her. "I've got a good lawyer."

About the Author

E. W. JOHNSON BEGAN HIS literary pursuits at age four, focusing on inane, vapid rhyming poetry. With no job prospects and a crushing rejection from the Hallmark greeting card company, he then opted for public education. His writing shifted to free verse prose and short stories and a first inept novel at fifteen. Penniless and chastised, the poet bowed to the sciences.

Entering medical training in 1980, Dr. Johnson, a board-certified internist, served as the town physician for a rural community in southwest Washington until 2018. When he moved to Hawaii, part-time writing finally became a full-time obsession, with four novels completed within the first six months.